Nicole Trope is a former high school teacher with a Masters Degree in Children's Literature. In 2005 she was one of the winners of the Varuna Awards for Manuscript Development. In 2009 her young adult novel titled 'I Ran Away First' (unpublished) was shortlisted for the Text Publishing Prize. *Forgotten* is Nicole's seventh novel. Her previous titles include the acclaimed *Blame, The Boy Under The Table, Three Hours Late, The Secrets in Silence* and *Hush, Little Bird*.

Other books by Nicole Trope

Blame
Hush, Little Bird
The Secrets in Silence
Roar
Three Hours Late
The Boy Under the Table

FORGOTTEN

NICOLE TROPE

ALLEN&UNWIN
SYDNEY·MELBOURNE·AUCKLAND·LONDON

First published in 2017

Allen & Unwin
83 Alexander Street
Crows Nest NSW 2065
Australia
Phone: (61 2) 8425 0100
Email: info@allenandunwin.com
Web: www.allenandunwin.com

Cataloguing-in-Publication details are available
from the National Library of Australia
www.trove.nla.gov.au

ISBN 978 1 76029 677 3

Set in 13.5/18 pt Minion by Midland Typesetters, Australia
Printed and bound in Australia by Griffin Press

10 9 8 7 6 5 4 3 2 1

For my mother, Hilary, who reads first

Chapter One

8.00 am

The bowl spins across the floor, ricochets off the cabinet and shatters into pieces, showering Coco Pops over every square foot of the kitchen. Malia watches as her five-year-old son, Aaron, stamps his feet, crushing the cereal into dust.

'I want Coco Pops with milk! I want Coco Pops with milk. Now, now, *now.*'

Small fists clenched and a face coloured with rage, he vents his fury at the world, at his dry cereal and, mostly, at his mother.

'Mind your feet!' yells Malia, matching his decibels, drowning out the television where puppet animals are

1

singing about a day on the farm. 'Now, look at this mess. Just look at this mess. I told you Aaron, there *is* no milk.'

Malia grabs her son by the shoulders and lifts him onto a chair, grunting at how heavy he is, while he attempts to kick her in the stomach.

'I want milk! I want milk!' He stands up, poised to jump.

'Sit down while I clean up this mess!'

As Malia steps towards the cupboard under the sink for the dustpan and brush she feels the sharp sting of a piece of the splintered cereal bowl pierce her foot.

'Shit!' she cries.

'You sweared!' shouts Aaron. 'Bad mum.' Tears stain his face.

'Just sit there and be quiet,' snaps Malia, sweeping up the Coco Pops and the shattered bowl, staining the kitchen floor with blood as she moves.

'Too much noise, too much noise,' sings Rhiannon, who had been sitting with her back to the kitchen, glued to the morning television show. She picks up the remote and turns up the volume.

'*It's a happy, happy day, when you get to work and play,*' sing the animals.

'Turn it down!' yells Malia.

She throws away the last of the mess and sits down on the floor to examine her foot. The splinter has gone deep, but a small piece protrudes, allowing her to pull it out. Aaron watches, momentarily silenced by the sight of blood.

Malia holds a piece of tissue against the wound and

takes a deep breath. This is not how she likes to handle the mornings with her children. She closes her eyes and resolves to take back control of the situation. Aaron sniffs dramatically, alerting her to his tears.

'You need to stop crying now, Aaron, and eat something or we're going to be late,' she says.

'But Mum …'

'We don't have time to argue anymore. You know that Mrs Epstein doesn't like you to be late.'

She makes sure her tone is light but firm—just the way the last book she read about raising children advised her to do. *Creating Calm from Chaos* is the latest in a long line of parenting books that Malia has downloaded. In the absence of her parents and extended family, who live in Melbourne, Malia has turned to the experts for help—all of whom have different ideas, although this has never stopped Malia trying to find the one expert who will help her be the perfect mother.

'Don't they all say the same thing,' Ian had laughed when she tried reading him a passage on dealing with tantrums in children.

'No, they don't,' Malia had replied.

'Yes, they do babe. Every book you read tells you that the best way to get through the day with three kids is to relax and take control. You just need to chill.'

Malia had given her head a shake, dismissing his opinion. Ian was usually at work when the children were at their most demanding.

3

'I'm sure Mrs Epstein has something wonderful planned for today,' says Malia to her son. 'You may get to do some painting. What do you think you'll paint a picture of?'

Aaron regards her sceptically; her change in tone has been too quick. He knows he's being handled.

Distract your child with questions and new ideas and soon the tantrum will be a thing of the past.

'I can make you some yummy toast for breakfast. What would you like on your toast?' says Malia, attempting to make toast sound like a treat instead of a poor second choice.

'I don't want toast. I *waaant* milk,' whines Aaron again, not willing to give up on his specific need for this morning.

'All you had to do was bring home some milk,' says Malia to herself, picturing Ian, at work in the car yard, holding a steaming cup of coffee, freshly made by one of the admin staff—all of whom were women and all of whom, she believes, probably have crushes on her blond-haired, blue-eyed husband. 'I don't see anyone but you, babe,' Ian always assures her.

Malia sees her own hand grab Ian's cup and upend it on his head. She smiles briefly at the image of her husband with coffee dripping down his beautiful suit, staining the crisp white shirt he was wearing this morning.

'Miiilk,' moans Aaron softly. Malia can hear that he's losing interest in his tantrum and she congratulates herself on sticking to the advice she has read.

Rhiannon turns around to see why her older brother

has stopped crying and Aaron seizes the opportunity to include her in his mission.

'I want milky Coco Pops,' he says, looking at his sister to encourage her to join the melee.

'I want milky Coco Pops,' seconds Rhiannon, jumping up and running to her brother. At three years old she is his willing accomplice against what they both seem to view as Malia's unacceptable expectations—things like eating vegetables and getting to bed on time.

'Eee!' she shrieks.

'What?' says Malia.

'My foot, sore, sore!' she screeches, already hysterical.

'Oh God, Rhiannon, stop jumping. Just keep still!'

'Milky Coco Pops!' shouts Aaron, ramping himself up again.

Malia takes a wide step towards Rhiannon, hoping to avoid standing on anything else she may have missed, and then picks up her daughter and sits her on top of the kitchen table.

'I want my dummy,' cries Rhiannon, pulling her foot away as Malia tries to examine it for a splinter.

'There's nothing there, Rhiannon!'

'Coco Pops, Coco Pops,' chants Aaron.

'Coco Pops, Coco Pops,' says Rhiannon, forgetting her sore foot.

Malia looks at her children and wishes just for a moment that she could join in the wailing as well. The pounding in her head is exacerbated by the feeling that she is moving underwater—from a lack of caffeine, she's sure. She wants milk for her coffee as well. She wants milk and coffee, she wants milk and coffee. She can't seem to think straight. The noise gets louder as Aaron and Rhiannon attempt to outdo each other.

'*We get up with the sun, we always have such fun,*' warble the animals on the television.

'Right, fine!' shouts Malia. 'We'll go and get milk. Put on your shoes and get into the car now.'

She snatches the remote control from Rhiannon's hand and turns off the television, silencing the animals.

'But . . .' says Aaron, momentarily stunned to have won the argument.

'Right now, or there'll be no milk and no breakfast at all.'

Malia looks at her watch. It's already seven forty-five and the traffic is going to make a five-minute trip to the 7-Eleven take at least twice that.

'Do I have to put on my shoes?' says Aaron.

'Yes.'

'I losted my shoes,' says Rhiannon.

Malia stifles the urge to scream. She closes her eyes and reimagines the morning with a full bottle of milk in the fridge and then she sighs as she catches the scent of a giant cup of coffee. 'Just get on with it, Malia,' she mutters to herself.

It takes another five minutes to get both children into the car and only as she pulls out of the driveway does Aaron say, 'What about baby Zach?'

Malia pulls back into the driveway and drops her head onto the steering wheel. 'Idiot,' she whispers. She's going to be late for work at the bakery. The kids are going to be late for school and day care. She hasn't even had a shower yet because at six o clock this morning Ian, the same Ian who forgot the milk, had pushed up against her in bed and instead of telling him to leave her alone she had given in, despite the fact that he still smelled like beer after stumbling into the house somewhere around two that morning.

'I need you,' he had said and she knew that meant a lot of money had gone into the pokies at the pub and very little had come back out. If he won he crowed about it, explaining his strategies and laughing at his luck, but if he lost he needed to conquer something else. Pushing Malia into sex was as close as he could get. 'Not pushing,' she admits to herself now, 'more like gentle coercion.' Even after three children and nearly ten years together, eight of them as husband and wife, Ian still manages to make Malia's stomach lurch just a little every time he touches her.

After she'd given in, Zach's cries had filled the house. 'Leave him, he'll be fine,' Ian had said. Malia had bitten down on her lip and endured her son's anguish and her husband's pleasure. Ian wasn't bothered by Zach crying; he never was.

She hadn't asked much of him, just a litre of milk bought on the way home from the pub. The empty bottle was still in the fridge, left there because it still contained a few drops and only discovered after all three children had been sound

7

asleep. The idea of a hot cup of tea, drunk in front of some mindless television show had carried Malia through dinner and bath time and story time and 'I want a glass of water' and 'I'm still hungry' and 'I'm not sleepy' time.

She'd had half a glass of acidic red wine instead.

Ian had not made it home for dinner. 'Work meeting, babe,' he had said on the phone, and she knew that was code, and not even very good code, for the pub and his favourite pastime. The pub was close enough to the house that if he did drink a little more than he should he could always walk home and pick up his car the next day. Something that Malia saw as a mixed blessing. He was already up to three nights this week. She had a speech ready to deliver when and if he made it home for dinner one night. It was the same speech she had delivered time and time again and so far it hadn't had much impact, but she still hoped to get through to her husband.

Please bring home milk, she had texted him.

Sure thing, he had replied. *Home soon*.

But Malia had rolled over in bed at 1 am to find his side cold.

'Maybe it was only fifty dollars or so,' she had tried to convince herself as Ian grunted and kissed her neck, before leaping out of bed to shower and dress.

It had only taken him fifteen minutes to get himself out the door to work, where someone else was responsible for buying the milk and a selection of breakfast pastries for the salespeople to indulge in.

'How much?' she had asked as he whirled around the bedroom finding clothes, and he'd at least had the good grace to hang his head and tell the truth.

'Just a hundred, but I was up by about two hundred at the beginning. Gotta go.' She had wanted to grab his arm and stop him walking out of the front door, had wanted to force him to speak to her, but Ian was focused on the day ahead and she knew that he wouldn't want to be late for work and his morning sales meeting.

Only when she had heard Aaron shrieking about the milk had she realised that Ian had not done the one thing she'd asked him to do. She had wasted futile minutes arguing with her son about choosing a different breakfast while she fed Zach.

In the car she lifts her head and takes a deep breath, 'Okay guys, stay here and don't move. I'm going to get Zach.' Aaron and Rhiannon nod and remain silent. They can sense her breaking point. Malia gets out of the car and goes back into the house, thinking that on any other day the sight of her two little blond-haired carbon copies nodding together would have made her smile, but today she can't even dredge up a grimace. Even as babies Aaron and Rhiannon had looked so alike that paging through photo albums is confusing. 'Is that me?' Aaron will ask. 'Is that me or Ri Ri?' Sometimes it will even take Malia a moment to work out exactly which baby she is looking at. If they were the same height Malia is sure they would be mistaken for twins. She is always amazed at the genetic mix that has gone into her producing three children who look exactly like their father but seem almost unrelated to her, with her black hair and dark brown eyes.

Malia unlocks the front door, wondering briefly about the wisdom of leaving her children in the car in the driveway. Anyone at all could walk by. She pictures the double garage with internal access that they would add to their home when they finally did the big renovation she and Ian have been discussing for years. 'Any day now babe, I promise,' Ian said month after month and year after year. The three-bedroom, single-level brick and fibro home in a suburb filled with families and only twenty minutes from the city had seemed perfect when she was pregnant with Aaron, but now it feels as though the family is almost bursting out of the small house, using every inch of space for children and toys and the other detritus of family life. Malia longs for a large ensuite bathroom with a big bath and soft towels and no children knocking on the door.

'Not this year,' she sighs as she makes her way down the passage to Zach's tiny bedroom.

Last night she had pored over the bills once again, hoping that she had somehow missed a loophole that would give her a little more time. But there was nothing to find except final demands and threats to cut off the electricity. She would need to ask Sean, her boss and the owner of the bakery, to pay her early, humiliating herself again, bearing his kind 'not a problem' once more.

Ian was having a bad month at work with one sale

after another falling through. He had only managed two sales so far and it was close to the end of the month. His commission from those sales was not enough to take care of all the bills. There were always bad months and they mostly seemed to be ill timed with the quarterly bills and the breakdown of major appliances. Malia can't quite remember when they went from being financially okay to struggling but lately it seems worse than ever. Even with her part-time job she never seems to pay anything off on time. 'A few good months,' she whispers to herself, 'just a few good months.'

Part of the reason she had agreed to sex this morning was because she'd hoped that it would put Ian in a mood to discuss what to do, but as she opened her mouth to say something he had turned on the shower. 'Sorry, babe, running late for a staff meeting and we don't need me to lose my job, do we?' So there had been no conversation and no time for her prepared speech on gambling, and all she had been left with was the knowledge that she had even less money to cover the bills than she thought she had.

It wasn't that Ian didn't understand their financial predicament; it was just that he believed—truly believed, as though he had a direct line to the universe—that he was going to win big, so big that he would be able to solve all their financial problems. This belief refused to be daunted by the science of slot machines, which explained the impossibility of ever coming out ahead.

'It has to happen for someone, Malia. Why not me?'

Even Malia believed it was possible when Ian talked about the powers of positive thinking and the benevolence of the universe. 'Good things happen all the time, Malia,' he would say, his blue eyes shining with absolute certainty. His persistent belief that amazing things were just around the corner for both of them was one of the reasons Malia had fallen in love with Ian in the first place. To him the world has always been filled with exciting opportunities and wonderful adventures and all he needs to do is be prepared and wait.

And he has proved himself correct in his thinking over and over again. When he applied for his current job he had said, 'I want this so I'll get it,' and he had. When they began looking for a home to buy Malia loved their house as soon as she saw it, attracted to the large front yard and the endless potential of the space, but it had been priced over what they could afford. 'It's meant to be ours, babe,' Ian said, 'just wait and see.' A month later the estate agent called them, letting them know the owners had lost a buyer and were willing to drop their price.

'Told you,' grinned Ian when Malia relayed the message. 'The good stuff happens and it may as well happen to us.'

His belief system felt magical and Malia couldn't help but be swept along with it, until it stopped working and then she found it harder and harder to remain in step with his way of thinking.

The realities of marriage and children meant someone had to be pragmatic. Even though he was two years older, he made her feel that he was decades younger than her thirty-three years. Becoming a mother had made her more cynical than she wanted to be, but raising children required money and all the positive thinking in the world wouldn't bring back fifty or a hundred dollars lost in a slot machine every week.

'I'm not sure you can out-think the randomness of pokie machines, Ian,' she would say. Sometimes he would agree with her but look so crestfallen at having to acknowledge it that Malia would feel bad for bursting his bubble of belief. But even if he did agree with her one day, he was usually back at the machines the next.

It was an addiction. Ian was an addict. Malia had read all the articles and visited all the chat rooms, but the fact that she knew what the problem was made little difference to Ian. 'There's always enough to eat, isn't there, babe, and I've never missed a mortgage payment, have I, even if I was a little late?' he would say whenever she urged him to get some help. 'It's my way of staying sane, Malia. You have no idea how much pressure there is at work.'

Malia understood his need to blow off steam after a tough day at work. His natural charm made him an excellent car salesman but the Walt White car yard where he worked was filled with men and women oozing natural charm. Competition was fierce. 'I always feel like complete shit whenever I lose a sale, and Walt always makes me feel like an idiot in front of the other guys and …'

'And?' said Malia.

'Nothing,' he would say, shaking his head, not mentioning the main reason he hung around in the pub, numbing his mind with pictures on a slot machine, which was that the domestic realities of children were never what he had wanted for his life. He rarely brought it up, but it was always there, always in danger of being spoken of.

Malia continually comforts herself that his gambling has never really gotten out of control, not to the point where the house is in jeopardy, but each month is a struggle and the bills get paid with only a little to spare. The extra few hundred dollars he spends each week at the pub could cover the water bill or the gas bill or a visit to the grocery store, and sometimes when Ian is relaxed and the kids are asleep, Malia broaches the subject with him, hoping to get him to see sense and maybe even agree to therapy so he can commit to change, but it never works.

'We always manage, don't we? No one has turned off the gas or the electricity, and the kids have everything they need. Please don't take this away from me, Malia.'

And implied in that statement was all that she *had* taken away from him. Mainly she had taken his freedom, his precious freedom. She had chained him down to a house and children when all he had wanted was a life where the only reason he got up to go to work every day was to save money to travel the world, visiting the best surfing beaches on every coast. 'I need more,' she told him when he asked her to marry him and he'd nodded like he agreed, but he hadn't really. Even marriage hadn't been part of his life plan, but when Malia told him that her parents would not accept her living with him without being married he proposed in a hot-air balloon, getting down on one knee, making the basket wobble and Malia shriek, 'Are you sure?' she asked before she said, 'Yes!'

'No way I'm letting some other bloke have you,' he had replied, making her laugh.

'I want kids, Ian. I really want kids.'

'Will they look like you?'

'They may look like you.'

'I'll love them anyway.'

But now Malia knew that for Ian the promises he had made, drunk on too much champagne, have often been regretted.

Seared in Malia's memory is one night, after Rhiannon had finally weaned herself at ten months old, when she and Ian were celebrating with a glass of wine that turned into two. Malia hadn't had a drink for months and she had felt the room tilt as she giggled at Ian's impersonation of customers at the car yard. She had closed her eyes and felt herself drifting into a doze when the folly of marrying a man who had little interest in children suddenly crystallised from a few words Ian voiced aloud.

'This is so nice, babe. It's been a long time since we talked like this. I forgot how much fun we can have when it's just you and me.'

'Until one of them wakes up,' Malia had said, feeling herself dropping into sleep.

'I thought you weren't serious, you know?' Ian had said.

'About what?' she had murmured.

'About having kids. I thought you would see that life was better without them, that I could change your mind.'

Ian had whispered the words and Malia had understood that he hadn't thought them through. Maybe the alcohol had released his tongue or maybe he needed to say the words out loud sometimes, to admit the truth to himself and to her. Malia had felt the shock of them sober her up. She had kept her eyes closed and dropped her head to the side, feigning sleep, rather than admit she had heard what he'd said. It seemed the safest option. The 'kids' Ian hadn't wanted to have were here now and the idea that he could still want to imagine them away made Malia profoundly uneasy. She had been sure that if she confronted him in the morning he would be deeply sorry for saying anything. When he was with the children his love for them was obvious. He made himself a human climbing frame as he walked through the door at night, spent hours pushing Aaron and Rhiannon on the swing set or playing cricket and soccer in the backyard. He listened to the same jokes from Aaron over and over again, laughing just as heartily each time. When he was home he read stories and managed to turn bath time into the most exciting part of the day. But lately, he was rarely home and on nights when Malia felt she would never get five minutes to herself she resented his freedom to come and go as he pleased, despite the responsibilities of fatherhood.

Ian loves his kids but sometimes he wants to be able to shift them off to one side so he can do whatever he wants.

'That's not how it works,' Malia tells him, but Ian has the luxury of not listening when he doesn't want to. He can walk out the door and pretend he doesn't even have a family.

'A nice Greek boy, Malia ... What would have been wrong with a nice Greek boy?' her mother had said after meeting Ian. But Malia wanted blond Ian with the smell of the sea permanently in his hair and his belief in the general munificence of the world.

Malia had met Ian at a New Year's Eve party at a restaurant near the river. She had been pressed up against the glass railing of the balcony, waiting for the midnight fireworks when she felt someone elbow her in the back. She had turned, laughing, assuming it was her friend Leigh, who had gone to the bathroom, only to find Ian grinning at her. 'Just because you're beautiful doesn't mean you get to be in the front row,' he said, his words slurring a little.

Malia noticed his lips first and without thinking she reached up to touch them, wanting to know if they were as soft as they looked. She pulled her hand away just in time and giggled at how forward she was being. It was not the way she had been raised to behave. The fireworks had begun and she had felt him behind her the whole time, pressing up against her a little, reminding her he was there.

He was nothing like any of the other boys she had dated

17

before, all of whom had mostly come from her family's large circle of Greek friends.

'But where does he come from?' her father had asked when she told her parents about him.

'He's Australian, Dad, I think his family came from England or Ireland. I don't know, we haven't really discussed it.'

'You haven't discussed it? What do you talk about?'

Malia had rolled her eyes at her father and wondered again why she still lived at home with her parents when she was working full time as head of marketing for a company that produced hand-made shoes. She was desperate to move out but every time she brought it up her mother went into hysterics about a 'woman living on her own like a dog'.

She and Ian talked about everything, about life and books and movies and art and philosophy. They discussed politics and how they would change the world if they could. His impressions made her laugh and he told her she was the 'most beautiful creature he had ever set eyes on'.

Being with Ian felt different. There was no serious discussion about marriage and work. No boasting of properties owned and plans for the future. There was just today and now and the freedom to do whatever they wanted.

Malia had grown up in a suburb populated by friends and family. Everyone knew everyone and there were times when she felt she could have been living in a small Greek village in the middle of nowhere. For years Malia had been chafing at her strict upbringing, at still being treated like a child even though she was in her twenties. The year before she met Ian she had gone to Europe with friends and had felt herself suffocating under her mother's lists of 'Don'ts'. Don't go out with strange men. Don't walk down dark alleyways. Don't drink anything you can't recognise. Don't try too many new foods. Don't go into nightclubs.

After yet another 'Don't' lecture, she had rolled her eyes at her mother and waited until she left the room to appeal to her father: 'Papa, she's driving me mad. I'm twenty-five already. Please make her stop.'

'Malia, my girl,' he had sighed, precisely folding his beloved Greek newspaper so he would know which article to read next, 'one day you will be a mother and you will understand what it means to love something more than yourself. What a wonderful, terrible day that will be.'

'But Papa ...'

'But nothing, Malia. You listen to your mother.'

Ian made a different life seem possible. He took her to Sydney to climb the Harbour Bridge and to Adelaide to taste wine. They travelled to Bali and Thailand and China. It felt like Ian had taken her out of her small village and shown her the world. It was only when she'd had Aaron, and Ian began his regular visits to the pub and the pokies, that Malia began to wonder if his desire for freedom was incompatible with her desire for a family.

'It'll all be fine, babe, don't you worry,' he said whenever they argued about how they were going to pay the bills.

Malia did worry, and in the last few years she had begun to understand that she would always be worrying alone. She had married a twenty-eight-year-old boy thinking he would turn into a man, but he never had. Just about every article she'd read on marriage held the truth that you can't change your spouse into the person you want them to be. This knowledge hadn't stopped Malia from marrying Ian, or Ian from marrying Malia, and she was sure that there were millions of people who'd made the same mistake.

But if her marriage was not brilliant, the poverty that would come with a divorce would be disastrous. And there was always the small problem of how much Malia actually loved Ian. Even today no one could make her laugh like Ian could, or make her as angry as Ian could or as happy as Ian could. If Ian was addicted to the pokies, Malia was addicted to Ian.

Zach is fast asleep in his cot. It's a wonder all the noise his brother and sister had been making hadn't woken him, but babies are like that. Sometimes a light breeze will wake them and sometimes they can sleep through a thunderstorm.

Malia rubs her eyes and sighs. Waking Zach now would mean that his whole schedule—as much of a schedule as a five-month-old could have—would be thrown off. She only has enough milk pumped for one feeding at day care. Now she would need more.

Malia picks up her son as gently as she can and is relieved to feel the heaviness of deep sleep. There's a chance she can get to the shop and back without waking him and then, if she gives him a quick top-up when she drops him off, she will be able to get through her shift at the bakery without worrying about him needing to be fed in between.

She hates that he has to be in day care. It doesn't seem fair when Aaron and Rhiannon both got to be at home with her until they were eighteen months. But last year Malia had been forced to admit that she needed to go back to work so she could always be sure of having a certain amount of money coming in. Ian's base wage was eaten up by the mortgage and the bigger bills. If he earned no commission at all for a month, they would be short of even food money. The few times that had happened had terrified her. Her father had always frowned on people who lived off credit, and she couldn't help feeling ashamed when she had to resort to buying groceries with her credit card. The job at the bakery, serving customers for a few hours a day, was a lifetime away from her job at the shoe company, where she had worked until Aaron was born. It required very little of her and it worked with Zach's hours in day care and Aaron and Rhiannon's days at school and preschool.

She makes her way carefully back to the car, where Aaron opens the door so she can slip Zach into his car seat. 'Thanks, my boy,' she whispers, and Aaron nods. Malia wants to stroke his serious face. He is used to being a big brother, but is not quite ready to give up being little, hence this morning's tantrum. His behaviour has been unreasonable, but Malia can see him trying to sort out his place in the family. He coped with one sibling, but two makes things difficult.

'Mum's tired, Aaron,' is a phrase he hears more than he should. The first year of school is an important one and Aaron wants to share everything with her, but the response is usually: 'Mum's tired, Aaron, can we read tomorrow? Mum's tired, Aaron, can you finish your spelling without me?'

It's only his first term but most afternoons he stands in the kitchen, holding his school diary, waiting patiently for Zach to go down for a nap or for Rhiannon to finish her tantrum, or for Malia to finish dinner preparation, or for her to finish her phone call to her mother, whom she speaks to nearly every day, keeping her up to date on her grandchildren who, according to her mother, 'live on the other end of the earth'.

'Just give me one more minute, Aaron,' she whispers while she listens to her mother detail what her cousins are doing or yells at him as she tries to get Rhiannon to eat her dinner.

'But you have to sign my diary, Mum. Mrs Epstein says you have to sign every day that we did my homework or I don't get my star sticker.'

Every night Malia goes to bed and vows to do better the next day, to become more organised and efficient in the afternoons so she can give him her full attention, but something always gets in the way, like Zach refusing to go down for his afternoon sleep or Rhiannon having a toilet-training accident. Getting milk for Aaron's Coco Pops won't make up for the fact that last night she had fallen asleep while listening to him sound out the simple words in his new reader, but it would have to do for now.

In the car she edges into the traffic and wants to squeal with joy when she catches a rare gap. Once she arrives at the 7-Eleven, she finds parking close to the store, mere steps away from the entrance.

'Okay, I'm going inside to get the milk,' she says.

'I wanna come,' says Rhiannon.

'No, you stay here with Aaron and Zach.'

'I wanna come, I wanna come,' says Rhiannon, her voice climbing.

'Shush, you'll wake the baby,' says Malia in a fierce whisper.

This morning is never going to end. She looks over at the entrance to the store. If she takes Rhiannon she knows that Aaron will have to come too because how can his little sister be allowed this treat without him. She knows if she picks up Zach a second time she will surely wake him, and she can't let that happen.

'Okay, both of you climb out quietly and stand next to the car.'

The children do as they are told and Malia also climbs out and then nudges the doors closed. *I'm ten feet away,* she reasons. *There are people everywhere. He'll be fine.*

She puts out her hands for Aaron and Rhiannon to take and then she stops. She shouldn't leave Zach in the car. It's a stupid thing to do. 'Wait …' she says, but before she can finish the command Rhiannon darts away from the car towards the store as another car pulls into the petrol station and seems to head straight for her.

'Stop!' shouts Malia and she moves away from the car, covering the distance to Rhiannon in seconds. She picks her daughter up and holds her tightly as the car stops in front of an open pump, nowhere near where Rhiannon was. 'We do not run away from Mummy, Rhiannon.'

''Kay, Mum, 'kay,' says Rhiannon and she kicks to be put down. Malia turns, relieved to find Aaron at her side. The doors to the store slide open and icy air washes over them, inviting them inside.

Inside Malia realises that she has left Zach in the car after all. 'Shit, shit, shit,' she says to herself. She looks down at her keys in her hand and tries to remember if she locked the door or not. She thinks about pushing the button but worries that the noise might wake Zach. She can remember berating her sister Cassie, who is older by four years, for being obsessed with not disturbing her first child's sleep.

'It's like it's the only thing you can think about,' she had said when Cassie yelled at her for calling during Sophia's nap time.

'Wait, Malia,' said Cassie. 'One day you'll have a baby and then you'll understand.'

'And one day you'll understand that we never see each other anymore because you have a baby and I work. You're my sister and we need to speak to each other,' Malia had replied and then she had hung up the phone, furious with her sister.

Cassie had called her the next day with a question about something she was cooking, and just as it had always been with her sister, the argument was over before it began. Only weeks after Aaron was born she had apologised to Cassie because she had finally understood about not disturbing a sleeping baby.

I won't be more than a minute.

She quickly finds the milk, glancing at her car over and over again as they wait in the check-out queue. Aaron is beside her, but as she gets closer to the counter Malia notices that Rhiannon has moved away.

'Ri Ri!' she calls. 'Time to go.'

It's a small store and she can hear Rhiannon singing to herself a few aisles away.

'Rhiannon, come now.'

''Kay,' says Rhiannon, and then Malia hears the distinctive sound of something breaking.

'I'll go see,' says Aaron.

'No, you stay here and give the man the money for the milk.'

Malia shrugs at the shop attendant behind the counter, but he doesn't meet her eyes. She had seen his mouth move with the word *Fuck* as the sound of glass shattering reverberated around the store. He knows he has something to clean up and Malia understands his irritation.

'Welcome to my life,' she would like to say, but is afraid that the words will come out sounding bitter.

She goes to the back of the store where Rhiannon has knocked over some jars of baby food, breaking one.

'Janelle, get out here!' she hears the man yell as he continues serving other customers.

'What are you doing, naughty girl!' Malia exclaims.

'For Zach,' Rhiannon says, pointing at the picture of a baby on the jar's label.

'Rhiannon, you know you are not to touch anything in the store.'

Malia picks up the unbroken jars of baby food and searches in her bag for something to clean up the mess when another store attendant appears next to her. 'Just leave it,' snaps the young woman, who has a mop in one hand and her phone in the other. Malia can't help noticing long, perfectly painted purple fingernails.

'I'm so sorry … I'm just … I'm sorry she didn't mean it. I can pay …'

The woman waves her hand at Malia, as if flicking away an irritation.

Malia stands up and again thinks about Ian at the car yard, sees that cup of coffee upended on his head. She takes a deep breath.

'I got the milk, Mum,' says Aaron, who has come to stand next to her.

'Right, let's go,' says Malia and she thinks about apologising to the attendant again but decides against it. The girl looks about eighteen and her eyes are fixed on her phone. Tap, tap, tap go the perfect purple nails.

It takes another few minutes to get everyone in the car and buckled up because Rhiannon insists on doing it herself. Malia rests her head on the steering wheel while she waits, grateful that Zach is obviously still asleep, thinking that she herself could fall asleep right there and sleep for hours. In the back seat she hears Aaron sigh and then the magical click that means Rhiannon is safely strapped in.

Finally they are in the queue to get back out onto the main road.

Coffee, here I come.

'Mum …'

'Not now, Aaron, I'm trying to concentrate.'

The traffic has built up in only a few minutes and cars scream past the service station. Malia feels her headache settle in.

This day is never going to end.

'But Mum …'

'What Aaron, what?'

'Where is baby Zach, Mum? Where is he?'

Chapter Two

'You see,' I whisper to myself as I walk away from the service station. 'Anyone can make a mistake. Anyone can slip up or drop the ball. Anyone.'

No one hears me speak. No one gives me a second glance. There is nothing to see here, nothing of interest.

I feel a surge of happiness at my invisibility on this busy street. I like being anyone and no one. I like being able to simply walk away from a place. The first thing I did when I was released was go for a long walk. I feel as though I will never get over the simple joy that comes from being able to walk and just keep walking. For the first few days I kept waiting to reach a fence or to have someone stop me. It's been two weeks now but I don't know if I will ever get used to being able to do what I want to do. I used to dream of travelling the world, of visiting every country on the planet. I was so jealous of the journalists at the magazine where I used to work because they had the privilege of flying to different destinations every week, but now I know that what I need from life is so much less than that. I just need to be able to walk.

This is not the nicest place to take a walk. I don't like being on a main road but now I'm glad I was here.

I don't think I'm going to enjoy my new home but I didn't have much choice. People with criminal records rarely do. I figured that a room in a house was a room in a house and there was no reason to suppose one landlord offering someone on parole a room would be any different to another landlord offering the same thing. At least where my room is now, I have access to the city and a job, although I don't think I need to look for a job right now.

I don't like to think about having a criminal record. It's not who I am.

I would have liked to have been farther away from the city, somewhere peaceful with more trees and less traffic, but I will find a way to move soon I'm sure. I am going to rebuild my life. I am going to begin again and I will be the person I was meant to be.

A man running to catch the bus speeds past me and clips my shoulder. 'Sorry, love,' he calls. I smile and nod to indicate I understand.

That *sorry* erases his mistake. I can't be angry with

him. He didn't mean it. He is late and stressed and he was running too fast to go around me.

But sorry doesn't always work.

I said sorry once. I said it over and over again but my sorry wasn't enough.

My mistake was too big.

Words couldn't erase it. Remorse couldn't make it better. All the tears in the world couldn't repair it. Nothing could change what had happened. Nothing.

Anyone can make a mistake and everyone does. People make mistakes all day long. Big ones and little ones. They cross against the lights because they aren't looking, or they reverse their cars into other cars because they're distracted. They forget to pay the telephone bill, or lose their wallets, or drop their glasses and step on them. They say things they don't mean to say and do things they don't mean to do and people get hurt every day.

Everyone makes mistakes, but not everyone gets punished for them.

I got punished.

One mistake and I will be punished for the rest of my life. One small slip and nothing will ever be the same again. I got punished. I got punished with police and nasty news articles and hate spat at me wherever I went.

'Isn't she that woman who...?' I thought I heard someone whisper when I was in the supermarket yesterday.

'Yes, yes, it was me!' I wanted to scream at all of them. 'It was me! Stare all you fucking like!'

I got a trial and a prison sentence.

But the world is filled with people who can get away with anything. There are rapists and murderers, child killers and criminals everywhere. There are people who beat their wives and kids and abuse drugs and alcohol and hurt everyone around them and they get away with it.

It's not about Karma or God; it's just random and mostly awful. Self-help books tell readers that their negative thoughts affect their lives, bringing bad luck and unhappiness, but I never thought that what happened to me could *ever* happen, and I certainly never believed that I would land in prison for it. I sent no negative thoughts out into the universe, only positive happy ones about how I wanted my life to be.

One mistake and the universe turned on me.

Why me?

That question has driven me insane for years. For five long years.

I'm sure this unpredictability is what drives humanity mad. How does a person know what they will be able to get away with? Terrorists blow themselves up thinking they're going to be rewarded in heaven. Fathers rape their daughters and, if they don't get caught, go on to rape their granddaughters. Men with millions steal from people with nothing and die in their nineties surrounded by their loved ones.

There was a woman who worked as the financial controller at the same magazine I did, and she was well known for refusing to have even a single sip of alcohol if she knew she had to drive. We went to lunch in the same group most days. People use to laugh at her. 'One glass won't hurt, surely?'

'I can't take the chance,' she would say. 'I know if I have one I'll want another and that's not a mistake I can afford to make.'

But one day, one very bad day, she gave in. She was tired and heartbroken over some man, and she went to a bar for lunch with friends—real friends, who should have taken care of her, not work friends—and she gave in to their entreaties to cheer herself up with some wine. One glass wasn't enough so she had two glasses, or maybe three, and then she went to fetch her child from school.

'Just over the limit,' said the policeman who stopped her. 'But you have a child in the car with you so it's very serious.'

'Please,' she begged, 'I'm sorry, it's been a bad day. I never do this. I will die of humiliation. My ex-husband will sue for custody. I'm always so careful, please, I'm sorry.'

Sorry doesn't always work.

She told me the policeman shrugged at her. Her problems were not his problems. Her life spiralled into chaos for months after that. At work all she talked about was her lawyer and the family court and her ex-husband suing her for custody. Her work suffered and people whispered about her at meetings and eventually they fired her. What had she done to deserve that? She made one little mistake, one silly mistake, and everything changed. She apologised to the policeman. He could have let her off but *sorry* doesn't always work.

Karma doesn't always get it right. It certainly didn't get it right with me. All I wanted to do was love and be loved. That doesn't seem like too much to ask of the universe.

I walk fast now. I am a long way from the petrol station already. She is probably regretting her mistake by now, regretting her slip-up.

It's not such a terrible thing that she's done—not at all. Millions of women all over the world have done the same thing … millions. I can imagine her thinking, 'I'll only be a few minutes. Nothing can happen in a few minutes.' Mothers think that all the time and get away with it.

I didn't get away with it.

The universe decided that I needed to be punished and now I've decided that she needs to be punished for being so careless, for not thinking about the possible consequences, for letting her guard down. Why shouldn't I get to decide that? Who decided it for me?

I was only at the 7-Eleven to buy a bottle of water but then I saw him all alone in that car, and he was so peaceful and so beautiful that I felt my arms reach for him. It was the Winnie the Pooh sunshade that drew me over to the car. I used to have one just like it. The door wasn't quite closed and without thinking I pulled on the handle. My hands moved automatically and there he was. All alone.

I was supposed to be looking for a job, but just like that I have one and it's the only worthwhile job in the whole world. I wanted to hold him. I needed to hold him, to feel his soft skin next to mine. When I opened the door I could smell his milky baby smell and I felt my knees buckle. There is no smell on earth more beautiful than that of a baby. I remember that smell. I thought I would never experience it again but there he was. The universe finally did something right. He looks like a lovely child. He looks like a second chance.

She shouldn't have just walked away from him. A good mother doesn't do that. She is obviously an awful mother. They said I was a bad mother but they were wrong. I can show the world the truth now. I can show everyone that I can be a good mother. Once I have him in my arms I know he belongs there. He fills up that space—that empty, awful space. 'It will be better if you come with me,' I whispered to him.

She almost got away with it. If I had left my room one minute later I would have missed her. The universe must be laughing about that.

I could see her watching the car as I walked up to the store, but then she turned away and I looked at the car she had been watching. And then I stepped in to show her the error of that decision.

I stepped in to punish her but I know I've also rewarded myself. I've balanced it out. I've made it right.

Maybe I'm Karma.

Chapter Three

'Ali, have you seen Mike?'

Oscar steps into the shared office and looks pointedly at the empty desk.

'What do you need him for, Ossie?' says Ali with a smile.

'Just a case.'

'I think he just went to interview that kid who turned up a couple of nights ago in the middle of a drug deal the Feds had under surveillance. He got dragged in with all the other perps. Mike's helping out the guys in vice—trying to get a different perspective.'

'Oh yeah, right, I thought he was done with that yesterday. Fuck.'

'In case you were interested, Ossie, I am also a fully fledged detective sergeant and I am sitting here twiddling my thumbs,' says Ali, lifting her hands to show him she is doing just that.

Oscar laughs. From the picture he keeps in his office, Ali knows that Oscar still looks like the boy he was when he started in the police force twenty-five years ago, with the same red hair, freckles and ears that stick out. He's also the best duty officer Ali has ever worked with, both as a new recruit and now as a detective.

'This one's not for you, love,' he says now, in a voice that would normally deter her from discussing the matter further, but the tedium is almost suffocating her. Before Oscar had walked into the office she had been contemplating putting her head down on the desk and taking an early morning nap just to pass the time.

'Oscar, I've been back from maternity leave for weeks. I'm as fit as I was before I got pregnant and Charlie is sleeping through the night now so I'm well rested. Why won't you give me a case? I'm not enjoying all this paperwork.'

'This one is not for you, Ali—trust me on this.'

'Why don't you tell me what it is and trust *me*?'

Oscar looks at her for a moment and then he scratches his head. 'I would be happier to wait for Mike. Everyone else is knee-deep in something. He'll be back soon, I'm sure.'

'Yeah, and he's going to need help on a new case.'

'It concerns a baby, Ali—a missing baby,' Ossie says. 'Okay?'

Ali opens her mouth to say something but for a moment her brain is incapable of putting a sentence together.

'It had to happen sooner or later,' she finally says to Oscar, in a deliberately accepting tone. 'I mean, I do work in the missing person's unit.'

'This is a very young baby, Ali. I think you can let this one go and Mike can handle it on his own.'

'I'll take it,' says Ali quickly. 'If it gets too much I'll let you know. It's not like I can avoid cases like this forever.'

'But a missing baby …'

'… may end up being a deceased baby,' says Ali, finishing the thought for him. 'I know the drill with missing kids, Oscar. I've worked in this department for a few years already. I understand that.'

Oscar may have been the first person to visit her in the hospital after Charlie was born but he's still her duty officer. The lines between the job and home blur for everyone in this unit, but now she wants them back again, bold and distinctive. She's a cop and a member of the team, just like everyone else. Being a mother doesn't render her incapable of professional distance.

'Okay … But Ali—'

'I know, I know. If it gets to be too much, I'll tell you. I promise I will. Give me the file and point me in the right direction.'

'Okay,' says Oscar, handing her the file. 'The mother is still at the service station where it happened, being interviewed by Constable Ahmed. It happened around fifteen minutes ago.'

Ali knows that timing is crucial in missing children cases, even more so when it's a baby. If a child is not located in the first twenty-four hours the trail grows more difficult to follow, details are forgotten and the parents begin to crumble under the strain. If one or both parents are responsible for the child's disappearance, they usually get a story together and are harder to trip up on the details after the first day. Either way, the quicker everyone is interviewed in a missing child case, the better.

Ali stands up and grabs her bag. 'Where am I heading?'

'Fairmont, the 7-Eleven on the corner. The mother went in to get some milk and left the baby in the car—or so she says. I need you to make an assessment as quickly as possible so we can issue a child abduction alert if the mother's story checks out.'

'If it checks out? We don't believe her?'

'We don't believe anyone when it comes to kids,' says Oscar and Ali nods. Without even thinking too much, she can summon up three or four cases from years ago, when she was starting out in the missing persons unit. She had found herself supporting mothers weeping for their lost children and feeling her heart break for them, only to discover that the tears were manufactured for the police and the media and that the only emotions were those of panic and guilt and fear of being caught.

Her skills are sharpened from all the weeks she has

spent looking for children who were already dead; she knows what to look for in body language and tone of voice, in reactions to toys owned by the child. She knows to listen for an inadvertent use of the past tense, to watch for a cigarette smoked with relief.

She's pretty sure she wouldn't be easily fooled by a lying parent ever again. *Don't get too cocky*, she reminds herself now. Every case is different.

'I'm on my way,' Ali tells Oscar, silently praying that this case will not end with a funeral. 'I'll text Mike to meet me there. I just need to visit the loo first.'

In the bathroom Ali stares at her reflection in the mirror. Her red hair has been falling out since she had Charlie thirteen months ago and it is now thin and bedraggled. There is very little she can do with it except stick it in a ponytail.

'Perfectly normal,' explained Dr Singh. 'Pregnancy gives you great hair, and then breastfeeding and everything else that comes with kids makes it fall out. And ...'

'And?' Ali had said, staring at her doctor, waiting for her to say the words.

'And,' said Dr Singh, 'you've had a lot of stress over the past four years and, even though Charlie is great and healthy, I know that you're going to be wound up for a long time.'

'Do you blame me?'

'No.' Dr Singh arched one of her manicured eyebrows. 'But I'm going to tell you again that you need to find something that will help.' She put up her hands just as Ali opened her mouth to protest. 'Not medication, I know you don't want that, but I think you quit therapy too soon. You need an outlet, Ali, somewhere to go or someone to talk to, especially because you're back at work now. Your job is not exactly a calming occupation.'

'Reuben, my husband, thinks I should try yoga.'

'That may not be a bad idea. In the meantime, get as much rest as you can, take a multivitamin, look after yourself. Think about going back to therapy.'

Ali had nodded like she was listening, but she was worrying about Charlie. He had a tooth coming and had been off his food. She had already taken him to his paediatrician that day and she had said he was fine, but Ali knew that you could never be sure. How could anyone ever be sure?

Her phone beeps and she looks down to see a message from Kady, one of the young women at Charlie's day care.

Charlie loves painting and the colour blue. He's having a good morning ☺

Below the message is a picture of Charlie, grinning, with a paintbrush in his hand. He looks like he has more paint on his body than on the paper pinned to the easel behind him. Just for a moment she is overwhelmed with the need to touch his dark curls and kiss his sweet-smelling neck over and over, making him laugh. She settles for stroking the picture on her phone instead. She forwards the text to Reuben, who responds with a thumbs-up emoji.

She smiles, feeling immediately lighter. Charlie has been

at day care for a month now and Sarah, the owner, has made sure that all the carers know that Ali needs to be updated every hour. It was the only way Ali had managed to go back to work. She had intended to stay home for years, but Reuben put a stop to that.

'You're driving yourself mad, Ali. You're thinking too much, reading too much, projecting too much. I can't take another call at work about how the baby looks funny, or his breathing is off. He's fine, and I think you're bored. You were never meant to stay home for this long—go back to work.'

'How can I do that? How could I ever leave him in the care of someone else if even I …?' Ali had not finished the sentence.

Reuben shook his head. 'Ali, you're going to turn into someone you don't recognise. You are not this kind of person and you can't let what happened change who you are. You work for the police, dealing with risk every day, but you've become someone who jumps every time the baby sneezes.'

'Of course it changed me. It changed you, too.'

'I know,' Reuben had sighed, 'but that's not what I meant. Of course it changed us, but I don't want it to cast a shadow over the rest of our lives. I don't want us to turn into over-protective neurotic parents who won't let their child out of their sight. I know you think you're doing the best for him, but what happens when he's five and goes to school, and then ten and wants to play soccer, and seventeen and wants to go out at night?'

'Maybe I'll be ready by then.'

'Maybe you'll be crazy by then,' Reuben had said, but he had smiled as he said it.

'Where would we even send him, Reuben? How can there be a day care good enough?'

'Okay, I haven't said anything because I know that you wanted to stay home until … I don't know … until Charlie can drive himself to school, but I have heard about somewhere he can go. Mum told me about it a few weeks ago. Before you say no—just hear me out.'

Sarah's day care was different to any other facility Ali had seen. For a start, they only took children up to three years old and their staff-to-child ratio was one to three. Their fees were very high, but Sarah ran her day care for parents who worried, parents who obsessed, and mostly parents who knew just how fragile a baby could be.

At the first meeting, Sarah had settled her bulk into an armchair and leaned forward, letting her glasses slip to the tip of her nose.

'So tell me,' she said, 'about you.'

Reuben had opened his mouth to say something, but Sarah had simply raised her hand. 'Tell me, Ali,' she had said again. 'Tell me about you.'

Ali had assumed that she was all talked out, that she would never want to tell the story again and that she had nothing left to say, but the words came rushing out. Maybe it was the way Sarah looked at her, or maybe she needed to tell the story to someone new, but her normal hesitancy with strangers disappeared and the words tripped off her tongue, surprising her once again at how much pain they caused even now.

'Of course you're a neurotic mother,' Sarah said when Ali had finished. 'How could you be anything else, but here we specialise in neurotic mothers. We have a full-time nurse and I promise you your child will be watched all the time. Charlie will have many eyes on him.'

'He's not sick,' said Ali, 'but ...'

'But neither was his sister, Abigail,' says Reuben.

'And now you can't let go of the worry,' said Sarah kindly. 'I understand. Think of this as an introduction to day care. We do it your way until you tell us to change things. If you want to be updated every hour you will be. If you tell us to do it twice a day then that's what we'll do. Some of the babies here need a lot of care, but Charlie will be watched the same way, and I promise that eventually you will be able to let go, just a little and then a lot.'

The first day she left Charlie in Sarah's care, Ali had held onto her phone all day, only daring to relax for a few minutes every time an update came through. More recently, she found herself surprised that another hour had passed. It was getting easier.

Coming back to work had been the next big step. She had sweated through the first day, checked her phone incessantly and written lists on why she should never have returned.

She had arrived late and left early and managed to do nothing other than rearrange her desk, but Oscar and Mike were happy for her to take her time. No one gave her anything to do, and every time someone walked past her office they looked in and asked, 'Going okay?' Ali had pasted a smile on her face and nodded. She'd eaten the muffin Mike got for her and drunk the coffee Oscar brought in and shared lunch with Peta, who spent her days befriending paedophiles on the internet so she could lure them into being arrested, and loved to talk about anything but her work. The next morning Ali had forced herself to get up and do it all again.

It was getting better with each passing day, helped by the continuous updates from the day care that showed Charlie enjoying every minute. She could feel herself relaxing and she had to keep reminding herself that she was doing what was best for him and for her. She was doing the right thing for her family.

What had happened was in the past. Charlie was getting bigger and stronger every day, losing his chubby baby cheeks and turning into a little boy. Now when she thought about her son she imagined him starting school and playing soccer and becoming an adult. When he was first born Ali hadn't been able to see past those first few terrifying months when she knew the worst was possible. She's been back at work for nearly a month and really ready for a proper case for a couple of weeks now. She had thought she would prefer something else, like an old person disappearing from an aged-care facility, but for some strange reason she feels like this is the case she was meant to start with.

*

Ali uses the time at traffic lights to glance at the file. The missing baby is a boy named Zach and he's five months old. Ali feels her stomach turn over. At five months a baby is still so small, still just learning how to be in the world, still so vulnerable, so defenceless. How must the mother be feeling? What anguish must she be suffering?

'Let him be found quickly, let the news be good,' Ali says aloud.

The mother's name is Malia, which sounds Arabic or Greek, but the children are Aaron and Rhiannon and Zach, which sound more Anglo. Maybe the father, Ian, had more influence with their names?

As she pulls into the 7-Eleven Ali sees that it has been cordoned off. There are three police cars blocking access from the road into the service station. The forecourt of the 7-Eleven is a chaotic parking lot. All the cars that must have been at the servo when the mother of the child noticed her baby was missing are still here, and all the occupants of those cars are being interviewed. There are at least twelve uniformed police, which means six police cars as well. Ali can see the people being interviewed speaking and gesturing as though explaining where they were when the alarm was raised.

Despite the number of people she spots the mother instantly, slumped on the step outside the store's entrance. Two children are huddled next to her, licking ice-creams. The mother is holding a cup of something, probably coffee, but she's not drinking it. She's staring out at the cars on the road. Even from metres away Ali can see she's been crying. Her gaze is blank, unfocused.

Here we go. Ali parks the car after one of the officers directs her towards a free space.

When she gets out she takes a deep breath and pulls her ID from her pocket. *You see, I'm holding it together. I am.*

She walks towards the mother, picking up snippets from the interviews being conducted as she does.

'And then she just started screaming, "Zach, Zach!",' says a woman, clutching the hand of a child nearly as tall as she is who keeps squirming to get away.

'I knew I had to call the police. You know, I mean, it's a baby,' says a man in a suit, using his mobile phone to gesture and point.

'Mrs Ellis,' Ali says as she reaches Malia Ellis.

'Yes.' The woman stands up, and Ali immediately notices the two wet spots on her T-shirt. She feels a small ache in her own breasts. She has only just weaned Charlie and sometimes she still feels like there is milk coming in.

'I'm Detective Sergeant Greenberg, I'm here to help,' Ali says.

'He needs to be fed,' says Malia Ellis. 'Who's going to feed him?'

The woman bursts into tears and Ali feels herself choke up as well. She takes a deep breath, 'I'm going to find him, Mrs Ellis,' she says. 'I'm going to find him.'

Chapter Four

Edna is irritated to be awake so early. Nine in the morning is early enough to get up but it's nowhere near nine and now she is awake and needs to use the facilities. Someone has been banging pots or pans or something in the kitchen downstairs so here she is, awake and annoyed already and on such a sunny day. She moves her toes up and down, getting her circulation going so she can get out of bed, while contemplating all the things that currently upset her. It's mostly to do with the new tenants in the house.

She believes that it's all very well behaving in a Christian manner, but she can't help feeling that not everyone deserves a second chance. She prefers the Old Testament way of thinking. An eye for an eye may seem somewhat violent, of course, but she's willing to bet few people got the chance to commit a crime a second time in those days. If she was in charge of things ... Well, she's not, but if she were things would be very different indeed.

Edna has never been very good at turning the other cheek. In her opinion, all that meant was you got the other cheek slapped as well. All this New Testament, love your neighbour nonsense was why she had to worry about things now.

When Mary, who had been a lovely friend as well as Edna's landlady, was running the boarding house, she had a strict policy about riffraff, but young Robbie seems to feel it's his duty to help every Tom, Dick and Harry.

Edna knows that Mary would be turning in her grave if she knew the kind of people her son was allowing to live in the grand old house. Edna remembers falling in love with this house the first time she saw it. Its beautiful arched windows and tiled roof spoke of a different time in history, when the suburb was filled with large gracious houses with sprawling gardens.

It hadn't been her intention to leave her little flat but suddenly the rent was more than she could afford on her pension, and her legs made it impossible for her to keep the part-time job at the button store—too much climbing up ladders to get to boxes stacked on high shelves. She could have waited for a place where the rent was subsidised by the government of course, but those places were far away from everything she's ever known. It frightened her to think of moving to a new suburb and having to find a new doctor to take care of her. She likes living so close to the city as well. Her own flat had once been part of a lovely old house just like this one so Edna had known she would feel right at home. Of course when Mary was in charge the home was freshly painted every two years and the carpets were always cleaned once a year and she maintained the garden. Robbie seemed more interested in getting new tenants in, even dividing up one of the larger rooms into two and making William and Nate share something too small for two people. He'd let things go in the two years since Mary died, and now the wallpaper was peeling and the paint blistering everywhere. Edna still wouldn't want to live anywhere else but she certainly didn't need to live with the kind of people Robbie was bringing in.

'We must help out our fellow man, Edna,' Robbie had said when she told him it wasn't a good idea to let criminals live in the house.

'And they're not criminals, Edna, they've served their time. The government has deemed them fit to go back into society and so should you,' he said.

'Well, I wouldn't want to interfere,' Edna had said and left it at that, but she was sure she heard him whisper *silly old bat* as she made her way to the stairs at the back of the house. That didn't sound very Christian to her. That was the problem with religious types—they thought they could pick and choose those to save, but it really isn't the case.

Edna had felt truly frightened when the first criminal had arrived. Robbie hadn't exactly sent round a letter to the other residents saying that the man was a criminal, but he had arrived right after the meeting where Robbie had told them he would be allowing *certain types* of people into the house. Only Edna had protested at that meeting. Solomon was dozing in his chair and William and Nate had shared a bottle of whiskey between them and couldn't be trusted to make sense. Albert, of course, agreed with Robbie. He worked at the St Vincent's charity shop and believed everyone deserved a second, third and fourth chance. Albert followed the New Testament.

You didn't have to be a rocket scientist to realise that the new resident had been in prison. He has shifty eyes and he's covered in tattoos—and not nice ones, either. Edna doesn't mind the odd tattoo. Paulo, the bartender at the local pub, has lots of tattoos, but his are nice. He has a rose and the words *Mum* and *Samoa* and a picture of his daughter on his arms, but this new resident has snakes and lions and a wolf with open jaws and pointed fangs. It's enough to give Edna nightmares.

Robbie introduced them one morning when they passed in the hallway. Edna was glad that the man was staying on the ground floor—well away from her. She would have hated to have to pass him on the way to the bathroom. The man's name is Luis and Edna knew immediately that she wouldn't like him, although so far he's been perfectly polite and always smiles when they see each other. And she has to admit, he does always open the door for her when she sees him as she's leaving the house ... But still, he used to be in prison.

Edna likes to keep to herself so she tries to time her cooking around the hours when other residents are out, although she does sometimes go into the kitchen in the hope of finding Solomon for a cup of tea and a chat. She and Solomon are the oldest residents in the boarding house and she knows he is going to have to move to an aged-care facility soon. He's forgetting things. Nothing big, but things like whether or not he's eaten dinner and what day it is, and there was that one morning he came out of his room without pants.

It makes Edna want to cry, it really does. 'The only alternative to old age is death,' Edna's father used to say. Edna tries not to think about what will happen to her when she gets to Solomon's age five years from now. Chances are she won't even make it that long, although she does come from a family with strong constitutions. Her mother lived until she was eighty-five and her father died at eighty-seven. Edna had been a late and only child for her parents so she was quite young when they died. It was hard for them to be older parents but at least they'd had the chance. Not everyone got the chance as Edna well knew.

Robbie would prefer all the old residents to leave. She knows he's just waiting to ship her off to a home where she will be surrounded by other people all the time and told what to do and when to eat. It's a horrifying thought. Edna made sure that her mother never had to spend even one minute in one of those places. She came to live with Edna and Harry after she'd buried her husband, who was five years her senior, and died in her own bed after her morning cup of tea, which was exactly the way Edna wants to go. Not having a daughter means that she can't be sure of that chance.

'Robbie can't force you to go anywhere,' Solomon said when Edna told him she was afraid of being forced out.

'He can raise the rent,' said Edna.

'He could but you could fight that.'

'I'm too old to fight anything, Solomon,' Edna had grumbled.

'He's getting money from the government for having the cons,' Solomon had said in one of his more lucid moments over tea and biscuits.

'I bet he is,' Edna had said, although she wasn't completely sure about that. Robbie was also a great follower of the New Testament.

Edna was used to being the only woman in the boarding house. Over the years other women had come and gone, but overnight everything had changed, and not for the better if you asked Edna.

'Getting a new resident in today, Edna,' Robbie had said a week ago.

'Oh yes?' said Edna. 'Another tattooed lout, I'll bet.'

'Luis is not a lout, Edna,' said Robbie. 'He's a man who's had a run of bad luck and now he's got a job and everything. He fixed the television last week so you didn't miss your program, didn't he?'

Edna hadn't replied, although privately she had ack-

54

nowledged that it was kind of Luis to make himself late for work so that he could get the television to work. Still, one swallow does not a summer make, her father used to say.

'Anyway,' said Robbie, 'the new resident is a woman. You'll like that, won't you?'

'Is she a criminal as well?'

'I can't say, Edna. I'm not allowed to.' He rubbed at his slightly greasy hair and gave Edna a little grin, pleased with his secrets.

'So that means she is. If you keep letting these people in we'll all end up being murdered in our beds. What would your mother say, Robbie?'

'My mother,' said Robbie, puffing out his chest and sucking in his stomach as though his mother were there telling him he was too fat, as she always did, 'would be very proud of me, Edna, and if you don't like it here you're free to go elsewhere. I'm sure you'd like to be in a place where you can get a bit of help with the cooking. Solomon's social worker is talking to him about a comfortable aged-care home right now. If you go along to the lounge room you can have a listen as well.'

'Don't you go shoving me out, young Robbie! I may be eighty, but I know my rights. I've never been late with the rent, not even by one day.'

'Relax, Edna. I only wanted to tell you that the new resident will be moving in next door to you. Her name's Jackie and I'm sure you'll get along famously.'

Robbie had walked away, leaving Edna to think about the kind of person she would be sharing her bathroom with. What kind of a woman got sent to prison? What could she have done?

Edna knew that it wouldn't be right to ask so she settled for hiding her valuables in case the woman was a thief. Once a thief, always a thief, her father used to say.

She always locks her door when she goes down the passage to the bathroom, but what if one day she forgets? The new resident might be a nice person who had made a small mistake, or she could be someone who liked to murder people in their beds and steal their valuables. If the new woman did happen to catch a glimpse inside her room, Edna didn't need her seeing her gold rings and the beautiful pearl brooch her father had given her on her eighteenth birthday.

She never has much cause to wear the brooch these days, but she does love looking at it. She runs her hands over the smooth pearls that always feel cool to touch even on the warmest summer day. It helps her conjure memories of Harry, who always said, 'You're fit to have tea with the queen when you've that brooch on, luv,' whenever she wore it.

She and Harry never really had the money for fripperies like jewellery and so, except for her wedding and engagement rings, the brooch has been her most precious possession. Occasionally Edna looks around the small room she has lived in for a decade and wonders how it was possible that a woman of eighty has collected so little in her lifetime, but she knew it did her no good to go down that path.

It had been easier to sell everything when she moved into the house at seventy. She had imagined that she would die in the little flat she and Harry had been renting all their married life, but suddenly the suburb was changing and the rent just kept going up. Harry had always had trouble keeping a job. He was a bit of a larrikin really. He liked a laugh and a drink and he never said a bad word about anyone, but he wasn't the most productive husband a woman could ask for. Her father hadn't liked him. He had called him a 'layabout', but he'd still given him a job helping in his furniture store. Harry was charming to all the customers and he always sold more than any other salesman, despite being late to arrive and early to leave most days. Her father was going to entrust the store to Harry—she knows he was—but before that could happen a huge department store opened up next door and overnight no one wanted to buy furniture from Queen Style Furniture anymore.

'Tastes change,' her father said the day he had to close the doors and admit he couldn't afford to go on. 'If I'd had someone in the business who really wanted to work we could have managed.'

'Harry made the most sales,' Edna had protested.

'It's easy to catch a fish once it's in the net,' her father said.

After that Harry had trouble holding onto anything for too long.

When he died he was only sixty and he hadn't worked for a while. He should have given up cigarettes and alcohol when he was younger. He knew his family had a history of heart problems. 'What's the point of living without the booze and fags, luv,' he said whenever she asked him to try and look after his health a bit more.

Edna had been keeping them both with full-time work at the button shop and a bit of cleaning on the side. She didn't mind working. It was good to get out of the house, away from the second bedroom with its single bed that would never be filled.

Sometimes she is angry at him for not leaving her with enough to get by without working, but then she remembers how much they used to laugh and how much fun they had, even on very little money, and she forgives him. Her parents had frowned on what they called 'silliness'. They were suspicious of people who laughed and joked too much.

It did hurt to have to sell her precious things so that she could move into the boarding house, but Edna mostly tries to think of what Harry had given her during his lifetime.

The big wooden bed with its carvings of flowers and fruit would never have fitted into her small room at the boarding house. She was lucky she had a single bed to bring with her, though on some days she saw it as a symbol of everything she didn't have and everything she had lost. The bed had occupied the empty second bedroom for years and Edna had changed the sheets every month, thinking that one day

58

it would be a splendid bed for a little boy or girl. Eventually she had turned the room into a sewing room and, though the bed made it seem cramped, she never wanted to get rid of it. She was glad she hadn't when it came time to move into the boarding house.

Her bed matches the wardrobe she had brought with her and, on her first night here, having familiar things around her had made the room seem less frightening, made the loss of Harry and then the flat where they had lived together seem less … less awful. Waking up that first morning had been hard.

Edna sits up and slips her feet onto the floor. She needs to get up now. It's quiet in the kitchen and, anyway, 'too much contemplation only makes you maudlin' as her father used to say. In any case, even though she's not happy about another criminal moving into the house, the new woman has turned out to be nothing like Edna was expecting. She's been in the house for a week now and Edna barely knows she's here at all. Jackie is a skinny slip of a thing with mousey brown hair and the habit of looking at the floor when she speaks. She is, as Edna's father would say, 'rather plain', having no features of any real interest. Her lips are thin and her eyes are small and her voice is too soft. Edna has to keep asking her to repeat herself if they run into each other in the hall and have to exchange a few words, but so far she's been all right. She spends her days out of the house—looking for work, presumably. Truth be told Edna is beginning to feel sorry for her. She looks so sad all the time. She would love to be able to ask her what she did to get sent to prison, but she knows it's best to stay out of it. 'Curiosity killed the cat,' her father used to say and Edna has always taken heed of that advice.

Chapter Five

9.30 am

Malia is certain that if she can pinch herself hard enough she will wake up from this nightmare. She came to the 7-Eleven for milk, and now her baby is missing and she is surrounded by police. The sun's heat increases minute by minute and assures her that she is, indeed, in hell.

'Go inside the store where it's cool,' Detective Greenberg had said, but Malia is convinced that she must remain outside, exposed to the elements, suffering just as Zach must be. She wants to sit here in case he is returned, in case the person who took him is watching her. It may be that they want to know she is suffering. Why else would they have taken her child? Who takes a child? Who steals a baby? Malia has been thinking about the people she knows, about the people in her neighbourhood, about the people where she works. Would any of them have taken her baby? Is there someone she knows who would kidnap a child? Her child? What if the person who took him wants to hurt him? He must be crying for her. Malia drops her head into her hands as she imagines her baby waking up in the arms of some stranger who doesn't look like her or smell like her.

'What do you mean *missing*?' said her mother when she called her. 'How can a baby be missing?'

It had taken Malia a full five minutes to explain what had happened.

'We will get on a plane right now!' her father had shouted in the background.

'When I first came to Australia,' her mother had once told her, when Malia was pregnant with Aaron, 'everyone left their babies outside in the garden. It's good for them to be in the fresh air.'

'Outside, without someone watching them?' Malia had asked.

'Of course, what could happen?'

What could happen? Malia thinks now as she recalls that conversation. She knows she lives in a different world to the one she grew up in. She doesn't live in a suburb populated by friends and family where everyone would be watching a child left outside. They know some of their neighbours but are only really friendly with Mrs Boulos.

There are predators on every corner according to the internet. And yet she had left her baby alone when such dangers exist. She is terrified for Zach and she is ashamed of herself for her stupidity.

'No, Mama, please tell Dad *no*. You don't need to come,' Malia had said as her father continued yelling in the background, now about finding his wallet. 'Just wait. They'll find him soon. I just wanted to tell you so that you heard it from me, in case it's … on the news.' She had swallowed hard, wondering at how it was possible that it would be on the news. Only tragedies are on the news, only tragedies. 'It's only been a few minutes, Mama, not even an hour.'

'Malia, we are coming. Don't tell me what to do. You need us now. Theo, call Cassie, tell her to come … tell her she must book the plane on the computer.'

Malia stifled a laugh, and then she was crying into the phone. Gut-wrenching sounds and tears that she had been holding back because she didn't want to frighten Aaron and Rhiannon. She was around a corner, away from the noise of the police and the eyes of everyone in the 7-Eleven. Now her children are being watched by every adult there, now after she has allowed one of them to be taken from her, now when it's too late. She has never seen so many police cars in one place. They keep coming in with sirens screaming. There are police examining the car and others interviewing the attendants in the store. The girl with the purple nails can be heard telling everyone that Rhiannon broke a jar of baby food. There are groups of police with sniffer dogs straining at their leashes so they can have a turn sniffing Zach's baby seat for his scent.

Listening to her parents yell about calling her sister, Malia had closed her eyes and tried to feel her father's arms around her, tried to feel his hands stroking her hair. 'Okay … okay,' she heard him saying in the background, 'it will be okay."

'We're coming,' her mother said. 'Right now. We will be there after lunch. There are planes all the time. It's nothing to find one. We are coming now.'

'Okay,' said Malia as she struggled to calm herself, knowing that there was no point in arguing with her mother. She wanted them here. She wanted to be able to turn to them and say, 'Make this right for me, fix it.'

Malia rocks where she sits and wraps her arms around herself. Only after she ended the call to her mother did she realise she hadn't called Ian. Her first instinct had been to call her mother, who she hoped would have some words of comfort. Ian never answered his phone during the day anyway, but she had called reception at the car yard and told them it was an emergency. When he was pulled out of his meeting to take the call she hadn't been able to explain to him what had happened at the service station. 'Just come here now,' she said.

Now she has a feeling that his presence will not be a comfort. Ian doesn't like to see her cry. He always says it's because he loves her so much, but Malia thinks it may be because her tears require him to do something, to say something that will change the situation and he knows he usually can't do that, especially because, these days, he is often the cause of these tears.

'Why Sydney, Malia?' her mother had asked when she and Ian told her parents that two years into their marriage they were moving away from Melbourne.

'Ian's been offered a job, Mama, a good job.' She didn't add, 'And the surfing is much better in Sydney, the beaches are better, and Ian is still harbouring thoughts of turning pro even though he's too old. And I want him to be happy because he's trying to be happy about the baby. He's really trying.'

And she wanted to get away. She wanted to be free of the daily visits from her mother bearing foods that would be good for the baby. She had moved to a different suburb and married an Australian man but she still felt trapped in her little Greek village. Sydney seemed to shine with the promise of a different life.

'So?' said her father. 'They don't need cars in Melbourne? The baby is coming. You need your mother and your sisters and your aunties and your cousins. You can't leave and be alone.'

'I won't be alone, Dad. I'll have Ian.' Those words came back to her over and over again as the years passed and she struggled through sleep-deprived nights with her children and anxious days worrying about money. She would fantasise about the way her life would have been if she had stayed where her family was instead of moving somewhere she didn't have a single friend. Her sister and cousins have, of course, all complained at one stage or another about the continual parade of relatives through the house, all of whom want to help with the baby.

'Mum just turns up and says to me, "Go and sleep now", regardless of whether I'm tired or not. And she brings Agatha with her, and the two of them look around my house and sneer, and then bloody clean everything I've just cleaned!' Cassie told Malia after her second child, a boy she named Nicholas, was born, only six months after Aaron was born.

'But it must be nice to have them,' said Malia.

'It is,' her sister said. 'I'm not saying it's not, and I know you could use them, but they're over every day. I'd like some time alone with my son.'

Malia clucked with sympathy over the phone, secretly wishing that she had the choice so she would not feel so alone.

'Mrs Ellis,' says the detective gently. 'I know you've gone over this a few times already with Constable Ahmed and Constable Evans, but I'm going to ask you to tell me again.'

Malia looks at the detective, whose red hair is tied neatly into a ponytail, and is conscious of the shabbiness of her own appearance. The detective is beautiful, with almond-shaped brown eyes and long lashes. She reminds Malia of an actress whose name she can't remember. Everything about her is perfect, from her make-up to her perfectly pressed blouse and fitted pants. She looks like a woman who fits in daily workouts and Malia wonders if she has children. She is wearing a diamond band on her left hand so Malia knows she is married.

She crosses her arms over her chest and begins again. She has told this story so many times the words are starting to lose their meaning. The constables have both made her keep repeating the same details, even though they have them written down.

'I didn't want him to wake up,' she begins. 'I was in the store for maybe five minutes, just five minutes.'

The detective nods.

'I kept watching the car. I looked at it every few seconds and the only reason I stopped looking was because Rhiannon broke something in the store, but that was only for a minute, one minute, sixty seconds, and then we were back in the car.'

'So you only took your eyes off the car for a minute?' asks the detective.

'Yes,' sighs Malia, 'one minute.'

'How do you know it was exactly a minute?'

'I … I don't know exactly,' says Malia, wondering how long it actually had been. Could it have been longer? It didn't feel like it was longer but now that she thinks about those moments, it wasn't as if she looked at her watch.

'So it could have been more than a minute?'

Malia looks at the detective and feels a flash of anger. 'It could have been a minute and a half,' she says stiffly.

'Mrs Ellis, I'm just trying to get the story straight. Bear with me, okay?' says the detective with a gentle smile. She reaches out and touches Malia's hand. Her hand is cool and dry and, in contrast, Malia feels like everything about her is damp. She is leaking milk and sweat and tears.

'So when you got back in the car, did you check on Zach?'

'No,' says Malia, shaking her head vigorously, feeling her stomach turn over. 'No, I didn't. I don't know why I didn't. I should have checked but I didn't think …'

'You didn't think?'

'I didn't think something like this was possible,' wails Malia, wiping her eyes and clenching her fists to try and control her tears. If she had checked it's possible she would have been quick enough to see someone walking away with Zach. If she had checked she would have called the police sooner. If she had checked she wouldn't have had to reverse the car back into the 7-Eleven and search through her car, screaming for her son while Aaron and Rhiannon dissolved into tears as they watched her become hysterical. If she had checked she could be at home right now.

'I should have checked,' she says.

The detective reaches out and touches her hand again. 'Okay, it's okay. Tell me what happened then.'

Malia explains how she looked through the car, how she darted up and down the street, how she ran from car to car in the 7-Eleven, banging on windows and asking people filling their cars with petrol to help. She is not sure who called the police but she felt overwhelmed with gratitude when a cruiser pulled into the station and the young policeman got out and came over and grabbed her shoulders to stop her frantic running back and forth and said, 'Calm down now and tell me what happened.'

She remembers thinking, 'If the police are here this will be sorted out in a few minutes. This will all be over soon and Ian is going to tell me how silly I am tonight at dinner. I should call Ian. Maybe I shouldn't call him yet. This will all be over soon. It will all be over soon. But it hadn't all been over soon and she had forgotten to call Ian, wanting only her mother.

'Okay, Mrs Ellis,' says the detective when Malia has finished speaking.

'Where could he be?' says Malia, knowing it's a ridiculous question but feeling the need to keep asking it in case the answer changes.

'I'm going to find him, Mrs Ellis. We have just about every single police car in the city looking for him. We've issued a child abduction alert, but you need to help me so we can find him. Is there anyone who may have wanted to take him?'

'Why would anyone want my baby?' Malia realises that she sounds stupid but she can't seem to think straight. This is not who I am, she wants to tell the detective whose flat stomach is emphasised by her grey trousers and tight black top.

It feels strange to be noticing what the detective looks like when all she should be concentrating on is Zach, but Malia finds herself aware of everything around her, as though she is a short-sighted person who has been given a pair of glasses. The ordinary petrol station has come sharply into focus because it is no longer just a petrol station. It is a place of danger and fear. The colours of the ice-creams on the signs outside the store are lurid pinks and greens, making them seem inedible. The concrete beneath her feet is not just grey but variations of grey and brown and black. She sees dark spots where petrol has spilled and stained, and a pump that hasn't been placed correctly back in the bowser.

Malia watches the police wipe their hands across their faces and tip their hats back, sees an angry red pimple on the side of the store attendant's cheek, which he picks at as he waits for instructions. The sky is a brittle, beautiful blue canvas with one lonely cloud that looks as though it has been pasted onto it. *And the detective*, Malia thinks, *looks like a movie star. Will she be able to find my baby?*

She pulls at her T-shirt. She still looks pregnant. After Aaron and Rhiannon were born her body snapped back into shape, but since Zach was born she has felt a continuous low-level exhaustion that refuses to go away.

'You're depressed,' Cassie told her the last time they spoke—only a week ago. 'Come home to Melbourne for a while. We'll take care of you so you can rest. Mum and Papa haven't seen your kids for ages.'

'I can't, Cassie. I have a job. I need to keep it.'

'You have a husband, Malia. *He* has a job. That should be enough.'

Her family had very clear ideas on the roles of men and women. Malia kept insisting that she was working to keep her mind occupied because she wouldn't cope with staying at home, but Cassie never believed her.

'You're too exhausted to occupy your mind,' she said whenever they talked about Malia's job, 'and it's not as if what you're doing is intellectually stimulating. You work in a shop, you serve people. You have a degree in marketing, but right now you need to be a stay-at-home mother—just until Zach is a bit older.'

'I don't need to be a stay-at-home mother, Cass. I need to get a good night's sleep every now and again. If Zach sleeps for a few hours, Aaron wakes up with a nightmare, or Rhiannon calls me for some water. Sometimes I think they're tag-teaming me. It's like they're trying to drive me nuts.'

'Listen May-May,' said Cassie, using the childhood nickname, which Malia knew meant she was in for a lecture. 'Your kids are not the problem. They're just being kids. If you felt you had other adults to support you, or even one other adult, you would be fine.'

'Ian's a good father, Cassandra,' Malia had said, sensing the words were hollow in her mouth but needing to say them anyway.

'Whatever you say, but I know you're not coping. You can talk to me about this. I'm here to listen. You don't have to pretend everything is fine.'

Malia had changed the subject then. She has never told anyone in the family about Ian's pokies habit, and she was afraid that if she kept talking about how she felt the whole story would come pouring out, shocking her sister and setting off a chain of events that her marriage would never recover from—beginning with her parents turning up on her doorstep to lecture Ian on his duties as a husband and father and demanding that he explain himself.

When they first moved to Sydney Malia had imagined that she would enjoy being separated from her parents, but she misses them terribly. When they came to visit, Ian spent more time in the pub than ever, claiming he was working. The house was small and Ian found his parents-in-law too much. Malia's father had a way of questioning Ian about his job that made him uncomfortable.

'So every car you sell you earn how much?' he would ask, making Ian blush.

'I'd prefer not to discuss it, Theo.'

'Why, Ian, you are ashamed?'

'Leave him, Daddy,' Malia would say, and that was usually Ian's cue to leave the house for a 'business meeting'.

'It's like your parents have no filter, they just say whatever they think,' he complained to Malia.

'It's not that they have no filter, Ian. They just believe that if you're part of the family you are happy to be open about everything in your life. Cassie's husband, Andreas, gets the same treatment. In fact whenever he sells one of the flats he's developed he calls my dad to tell him how much money he made. Papa likes to know his daughters are being taken care of.

'Yeah, well, it's rude to ask. My parents would never question me like that.'

Malia saw no point in replying to that comment. Ian's parents were an anathema to her and to her parents. They lived in Melbourne but were divorced, and while Ian's mother, Heather, would sometimes come up for a few days at Christmas, his father barely ever saw his grandchildren. When she and Ian were first married Malia called her mother-in-law daily—as her mother had told her to do—until she realised that Heather was uncomfortable with too much contact.

In addition to being grilled about his job, Ian disliked the way Malia's mother had something cooking on the stove all day long so that when she left the family had weeks of meals in the freezer.

'We're quite capable of bloody cooking for ourselves,' he grumbled.

'You mean I'm quite capable,' Malia said. 'I haven't noticed you volunteering to make dinner.'

'I don't know how to cook.'

'You could learn. I wouldn't mind if you managed some basic things.'

'Come on, babe, one of the things I love about having a Greek wife is the fantastic food.'

'Maybe I'm tired of having to cook something fantastic every night.'

'You know every time your parents come to visit, Malia, you …'

'I what?'

'Nothing, nothing. I really hate fighting with you. I know you're tired and I'm stressed at work right now. You know how it is. I love your parents and I'll enjoy everything your mother's made.'

Since Zach was born Malia has compensated for her exhaustion by eating at work all day long, where there is never a shortage of baked goods: Sean is continually trying out something new.

'What do you think about peanut butter and caramel brownies, Malia? What about cream cheese brownies? Try these mint chocolate chip cookies.'

She can't resist the sugar, or the way Sean's face lights up when she compliments a new recipe …

'Mrs Ellis?'

Malia turns back to the detective. 'Please call me Malia.'

'*Malia*. And I'm Ali. I'm going to need you to give me as much help as you can. Some of my questions may sound silly or rude or seem to have no point, but I can guarantee you that I want to get Zach back in your arms as soon as possible.'

Malia nods. 'There's no one who would want to take him. I mean, no one that I know.'

'How about your husband? Is everything okay between the two of you? No arguments or anything like that?'

'No,' says Malia, 'we're fine.' *Are we fine?* 'Ian is not the type to do something like this. He's not very fond of babies. I mean he loves his kids … He's just … you know?'

'Have you called him?'

'I did. He was in a meeting but he's on his way. He'll be here as soon as he can. I should call my work, and school and preschool.'

'Yes, good idea. We may need to do a media appeal so we can reach as many people as possible.'

'But isn't that what the alert is doing? I really don't want to talk to anyone.'

'You may have to. Sometimes an appeal from the mother lets whoever took the child know that they're being missed, lets them know that everyone is looking. But we'll take it one step at a time.'

'He's due for a feed at ten,' says Malia. 'It's so hot. He needs his milk.'

'I know,' says Ali and she gives Malia's shoulder a quick squeeze. 'I know,' she says again.

A blue Toyota sedan tries to pull into the service station. Before he is turned away Malia says, 'That's him, that's Ian.'

Ali motions at the uniformed police to let Ian in and one of them reverses a car to open up a space.

Once he's parked, Ian gets out of his car and runs towards Malia. 'What's happened?'

Ali steps forward. 'Mr Ellis, I'm Detective Greenberg and I'm here to help you get Zach back as quickly as possible.'

'Jesus,' says Ian. 'What does that mean? Where's Zach? What happened?' He looks around and spots Aaron and

Rhiannon sitting together on the side. 'Why aren't they at school?'

'They came with me,' says Malia. 'We needed milk and they all had to come and I went in for a minute, just a minute and then someone … someone took Zach.' Malia listens to herself say these words, trying to understand them. 'Someone took Zach. They took him out of the car. He was in his seat, strapped in, and they just opened the door and took him.'

'Why was he in the car alone? You know not to do that! Oh God, Oh God, he's so little. Who could have taken him? How can this happen? I don't get it, Malia, I don't get it.' Ian buries his face in his hands and then he turns to Malia and puts his arms around her, squeezes her tightly. Malia feels her body stiffen. She does not wish to be comforted by Ian, does not wish to comfort him. She realises she is angry now. Angry with Ian. In fact she is furious. She waits until he lets go of her and then she steps back, away from him a little.

'Mr Ellis, can I suggest we all try to remain calm,' says Ali.

Malia watches as Ian asks the detective the same questions again. His face is pale and his lips tinged with blue as though he is having trouble breathing. *He is afraid*, thinks Malia, and she wants to feel compassion for him, wants to be able to stand with him as they wait for their baby to be returned to them, but she finds that she can't.

Ian listens as Ali explains quietly and methodically

exactly what happened. She goes through it twice before Ian indicates that he understands.

The day is getting hotter, and Malia can hear the children starting to whine about being thirsty and bored. 'I'll get them drinks,' she hears someone say.

In her head one question swirls around and around and she feels her lips start to form the words as she realises exactly why she is so upset with Ian, with him touching her, with him being here, with his judging her for what has happened, because he must be judging her just as she is judging herself. Her father was an accountant before he retired and every night on his way home from work he would call her mother and ask, 'Can I stop at the store and bring you anything?' and even though her mother had probably been to the grocery store that day the answer would inevitably be, 'Yes'. It was always something small, never more than an item or two and even though her mother could usually wait until the next day to get what she needed, her father seemed to enjoy doing this small thing for his wife. He walked through the door every night with something to give his family. It occurs to Malia, as she watches her handsome husband in his well cut suit speak to the detective, that this was how she had pictured her husband would behave. This is what she had expected from the man she married, from the father of her children, but this is not what she has. This is not what she has ever had. She cannot say this to Ian and so she says the only thing she can coherently say: 'Why didn't you get the milk?'

She says it again, louder, as she walks towards Ian and the detective. 'Why didn't you get the milk?'

'What?' says Ian.

'Why didn't you get the milk?' She gives Ian's shoulder a shove.

'Why didn't you get the milk?' she shouts again, this time shoving him so hard that he has to take a step back. Then she hits him on his chest.

'Malia, what are you doing?'

But her voice only rises with each repetition, and each time she hits Ian she feels the force increase and the power behind her rage and her dread. She knows that everyone at the 7-Eleven must be watching her, but she can't stop. It can't be that she is responsible for losing her baby, for allowing her baby to be taken from her. Someone else must be responsible. Ian is responsible. This is Ian's fault.

'Stop it!' shouts Ian and he grabs her hands. 'I'm sorry. I ran out of money. I didn't have any money.'

He forces Malia's hands behind her back, holding her there while she butts her head against his chest. Her rage dissipates into tears because she knows she is the only person to be blamed for what has happened.

Malia feels another set of arms around her and she realises it is Ali. Ian has already released her, and is walking away towards the children. Malia is conscious of her wet T-shirt and her sweaty body, but she breathes in the sweet scent of flowers that surround the detective even on a boiling summer's morning.

'It's okay,' she hears Ali say, 'we'll find him. We'll find him.'

And even though she knows Ali is just trying to calm her down, Malia feels the fight go out of her. It will do her little good to get hysterical. Ali sounds so sure of herself, so capable. 'How do you do that?' Malia would like to ask her. She spends so much time questioning every decision she makes that some days there seems to be no time for anything else.

'We'll find him,' Ali says again and Malia nods, taking a deep breath, before heading back to sit with Aaron and Rhiannon who are now drinking Cokes. Both of them have climbed onto Ian's lap, taking refuge in his presence.

'The man said we could have them,' says Aaron, waiting for her to take the drink away. Malia can see that he is surprised at the rare treat.

'You can,' says Malia. 'You can have whatever you want.' She sinks down onto the concrete step near her husband and children.

'You hit my dad,' says Rhiannon, looking at her pink thongs, adorned with butterflies, as she strokes Ian's hair.

'I didn't mean to,' says Malia, and she sniffs and wipes her eyes.

'Don't cry, Mum,' says Aaron, patting her on the arm. 'Zach will be back soon.'

'I know, baby,' says Malia. 'It's all going to be okay.' Aaron gets off Ian's lap and scoots right up to her and puts his head against her shoulder. 'It's going to be okay,' she says again.

It is nearly ten o'clock. Zach's last feed was at 7. The longest he has ever gone without milk is three and a half hours. He should be going longer than that by now, according to all the books Malia has read, but none of her children ever managed the magical four hours between feedings. 'Where are you, baby?' she whispers, looking up at the blue sky. 'Who has you? Where have they taken you?'

She folds her arms across her knees and rests her head.

'Please, God, keep my baby safe,' she whispers loud enough for only her to hear. 'Please, God, bring him home.'

Chapter Six

It was so easy to take him. Too easy. I felt like it was the right thing to do. I feel like I rescued him. I rescued him and I will give him a better life, one with a loving mother and father. He will have me and Marcus. Marcus—my lover, my husband, the father of my child. Marcus—my heart. Marcus and I will be better parents to this child than she was. A baby will bring Marcus back to me.

Children should never be left alone, especially in a car. What was she thinking? If it had been the wrong thing to do surely someone would have stopped me?

I stop walking and look around a little bit, trying to orient myself. I am far away from where I found him but I still recognise this part of the neighbourhood. I am close to where I live now. I've been walking these streets for a week already, admiring the few big old houses that haven't been pulled down to make way for large blocks of units. Some of the trees on the streets around here must be hundreds of years old. They have stood here since before the first house was built. I won't get lost here. I know my way.

His car seat was different to the one I was used to, but I managed to get it undone and he didn't cry at all. He just snuffled and buried his head in my shoulder, making my heart flip. Oh, the beautiful, precious weight of him. It's been five long years since I had a baby in my arms and I have felt that loss, that awful, terrible emptiness for every hour of every day of those five years.

I never knew I would feel that way. I didn't know that the ache goes on through the weeks and months and years. The ache, the nightmares, the visions—there is no end to them, no light, no tunnel to go through. No point when it is all over and the memory becomes bittersweet. It never ends.

Compared to that pain, prison was easy. I will not forget the taste of fear in my mouth on the first day I spent in prison. Fear tastes oily, slimy—it turns your stomach. As the van I was in drove through giant metal gates and into the Haywood Women's Correctional Facility, it didn't seem possible that I would survive such an experience. There are no trees around the prison, just a road and buildings. There was some grass, but in summer it turned brown and died. The dust got into your throat when you walked around the yard. There were high walls and fences and barbed wire and guard towers and small cells for each woman. In prison I had to follow the rules. There were bells that rang all day to tell me when to get up and when to go to sleep and when to eat. I woke with the shrieking sound of the bells in my ears today, not realising that I was in a room in a boarding house, and that the sound was only inside me. That's happened every day since I left prison. But the bells don't bother me as much as the nightmares do. Even now, so many years later when I have been set free, the nights are still hard. I see her in my dreams, always reaching out for me.

In prison I had to keep my head down and stay out of the way. The other women in there were waiting for me to do something or to say something—anything to justify them attacking me with kicks and punches and maybe even a sharpened toothbrush or two. Everyone I looked at in prison held their hands in fists, ready to hit.

One of the guards, Helen, warned me to be careful on my first day. 'This is not going to be easy,' she said. 'There are a lot of women in here who believe you did it on purpose. Stay out of the way and keep your head down because we can't be watching every minute of every day.' My lawyer said something similar to me after I was sentenced. 'Keep out of everyone's way,' he whispered before the police took me away, but I wasn't exactly sure what he meant until Helen said more or less the same thing. The other prisoners hated me before they met me.

I witnessed some of them beat another inmate once. They didn't know I was there, but I saw the way they used their hands and feet. I heard the smack of fists hitting flesh and smelled fear and blood. It was horrifying. Eventually the victim was curled into a ball, still, waiting for it to be over. I'm not sure I would have lived through such a thing. I'm not sure I would have wanted to.

It was nice of Helen to warn me about the other prisoners but even though she seemed kind, I saw her lips curl a little at the idea of what I had done. People don't discuss their crimes in prison, but my crime wasn't a secret I was able to keep. The details had already made their way through the whole place—first heard on the television news and then whispered from ear to ear.

'They're very sensitive about crimes against children,' Helen said, 'especially babies, so be aware—don't drop your guard.'

I hoped that Helen was in the camp that thought I had made a mistake and that was why she tried to protect me or warn me. There were a lot of people who knew that was all it had been—a mistake. Strangers seemed to understand more than those who knew me. Some women sent me emails, although I have no idea how they got my address. They told me they knew what I was going through and wished me luck with the trial. They said they knew what happened to me could have easily happened to them. I was grateful for their support.

Not everyone was supportive, and there were those

who were almost frightening in their wrath against me. I read everything on the internet, read all those arguments housewives across Australia were having about whether or not I had done it on purpose.

Those who were against me were vile, tapping out one hundred and forty characters, calling for the death penalty to be brought back, shouting for a violent end to my life.

I enjoyed reading comments from the women who were on my side, who believed me, who understood the truth. The problem was that there were not enough people in that camp. Not enough people who looked objectively at their own lives and understood what I had done. Everyone had an opinion, and it seemed to me that the whole country went back and forth over my actions, chewed them over, spat out their ignorance and left me with no chance of an impartial collection of people to judge my actions.

The jury were, unfortunately, in the wrong camp. 'Guilty,' they declared, and I knew while they had salivated over *murder* they had to settle for *manslaughter*.

It didn't matter that I had cried every day in court, or that my lawyer brought up one person after another to say what a wonderful mother I had been. My own mother was reluctant to speak for me, but she agreed to do it and she did her best in the end—she really did. She was heartbroken over Ella, just heartbroken, and she was afraid that she would end up crying on the stand about how she had lost her first and only grandchild, but my lawyer convinced her it was important the jury see that my mother loved me.

We were sitting in his office when he said this. My mother kept calling him Sam, as though she knew him as a friend, and I kept calling him Mr Booth so that she would understand we had to be formal, but I guess she was paying so she could do anything she wanted to do.

'Of course I love her,' said my mother.

I must have snorted or laughed or something because she turned to look at me. 'Something funny?' she asked, and I saw an expression on her face I hadn't seen since I was little. I shook my head.

It was interesting to listen to her talk about me in court, saying she was proud of me and describing what a good person I am.

Having her sitting in the witness box gave me a chance to study her from a distance. I imagined that she was someone else's mother. She was beautifully dressed in a pale blue skirt and matching top, and she'd had her hair done, knowing, I'm sure, that she would be photographed on her way in and out of court.

My lawyer asked her to describe my childhood and she said, 'It was a little stressful because her father and I got divorced when she was only two, but we got through it together, and I knew she would make a wonderful mother.'

I had to bite down on my lip and close my eyes when she said that because I wanted to jump up out of my chair and run over to her and put my hands around her neck. I wonder what Twitter would have made of that.

On and on she went about how close we were and how

86

happy I had been as a child. While her words filled the courtroom, my body filled with rage. But I knew I had to sit there and listen to her spouting her bullshit since there was no way I wanted her to talk about how she used to lock me out of the house at night when I was eight or how sometimes she decided that my voice was irritating her when she'd had a bad day at work and that I should remain silent for the rest of the night. I would never have wanted people to know about how she used to come home from having dinner and drinks—many, many drinks—with friends and grab the belt without even saying 'hello'.

'Do you know what my life could be like if I didn't have you? If you weren't around? If I hadn't let your dog of a father get me pregnant?' I can still hear the whistling swish sound her belt made as it moved through the air towards me.

My 'dog of a father' went out for the proverbial pack of cigarettes one day and never returned. Although he left to play golf. All he took were his clubs and the clothes he was wearing. I think that bothered my mother most of all, the idea that he wanted to get away so much that he didn't even return for his things.

Sometimes my mother would hear about him through her grapevine of old friends. 'He's in America' or 'He's in the UK' or 'He's somewhere in Europe'. He just dropped out of our lives. Men can do that when they've had enough of their children but women can't. Women aren't supposed to leave their children. Women are supposed to love their children.

The truth about my childhood was not fit for court. It would hardly have helped my situation.

It all stopped when she met my stepfather. I was twelve. She turned back into the mother she had been before the divorce, the mother who was, by then, a distant memory I could only recall at the smell of a baking cake. Now she likes to pretend that none of it ever happened. 'Don't be ridiculous,' she used to say when I accused her of some misdemeanour from my childhood. She was a different woman with a man in her life, expertly concealing the truth of who she was and how she felt, and I have wondered if it is possible that my father saw this concealment where Colin—her second husband—has not; if my father left because he understood that she was someone else entirely. I should have learned from her. If I had known how to pretend like she does I may have been able to conceal my desperation and anxiety from Marcus, but I was too busy trying not to be like her to understand that a woman needs two faces if she is to keep a man in her life.

She went back to university and became an upstanding member of society, and everything else was glossed over. Colin's money made that easy. She embraced the beauty of subjective memory in conversations with me, but the truth is still lodged inside her somewhere. When I asked her to testify on my behalf she said she'd rather not. 'I miss my granddaughter so much I worry that I'll say something that will hurt your chances of an acquittal,' she explained. 'Sometimes you seemed so angry at her.'

It was true that she loved her. I think she saw my daughter as a second chance, as a way to raise a child who didn't know she would think nothing of throwing a glass at someone's head.

My mother liked to babysit. Sometimes I would drop my daughter off and hang around for a bit to watch how my mother would sing and dance around with her, making her giggle in that cute way babies do, and I would want to be grateful that she adored her grandchild but mostly I felt a sort of seething anger. *Why not me?* I thought but never said.

After Sam spoke to her she said she would think about testifying.

'You owe me,' I said and her face paled and she nodded her head. She didn't argue with that. She knew what I was talking about and she may have been afraid that I would tell Colin the truth. She told the jury that I was a loving mother who only wanted the best for her child.

It didn't matter. Nothing nice anyone said about me mattered because in the end it all hinged on some web searches I'd made on my computer.

I like to be prepared. I feel better when I've done all the research, when I have all the facts. I spent my whole day checking facts as part of my job for the travel magazine before she was born. It's what I did and who I am. So just like I made sure that the journalists had all their inform-ation correct for their articles, I made sure that I had all my information correct when it came to having a baby and raising a child. I searched up information on all the things mothers usually search for and then, just to see, I looked up other things that interested me.

I'm sure there is not one single human being who owns a computer who would be happy to have their search history scrutinised. Everyone looks up things they shouldn't.

Marcus looked up porn all the time. I thought that once you were married you gave up that sort of thing, but Marcus said he used it to relax.

He likes skinny women with clean-shaven vaginas and balloon breasts floating on their chests. He likes mouths that open wide in joyful bliss at the sight of an enormous cock. His eyes glaze over watching women smile as they are covered in sperm.

'Do you want me to get my breasts done?' I asked him once when I caught him in the middle of one of those searches. But he shook his head and laughed at me. 'Why would I want you to look like that?' he said.

'Because it's what you like.'

'I love you, I'm just looking at this.'

That's all I was doing when I typed those words into the computer. Just looking. Everyone looks at things they shouldn't, it's human nature and the internet caters for every thought, every feeling, every strange idea you've ever had. It's not all cats and giggling toddlers. I like to have all the information I can.

I had also researched other things, like the perfect time to wean a baby and ways to get a baby to sleep, the best pram for a newborn, what to do about colic, what cream to use on nappy rash, baby milestones, the best time to start solids, the best time to send your child to day care, what to do if a baby has a fever, how to get a baby to stop crying ... I had researched everything, but the police and the jury paid no attention to those searches.

I'd researched divorce as well. I didn't want to have to research it, but after four years together Marcus said, 'Get your ducks in a row because I'm getting myself sorted on my end.' I didn't want to believe him. I didn't understand why he was so unhappy.

'I've told you again and again,' he explained. 'I can't deal with your anger, your jealousy. I have to be able to leave the house and you're not even letting me go into the garden without giving me the third degree. Ever since we came back from our honeymoon you've been like this and I don't understand why, and now that we have a child it's worse.'

'It's because I love you,' I told him. 'I'm interested in everything you do, I want to know.'

'You want to know too much. You're suffocating me. You can't call me at work all day long. I have to be able to talk to my clients without worrying about you interrupting me.'

'You're an architect, Marcus, not a doctor. I get lonely now that I'm home with her. I just want to talk.'

'You were calling me before she was born, before you were home. You almost got yourself fired because you spent so much time calling me. It's like you don't see anything wrong with your behaviour. You need to see someone, talk to someone about why you feel the need to monitor my every move. I've never given you any reason not to trust me, have I?'

'You watch too much porn.'

'Not this shit again. I just like to look. I'm a fucking man and we all like to look. It has nothing to do with how I feel about you. I've told you that over and over again. It's not a reason not to trust me.'

'It's not that I don't trust you,' I lied. 'I like talking to you, I like hearing your voice.'

I couldn't explain it to him, not without revealing the truth about myself, the truth that I'd always known.

'You are an annoyance, an irritation, you're not worth my time,' my mother taught me. 'Having you has ruined my life.'

And when I got older and looked in the mirror, I understood that I was not even worthy of being looked at. Wrong-shaped body, too-small eyes, thin lips—nothing about me is right. I don't look like the women in the magazines and I don't look like the women getting fucked for a camera on the internet. I didn't know how Marcus could find me attractive, how he could want to touch me when I was so obviously not what men were supposed to want. How could I trust him when he was everything I wanted, and the only thing I wanted, but I was nothing that anyone could want?

I would have felt stupid saying, 'How on earth can someone like you be in love with someone like me? I'm nothing and you're … you're everything.'

I wanted to say it to him, but I was afraid that if I did he would realise how he actually felt and say, 'You're right, I don't love you. This has all been a huge mistake and I don't think I ever loved you. I only ever pitied you.'

I never said it, of course, but I needed to check in with him all the time to make sure that he still loved me, that he hadn't realised his mistake. That's all I was doing, but he hated that I needed him so much. At home at night he would sit down on the sofa and I would drape my body over his and it wouldn't even take five minutes before he had an excuse to get up again. 'I need a drink' or 'I'm tired and going to bed' or 'I'm too hot to sit like this'. Sometimes I would follow him when he walked away from me. 'I'm going to the bathroom, why are you following me?'

He changed, not me. When we were dating he called me all the time, sometimes five times a day, to tell me that he was thinking about me. I'd never been treated like that before. I was used to drunk sex with boys from bars, boys who regretted touching me in the morning when the booze glasses cleared. I was used to men like Douglas, who told me, 'Relationships are like partnerships—if the basics are agreed upon then attraction will follow.'

I had never experienced anyone like Marcus before— not his beauty, not his devotion, not his level of interest in who I was and what I thought and felt. It was intoxicating to know that I was on his mind all the time. I daydreamed about him all day long, dreaming myself into car accidents, when I mindlessly hit the accelerator instead of the brake. I loved the way he looked at me—but I still didn't believe it. Even when he asked me to marry him I didn't believe it.

My mother and stepfather didn't understand, either. 'Is it money he's after?' my stepfather asked when I told them the good news.

'No, Colin, it's me he's after—he *loves* me.' I wanted to claw at him and smack the condescending smile off my mother's face. Her pretty, pretty face.

'Sweetheart, please don't get upset,' said my mother, using the sugary tone she'd used since the day she met Colin. 'We love Marcus, he's a good man, a beautiful man, but we're worried for you. We want someone to love you for you and not because you're going to inherit a lot of money one day.'

'Me and Colin's other children,' I said.

'You're all my children,' said Colin, but that wasn't the case in the end. He refused to even come to court when I was on trial. Then I went back to belonging to my mother and my absent father. Now that I am out of prison neither my mother nor Colin want to hear from me but I'm sure they will change their minds when they realise that I have started again, when they see that I have this beautiful baby and Marcus is back in my life.

I didn't speak to them for a week after I'd told them I was engaged—not until they called to apologise and offered to pay for the wedding. They wanted to buy us a house but Marcus wouldn't hear of it. He wasn't interested in Colin's money. 'We'll rent until we can afford something,' he said but we weren't together long enough for us to find our dream home. I don't know what it was that drew him to me, and because I don't understand it I'm sure it's possible that it's still there, still inside him. It's still inside him like he's still inside me, wrapped around my heart, part of my soul.

'You're so lucky to have parents like yours,' Marcus once told me.

'Yes,' I agreed, 'very lucky.'

It was a beautiful wedding on a perfect spring day. Marcus looked like a movie star, like a photograph. Everything about him was perfect. His hair fell over one eye in gorgeous black curls and his green eyes shone with joy. His perfect white smile made even the photographer blush, and I could see the green-eyed monster sitting on the shoulder of every woman there. 'You'll see,' said my mother, 'a good man changes everything.'

'Colin certainly changed you,' I replied.

'I know, sweetheart, aren't we lucky I found him.'

Things changed after the honeymoon, or perhaps things changed *on* our honeymoon. I'm not sure now when it happened but I know that I suddenly started seeing the way he looked at other women. Because he did look. He looked all the time. In the middle of a conversation with me he would stop speaking and his head would turn and I would have to follow his gaze, only to find it on another woman.

'I don't notice I'm doing it,' he told me. 'It means nothing.' But once I'd noticed it, I couldn't seem to see him doing anything else.

'Is she prettier than I am?' I asked when I saw him glance at a thin, blonde woman getting out of the hotel pool.

'Nothing compared to you, babe. I love you, only you. Don't worry about it.'

But how could I not worry. I was so careful by then with how I looked. My hair was perfectly cut and everything I wore perfectly suited my body. My nails were long and shaped and I knew how to draw out every ounce of beauty I had with make-up—and still he looked at other women. I couldn't make myself beautiful enough to deserve Marcus.

I began to worry that there were women in his office that he liked more than me. I had seen them at a Christmas party, seen how they sidled up to him and pushed their chests out, touching him lightly on the arm. They would look me up and down and I could almost see them shaking their heads. 'What are you doing with this chunky, ordinary woman,' I could see them thinking.

I started dropping by for lunch and phoning just to check. It drove him crazy, I know it did, but what else was I supposed to do? I had to protect my marriage—especially after I got pregnant.

You have to love the mother of your child, you have to. I let it happen because I didn't know what else to do. I could feel him slipping away from me.

'When are you two thinking about children?' Colin asked us one night over dinner. Marcus had laughed and said, 'Not for a long time,' but I saw how his eyes lit up at the idea. I didn't know what else to do.

The baby was supposed to save our marriage, but being home with her only made things worse.

'I told you to join a mother's group, to meet up with your mum, anything,' said Marcus when he berated me for interrupting him during the day. 'I've told you over and over again that this can't go on.'

'I don't like mother's groups, they're boring.'

'Maybe you should go and see Dr Burns, tell her how you're feeling. Maybe you need something to help you feel better. Lots of women suffer from postnatal depression— it's nothing to be ashamed of.'

'I'm not depressed, Marcus, I just want to speak to my husband.'

He threw his hands up and walked away from me. I didn't know how to make him love me again.

I went back to work instead when Ella was six months old, but that didn't help either. I couldn't concentrate. I was too tired. So I called him again. I wanted him to be kind to me, to say something nice, but he just got angrier and angrier.

'I've had it,' he said. 'I can't live this life.'

'Please, Marcus,' I begged, 'I'll do better, I will.'

He didn't want to listen anymore.

*

The press called me a psychopath, but they should have used that word on Marcus. And though he's the cruellest man I know, I can't stop loving him. I just can't. I can close my eyes and conjure up the way he smelled, even after five years apart. I want to touch the smooth skin on his chest and kiss his neck the way he liked. I want to be near him, with him and only him.

Once I have a job I'll save up the money to get my breasts done. I'm skinny now and I can dye my hair blonde so I'll look just like the women he likes to watch moaning on his computer. That'll make him happy. That and a baby.

In prison there was one woman named Marjorie I would occasionally speak to. She had been given a seven-year sentence for manslaughter after she stabbed her ex-husband twelve times with a large kitchen knife. She only told me the reason she was in prison after we'd known each other for a year. The other women didn't like the fact that she spoke to me but she didn't care. Her three children were in foster care and she didn't think she would ever be able to have them live with her again. 'I don't care what those other bitches think,' she said. 'I know that sometimes terrible things happen without you meaning them to. I'm sure I didn't mean to kill him but I was drunk and so sad and he was all up in my face about how much food was in the fridge and I realised that he was never going to leave me alone to live my life.'

'But you were divorced,' I said. 'You didn't have to see him anymore.'

'Yeah, but we were tied together forever because of the kids. I had to see him every time he came to pick them up and drop them off and he would call me to discuss them and I was always afraid he was going to hit me again. I couldn't stand living with that, you know. I just wanted him gone.'

I wondered then what would have happened when Marcus and I were divorced if we had still had a child together. *Would I have been able to make him love me again?* He would have had to see me all the time. *Could I have made him love me again?*

It's such a hideous word—divorce. Sounds like die and force. Forced death. It was Marcus's choice, Marcus's decision, and though I would never tell him I do believe that what happened was his fault. I was under so much pressure, so much stress.

My heart felt like it was literally breaking in two. I even had pain down my arm one day and I thought I was going to die, but the doctor said it was only anxiety.

'Only anxiety?' I said to him. 'It feels like death reaching out for me.'

Some days the pain was so bad I couldn't breathe, but because of her I still had to get out of bed and do all the things a mother has to do, and then I had to go to work and be polite to the writers at that ridiculous travel magazine, with their stupid questions about the size of Greenland and the amount of rainfall in the Amazon Basin. I couldn't just stare at the television or sleep while I tried to work out how to save my marriage.

It was all too much. That's what my lawyer argued. 'She was a woman on the edge,' he said. I liked him because he looked like a grandfather with his white hair and paunch. I thought he seemed like the kind of man other people would believe.

'She had a full-time job and a young baby,' he told the jury, pausing to ensure they were listening, 'and a husband cruelly demanding a divorce! She was sleep-deprived and depressed. It's no wonder it happened. We expect too much from women today. We expect them to do it all and it was too much for this young mother who had no help from anyone, including the man who should have been her greatest support.'

It made perfect sense. I saw the jury looking over at me and I realised that I was nodding as he spoke. *That's it*, I thought. *That's exactly what happened.*

But Marcus got angry and the prosecutor had to tell him to sit down. 'It's not true!' he shouted.

I felt sorry for him then because he started crying. He missed her so much. He was a good father, an involved father, but he was a bad husband. Marcus was different to my father because he didn't want to leave his wife and his child, just his wife. I suppose that makes him a better man than my father but he never should have asked me for a divorce. It put me under an enormous emotional strain— it's no wonder I made that mistake.

He'll be a better husband this time, I'm sure of it.

The jury didn't believe my lawyer. The other searches I

had done on my computer didn't seem to matter to them. I thought that once you erased your search history it's gone, but I was wrong about that too.

'Nothing is ever gone,' Marcus said to me after we'd been told what the police found on my computer.

'What about love?' I asked. He didn't have an answer for me.

I made a mistake. Just like she did when she walked away from her baby and left him for me. I'm sure she was distracted by her other children. I watched the girl run away from her. I could pity her, but I don't. Not enough people felt pity for me.

It's hot today. A car can reach 50 degrees Celsius in just ten minutes on a day like today. There are some days in a Sydney summer when it feels like someone has turned on a giant furnace designed to roast us all.

The day I left her was like that. Road-melting heat. Skin-burning heat. Dehydrating heat. Murdering heat.

I shouldn't have left her. And she shouldn't have left him.

Chapter Seven

Ali hands Malia another cup of coffee. She knows she isn't drinking them, just holding one cup after another until it turns cold and has to be thrown away.

Without having to think too much Ali can summon the sour taste of all the cups of coffee that were handed to her after Abigail died. People had no idea what to do so they kept giving her things to drink and she had no idea what to do either so she kept drinking them. She hasn't had coffee for four years now. The taste reminds her of grief.

'Fucking security cameras are broken,' says Mike, coming out of the 7-Eleven.

Ali has been making the rounds of all the officers interviewing people and checking to see if they have anything before she releases those who were here when the baby was found to be missing. She knows that the people who were not here are the ones they are really interested in but in her experience someone always sees something that can be of help—except today. Today no one has seen anything.

'Shit,' she says softly to Mike. 'Have we got someone checking the street cameras?'

'Right now,' replies Mike. 'There are two that may be of help—one outside the other station across the road and one outside the pathology lab over there. Otherwise it's a bit of a stretch of nothing until the shopping centre. It may take a while.'

'Isn't it always the case with cameras? They break and everyone knows they're going to get around to fixing them, but no one does, especially around here where the most exciting thing that ever happens is a bird flying into the store window.'

'And the ones inside are directed at the cash register and the candy aisle. Seems they have a lot of kids coming in from the school up the road and not everyone is carrying money,' says Mike.

'It would have made everything so simple,' says Ali.

'Maybe, but the outside ones aren't pointed at the car anyway. They're directed towards the bowsers.'

'Yeah, but they still might have caught something. Are we going to be able to trace all the customers here at the time without the camera?'

'Quite a few paid on credit card so we're looking into that. Some paid with cash, though. We've got the tech guys on it. Shouldn't take too long and the banks are cooperating so we should have a workable list of names soon. I've already sent two teams out to start interviewing the people we have identified because they're regulars and the guy behind the counter knew their names. It was pretty busy this morning.'

'Good, anyone interesting? Anyone with a record?' asks Ali.

'Not so far, we haven't had any pings on the database. Ossie has authorised the social media appeal so the information is up on Facebook and everywhere else. Ossie is speaking to the press and the next thing we need to do is film Malia and Ian—do an appeal.'

'I had hoped we would have found him before any of this became necessary,' says Ali.

'Yeah well …'

Ali sighs, 'Yeah well.'

'You doing okay?'

'Fine. I know Ossie was worried, but I have to get used to this again, Mike. It's my job.'

'I know but you just got back.'

'And I'm fine.' Ali tries to keep the frustration out of her voice.

Mike's phone rings and he answers and listens for a moment. 'Okay, and what about the other couple? Yeah … yeah … Let me write that down.' He pats at his pockets for a pen and, when he finds it, tries to use it to scribble something in his notebook but it doesn't work. Still holding the phone he shakes his head at her and walks back to his car to get another pen.

Ali feels irritated that she will not know what he's hearing until he tells her. Before Abigail died, Mike had been quite happy to let her take the lead on a lot of cases, even though he was senior. She feels like she's a rookie again, waiting to be told what to do.

They're only trying to help. Reuben with his endless texts and Mike with his gifts of chocolate and Ossie with his gentle, solicitous enquiries—they're only trying to help, but she needs them to stop fussing and let her get back to being the kind of cop she had been before.

She would like to yell at them all to stop, but then she remembers what it was like in those blank, dark days after Abigail died. It's their way of grieving for her and with her. She's sure that Mike never expected her to return to work at all. She didn't go back until she was pregnant with Charlie and then she was only on administration, before leaving again to have him. It is only recently that she has begun to feel ready to do her job properly, not because she has managed to somehow get over losing her daughter but because she knows that a choice had to be made between her live child and the child who died. Work keeps her mind occupied and, even though the paperwork has been tedious, she has still needed to concentrate. Reuben was right about her returning to work, about her needing something else to think about.

He had gone back to work two weeks after Abigail died

and she can remember resenting him for finding a way to get out of bed so soon.

'I'm the boss, Ali. I can't just leave the work to other people.'

'Don't you miss her? Don't you think about her every day, every hour, every minute?'

'Of course I do, Ali, you know I do, but other people rely on me. I have to work.'

She had not understood or perhaps she had not wanted to understand. When Charlie was three months old she had stopped in at the office to show the baby off because Reuben said that everyone wanted to meet him. While Reuben took Charlie around the office, letting everyone cluck over him, Ali had a cup of tea with Shayna—Reuben's administrative assistant.

'I'm so happy for you both,' she said. 'I never thought he would recover.'

'You didn't?' asked Ali.

'No, I knew he needed to come back to work, but for someone whose door is always open ... for nearly a year there was always one period of every day where it would be closed and then we would all know he was in there, staring at his collection of pictures of Abigail.'

Ali had swallowed hard, taking a large sip of hot tea and chastising herself for ever thinking that Abigail's death was easier for Reuben to handle.

She had imagined that having Charlie would somehow allow her to tuck Abigail away in a corner of her mind.

Instead she can't help comparing the two of them. Abigail smiled at six weeks but Charlie smiled at five weeks. Abigail could almost sit by herself at four months old, while Charlie could roll over. Abigail never slept through the night and Charlie slept through the night from four months old—well, not through the night, but from eleven until five … Abigail was a fussy baby who could cry for hours at a time without Ali knowing what she wanted, but Charlie is placid and easy, and before he could make himself understood he would alert her to his hunger with a bleat, like a lamb.

Charlie looks like Reuben, with the same dark eyes and curly brown hair, but Abigail, with her blue eyes and fine red hair, looked like her.

The comparisons should stop there because Charlie is thirteen months old and Abigail will always be five months and one day. Instead Ali finds herself thinking about when she would have started crawling and walking, and when she would have said her first word.

Ali takes a deep breath as she feels an imaginary punch to her stomach. It's lighter now, more like a tap, but the first few months after Abigail died it would force her to sit down, wherever she happened to be. There would be pain in her stomach and her legs would collapse.

The pain foretold a crushing wave of grief that would leave her stunned. It came without warning, like the time she made her first outing to the grocery store since Abigail's death. Ali thought she'd been doing fine, but then she found a car park and got out to open the passenger door to collect Abigail, only to find an empty back seat. She had felt that punch and sunk to her knees, tears staining her face. When a passing man stopped and asked her if she was all right she couldn't answer, and he'd called an ambulance.

Ali had been ashamed of her behaviour, of her weakness, but there was nothing she could do about it. 'It will take as long as it takes,' her therapist, Lou, told her.

She had begun seeing Lou a month after Abi died. She hadn't wanted to. She wanted to stay in her bed, curled around one of Abi's blankets, but one morning Reuben's mother had arrived with an old friend in tow.

'This is Lou,' said Joan.

'Short for Louise,' the woman with spiky grey hair said.

Ali had sat up in her bed, resentful at being woken, ready to bolt for the bathroom, but before she could say anything Joan walked out of the bedroom, leaving her alone with Lou.

The woman sat down on the bed. 'What a terrible time you've had,' she said, covering Ali's hand with her own, and Ali had nodded and burst into tears. Lou had sat on her bed for over an hour, listening to Ali talk, and it was only when she got up to leave and handed Ali her card that she realised she had actually had her first therapy session. The next week she had managed to get herself out of bed and into Lou's office, and for a year after that she went every week.

'I'm not this person,' Ali said in the session where she told Lou about her legs failing her. 'I'm stronger than this.'

'Correction,' said Lou, 'you *were* stronger than this. Now you're a mother who has lost a child. How can you be anything except weak right now? Accept it, move through it, and your strength will come back.'

Abigail made Ali realise that she was capable of loving something beyond reason, that it was possible to think about the collection of sleeping pills hidden in her underwear drawer and imagine using them to make the pain stop. She had never mentioned the pills to Lou. They were her last resort and just knowing they were there helped. Now she sometimes has moments of terror when she thinks about the possibility that she may have swallowed all those pills and that now there would be no her and no Charlie and Reuben would be utterly broken.

Abigail made her realise that she was not protected and invulnerable because of her work but *more* vulnerable because she'd had a child and given her heart to that child.

Abigail made her realise that she could break.

'You okay?' says Mike, drawing her back to the present. 'You look like you're in pain.'

'Yeah, I think I pulled a muscle at the gym yesterday.'

Mike nods, even though he looks like he doesn't believe her. They both turn to study Malia, huddled together with her two children.

'She won't leave,' says Ali, 'and she won't go inside, and the kids won't leave her side.'

'So,' says Mike, 'everyone is calling in and so far the teams we have doing the legwork have managed to find and interview four different groups that were here at around the same time.'

'And?' says Ali.

'And nothing. Everyone interviewed was shocked and concerned and they all check out. They're either at work or home and if they are home their houses have been searched and nothing has turned up.'

'I thought that might be the case.'

'Any reason to suspect the parents?' says Mike.

'If there were I'd be surprised, although ...'

'Although?'

'She only came to the store to get some milk. It was supposed to be his job—something he did on the way home, but he said he didn't have enough money on him after the pub. You don't need a lot of money for milk and he could have added some stuff and used a card. Why didn't he just get the milk?'

'Maybe he's lying and he doesn't want to tell her he forgot.'

'No,' says Ali, 'it's something else. Maybe he couldn't use the card because he'd maxed out his daily allowance.'

'How the fuck do you do that at the pub?' A pause. 'Fucking pokies.'

'You know you don't have to use the word *fuck* in every sentence, don't you, Mike?' says Ali with a grin.

He has backed up her hunch. It's part of the reason why they work so well together. She hadn't imagined they would be able to at first. Ali made detective five years after Mike did and she saw him raise his eyebrows at Ossie when he introduced them. *Tread carefully, be patient*, Ali had said to herself, but as always her mouth hadn't been paying attention. 'Is there a problem?' she'd said to Mike after Ossie left the two of them alone to get better acquainted.

He had looked her up and down without even bothering to conceal it. 'It's not that I mind ending up with the station Barbie doll, but …'

Ali had known right then that she had two choices. She could have reported him for sexual harassment and generally being an arsehole, or she could just laugh. She knew how the people she worked with referred to her. It was the red hair and her vague resemblance to a famous actress, but she knew who she was and she also knew that she loved her work more than anything. Plus she had her eye on Ossie's chair …

So she laughed, which made Mike laugh. He had that weathered look that some men get from drinking too much and smoking too much and thinking that salad was a nice suggestion but didn't count as a food. For some reason they just clicked.

Ali was willing to learn and Mike was happy to teach, and after a while they had developed a connection that most detectives dream of. When Ali was pregnant with Abigail, Mike became so overprotective that Ali took maternity leave a month early. She didn't think Mike could take the strain of worrying about her anymore. And when Abigail died, Mike had come over that night and fought his way through the mass of friends and relatives to enclose her in a hug that lasted five minutes.

'I've spoken to the coroner,' he'd said when they had a few quiet moments together. 'They have to do an autopsy but he's going to expedite the process. I know the detective coming to interview you. She knows who you are.'

'We have to do everything by the book, Mike,' Ali had said. She had been on cases as a constable when there had been the unexplained death of a baby. She knew she would be asked over and over again about what had happened that day.

'Are you with us, Ali?' says Mike.

'What?' says Ali, glancing about the 7-Eleven car park. 'Oh yeah, yeah, just thinking. Maybe you should talk to him, ask him about his night at the pub?'

'Okay,' says Mike. 'I'll go and see what he has to say.' Ali gives Mike a grateful smile. Technically he should be calling the shots, telling *her* what to do.

She can see that the children are getting whiny. Malia is trying to calm them but it's too hot.

She watches Mike amble over towards Ian and begin the conversation. Ian steps away from his family and then throws up his hands.

'Just fucking find my kid!' he shouts.

Mike steps back, and stands up straight. It makes him appear taller, brings attention to his wide shoulders and for some reason makes it more obvious that he is carrying a gun. It's a non-aggressive move but it makes people aware of who they're speaking to. Mike's movement works because Ian lowers his hands and Ali can see him apologising. Mike backs off and returns to where Ali is standing.

'So something went down last night but he's not ready to discuss it,' says Mike.

'I can see that,' murmurs Ali. 'You may need to get him alone and give it another shot.'

'Obviously,' drawls Mike.

'Sorry,' says Ali, 'not telling you what to do, just thinking aloud.'

'Relax Barbie … no offence taken.'

Ali smiles and looks down at her shoes. She doesn't want anyone at the 7-Eleven to see her grin. The first two frenetic hours after the baby was taken have passed. In the beginning constables were everywhere, shouting instructions into their two-way radios, but now things are quiet. The customers who were here at the time have been sent home with instructions to call if they remember anything else. Mike is getting continual calls from the teams out on the road and every time his phone rings, Ali hopes that there is something worth reporting.

The sniffer dogs are out on the streets and all stations

across New South Wales have been alerted, as have major train stations and the airport.

They would give Ian a little time to calm down, hopefully to make him think they had no interest in him beyond being the child's father, and then Mike would need to talk to him again. If he was somehow involved, Ali knew that a little time spent simply watching Ian before they spoke to him again would be helpful. So far he's upset but he's not displaying any behaviour she would normally associate with someone who has something to hide. He's not checking his phone, or biting his nails. He's not pacing or trying to find reasons to leave the 7-Eleven. His emotions seem to fit the situation—he's alternatively worried, upset, hopeful, just as his wife is.

Ali knows that they don't want to get forceful with anyone in a situation like this, but they do need to discuss Ian's lack of money at the end of the night. If you found yourself without even enough money to buy some milk after a night on the machines, you had a problem. What Mike and Ali need to figure out is if Ian was using the money his family needed to pay the bills on the pokies or if he was using money borrowed from the kind of people who didn't send polite letters asking you to repay your loan. Taking someone's kid was not their usual mode of operation, but you never know. All angles have to be covered.

Mike's mobile goes and he answers, nodding as he listens, and then turns the screen to Ali.

'One of the teams is at a house where there's a baby,' he says urgently, showing Ali the picture of a child taken with an officer's mobile phone.

'Not him,' says Ali, who has been studying the pictures Malia has sent her from her own phone—pictures of Zach smiling and Zach sleeping and Zach lying on his stomach and on his back and Zach eating his first mouthful of solid food. Malia has chosen a picture of Zach in a blue Babygro for the social media feeds. 'It matches his eyes,' she had said, and then she had covered her face with her hands.

'Not him,' says Mike into the phone.

'I didn't think so,' he says when he hangs up, 'but I just wanted to check.'

'They have pictures of him, don't they?'

'They do, but that baby had blue eyes as well. I think they just wanted to make sure.'

'It didn't even look like him, Mike.'

'I know, but babies do sometimes seem quite similar.'

'Rubbish.'

'Ali, calm down. All I did was make sure.'

Ali rubs her forehead, 'Sorry, it's just …'

'I know, Barbie, I know.'

Chapter Eight

Edna opens the bathroom door and steps out into the hallway. A morning bath was just the thing to make her feel ready for the day. The hot water has soothed away all those little aches and pains that seem to arrive as she sleeps. It was certainly worth a late breakfast although she feels rather hungry now.

In her bedroom she puts her things away and applies a little face powder and rouge. She feels better when she is bathed and dressed even though she is sure few people would care if she spent her days in a housecoat and slippers.

Jackie's door was closed when she went past and it didn't sound like she was in her room, so Edna assumes she must be out of the house again, looking for work or visiting her parole officer. Edna knows about parole officers now

117

because Luis has to check in with his once a week for the next three months. She heard him discussing it with Robbie—not that she likes to eavesdrop but sometimes it can't be helped. She was in the kitchen getting a cup of tea and Robbie and Luis were in the television room, which was right next door, so obviously it was easy to hear what they were saying.

She thinks about last night and the sounds she heard coming from Jackie's room. Such terrible sounds, like an animal in pain. At one point she had hauled herself out of bed and groped her way along the dark passage to Jackie's room, intent on knocking on her door. She had no idea what she would say or do if Jackie opened the door, but she felt she had to offer comfort. *Doesn't everyone need comfort when they are distressed?*

Jackie hasn't mentioned any family and no one has visited her so Edna has assumed she must be alone. She knows what it's like to be alone and distressed and even someone who's been in prison must sometimes want some comfort. Edna couldn't remember the last time she had cried— probably when Harry died, but even then she had managed to keep her distress private. 'No use showing the world your heart,' her father used to say, and though Edna had often wondered why that was the case she had always tried to put on a good face when she was out in public.

Last night she had stopped outside Jackie's door and raised her hand to knock before she felt the terrible weight of indecision. What if she offended Jackie? What if the woman was angry? What if she simply laughed at her for her concern?

After a moment Edna had lowered her hand, turned away and returned to her room. Jackie could be crying over anything, and Edna was sure that she wouldn't want to tell all her secrets. It was best just to leave her to it and hope that she managed to sort it out on her own.

Edna makes her way downstairs for her breakfast. Most mornings she has breakfast with Solomon, but she had known he wouldn't be there today because he had spent the night at the aged-care facility to see how he likes it. 'Don't go,' Edna wanted to tell him, but she knew that he really had no choice in the matter. Two days ago he had left the house for his usual walk to the park, but he'd somehow got himself lost and had been brought back by the police.

'I felt like a foreigner in my own city, Edna,' he told her afterwards as he tried to guide the teacup to his lips with shaking hands. 'Imagine that—just like a foreigner. I couldn't recognise anything at all.' It was time for him to be somewhere where other people could take care of him.

Edna eats her fruit and oats in the silent kitchen, missing Solomon and his cheery 'Morning, luv.' She feels a little blue today and doesn't like the idea of spending the day alone.

I'll pop into the pub for lunch, she thinks. *Treat myself to a G&T and one of the steak sandwiches.* She cheers up immediately once she has decided this. Paulo, the bartender at the Rose Hotel, is always up for a chat. She would tell him about Solomon leaving and about the new woman in the house. He was always interested in the boarding house and its residents.

Humming to herself, Edna reads a newspaper left behind by one of the other residents. She takes her coffee into the living room and switches the television on to the morning show, hoping to catch the end bit where they repeat the news.

She likes to watch Channel 9 because the newsreaders are always so well dressed. If it's a man he's always in a smart suit and if it's one of the women she's always in beautifully tailored clothes, always elegant and smart.

'Once again,' says the newsreader, concern darkening her blue eyes, 'police have issued a child abduction alert and we are appealing for anyone who was in the vicinity of the Fairmont 7-Eleven—corner of Marlborough and Watson streets—to come forward if they have any information on the missing baby.'

'Oh my,' says Edna as a picture of a baby in a bright blue romper suit comes up on the screen. *Zach Ellis*, reads the writing at the bottom of the screen, *five months old*.

Then there is a picture of the service station where the baby was taken from. 'I know where that is,' says Edna, shocked to be able to identify a crime scene. There are police standing together in groups, all speaking into their phones. Then there is a picture of a red car with the door open and an empty blue baby seat.

Edna wonders where the mother is. 'Poor woman,' she says. 'What on earth is this world coming to?'

She remembers the time when mothers would just park their prams in their front yards so the babies slept in the fresh air. No one would even think of stealing a baby from someone else. It was all so different now with high fences everywhere and horrifying stories on the news every day.

'If you have any information at all please call Crime Stoppers,' the newsreader continues. A telephone number scrolls across the bottom of the screen. Edna grabs a pad and pencil from the small table next to the couch and writes down the number, although she has no idea why she does this.

While the service station isn't terribly far from the boarding house, it is a bit too far for Edna to walk to. Still, it feels like crime is creeping towards her—and not just because Robbie is letting in the riffraff.

'Who would steal a baby?' she says to the empty living room. She feels much better when the news ends and the man selling vacuum cleaners comes on. He's also always nicely dressed.

She'll ask Paulo if he's heard about the missing baby. He's sure to know more than anyone else. He has a way of collecting all sorts of interesting titbits.

She smiles to herself in anticipation of a good lunch and a G&T.

Chapter Nine

10.30 am

The morning sun beats down on everyone gathered at the 7-Eleven. Malia has moved Aaron and Rhiannon into a shaded area under an overhang of the store's roof. She doesn't want them sitting inside the store where there are so many things to touch or break. The broken jar of baby food has been cleared away and its contents retrieved from the garbage and inspected by the police, as though it may have held some answers.

If not for Rhiannon's curious fingers they would have returned to the car before Zach was taken. If not for Rhiannon wandering away from her side Malia would have been able to watch the car the whole time and seen the abductor—perhaps thwarting the attempt to take Zach. She feels a momentary flame of anger at her daughter but it dissipates quickly. Rhiannon is three years old. Malia is old enough to know better, old enough to understand that there are no safe places.

She is aware of where the fault lies, but she can't help but unpick the morning, focusing on each critical moment that led her here. If not for the broken jar of baby food … If not for Rhiannon wandering away … If not for the long queue at the check-out … If not for the children wanting to come into the store … If not for Zach being asleep … If not for the lack of milk … If not for Ian fucking up and not doing the one thing she asked him to do …

Both Aaron and Rhiannon are sitting quietly, which is so unusual for them that Malia touches their foreheads with her lips in case they both have temperatures. But they are fine, only stunned by the heat, by the chaos, by Malia's breakdown and her subsequent silence, and mostly by the disappearance of their brother whose presence they were both only beginning to get used to.

Malia looks at her watch again, as she has done every five minutes since she reversed her car and got out, hysteria rising, to search the rear-facing car seat for her son. The shade cloths featuring Winnie the Pooh holding hands with Piglet on the back passenger windows of the red SUV were meant to protect the children from the sun, but today Malia deeply regrets their existence. She would have seen Zach was missing, even though the windows of the car are tinted.

Once she had screeched to a halt in the middle of the petrol station, cars had backed up behind her, horns blaring and people shouting through open windows. Only when she had begun screaming, 'Zach, Zach, where are you? Where are you? My baby, my baby!' had the shouting stopped and one person after another got out of their backed-up cars to see what the commotion was about. She had looked wildly around the service station when she could see that he wasn't anywhere in the car and then she had run to the parked cars, banging on their windows, begging for help.

He's been missing for two and a half hours. He'll be thirsty now. He was due for a feed half an hour ago, and he hates to be kept waiting. Sometimes it seems that Zach is aware that he is a third child and knows he has to make a lot of noise to be noticed. When he is hungry he doesn't just cry, he bellows.

'Good lungs,' the obstetrician said as he placed a squalling Zach on Malia's chest just after he'd been born.

'Doing my fucking head in,' was how Ian described it.

Malia knew that whenever Ian said something like that it was a clear sign that his next words would be: 'Just going out for a walk.'

What have I been doing all these years? she thinks now as she watches Ian pace up and down the forecourt of the 7-Eleven, talking to Walt, explaining why he won't be in, although Malia is sure Walt must already know. Social media has the story and most people would have seen it on their feeds by now. Ian probably just needed a distraction and it's not like there's a handy pub for him to pop into. Malia shakes her head, wondering at how she could think Ian capable of wanting to go to the pub now; but then he's been capable of going to the pub at just about any time in the last couple of years. He went when both Aaron and Rhiannon had stomach bugs and she was nine months pregnant with Zach. He went when she told him her aunt was ill in hospital in Melbourne—presumably to order some flowers to be sent but he was gone for at least three hours. He went after they had a massive argument last week about the electricity bill being overdue.

He goes because he doesn't want to be with me, with us. He goes because he's unhappy.

'I can't go through all of that again, Malia,' Ian had said when she told him that she was pregnant for a third time. 'We've just managed to get them both sleeping through the night and soon Ri Ri will be toilet trained. We're nearly out of it and anyway I thought we agreed on two kids. You promised me that you were done after Rhiannon.'

'I was. It's not like I planned this.'

'No?'

'No, Ian. I'm on the pill. You know I'm on the pill. It doesn't work one hundred per cent of the time. It's not like this is an immaculate conception. I didn't get myself pregnant.'

'We've just started getting our lives back,' Ian had whined, and Malia had bitten down hard on her lip to avoid saying, 'What do you mean *we*?' As far as she could see Ian's life had not been terribly affected by the arrival of his children. They had never really had another discussion about having children once they got married. After a couple of years, Malia had said, 'I'm going off the pill.' Ian had shrugged his shoulders and Malia had considered the matter discussed.

She should have made sure, she should have sat him down and said, 'This is what I'm doing. Are you okay with it?' But he may have said 'No', and then what would she have done. Would she have left him? Would he have said 'Yes' if she threatened to leave him? She doesn't think she could have given up on her desire to have children but she wouldn't have wanted to lose Ian either.

'You don't have to have this baby,' he said at the end of a long night of discussion about her third pregnancy.

Malia had imagined telling her parents that she was having an abortion, had seen her father shaking his fist and her mother growing pale and crossing herself. A baby was a gift, a blessing, a joy. She knew she could have kept it from them. They would never have to know, but the secret would have sat between Malia and her parents, colouring everything she said to them.

'I can't do that,' she'd said to Ian. 'I can't.'

Ian had left then. She had known he was off to the pub to stick more money in the pokies. When he was gambling he didn't think about anything else. He watched the lines go around and around and waited for three pyramids, or three sombreros, or three *anything* to appear so his free games would begin.

Malia had watched him at the machines when they were first dating. His eyes glazed over and he mumbled to himself; words she couldn't hear. Then it had all been a bit of a laugh, something to do for five minutes before they went for dinner, but now it was the only reason he ever walked into a pub. He didn't even drink very much.

That night Malia had gone to bed with her hands cradled protectively around her stomach, safeguarding the child she would not give up. She had felt Ian climb into bed with her as the sun was rising.

'So how are you feeling?' he asked her the next morning when he finally stumbled out of bed. 'Are you as nauseous as you were with the other two?'

'I'm okay, just a bit sick but not as bad as last time,' she had answered, stunned at his gesture, at his acceptance.

'Are we going to be okay?' she asked.

Ian had put his arms around her. 'We're always okay, babe, you and me and Aaron and Ri Ri and whoever this one is.'

Malia looks at her watch again. Zach has been gone for one hundred and seventy minutes. It doesn't sound like long, but it feels like she has been sitting here in the sun her whole life.

Her head is buzzing and her stomach is rumbling, but she knows she would not be able to force even one mouthful down her throat. She feels like she's in the middle of a nightmare. She might be going mad.

She can't talk to Ian; can't even look at him. He's tried to apologise a few times but he can see she's not listening. How can you apologise for something like this? All he had to do was get the milk and Malia would be standing behind the counter at the bakery right now, handing out sample bites of Sean's latest creation.

'Oh God, is there anything I can do, Malia? I can close the shop, come over right now and help look for him,' Sean had said when she called him after she had called the children's schools, and told him what had happened.

'No, no,' she'd replied. 'The police are here. I think every cop in the city is looking for him. I'm just sorry to leave you short-staffed.'

'Forget that, Malia. All that matters is Zach. I'll be thinking of you, honey, praying for you.'

'Thanks, thank you,' Malia had said as she felt her throat clog with more tears. Lately Sean had been using endearments more and more. He called her *love* at first and then *darl*, but now he was onto *honey*, which crossed the boundary somehow.

He was getting more personal as well, telling her when he thought she looked nice, bringing her something to eat or drink whenever he could, touching her as he walked past her—just a quick shoulder squeeze or massaging her neck if he saw her try to loosen her muscles. They were friends and she knew that if she had said something he would have stopped immediately, but the first time he gave her a five-minute neck massage she had relaxed and said, 'That's better, thanks,' when a customer walked in and he had to stop. She didn't want Sean to go back to being just her boss.

One night when her parents were visiting, as they did every July for three weeks, she had stayed back after the bakery closed to help him with the accounts, and when the hours hunched over paperwork had led to her neck seizing up he had stood behind her, his big hands warm on her neck, smoothing away the tension. They had been talking as his hands moved at first, discussing one of their suppliers, but after a few minutes both had fallen silent, aware of the air thickening as Sean's hands moved down her back, touching more than he should.

Malia had closed her eyes and let her head rest against Sean's stomach but then he had whispered her name, jolting her back to where she was, and she had stood quickly and told him she needed to go. Sean had flushed and they'd both looked away, aware that things had almost gone too far.

Malia knows she should stop it, knows she should say something, but she doesn't want to. She won't allow herself to explore her feelings for Sean because that would mean admitting that sometimes she wanted to be Sean's *honey*. He worries about her and cares about her. He notices when she looks tired and asks after the children all the time.

Every day for the past few months she has gone into work and fantasised about Sean wrapping his muscled arms around her and saying, 'Don't worry, honey, I'll take care of everything.'

He makes Malia feel cherished, and the way he says 'There she is' whenever he sees her gives her a little lift at the beginning of each day.

Sean had never had children. He had been married to his wife for twenty years, ten of which she had been sick. 'It started with breast cancer,' Sean had told her, 'and we thought we had beaten it, but it came back and then it came back again.'

Malia could see that Sean was one of those men who would have been a wonderful father. She knew what she was doing was dangerous because she was encouraging him, encouraging him to listen to her and talk to her and laugh with her. She confided in him too much and he knew most things about her life, except for Ian's pokies problem. Malia couldn't bring herself to confess that to anyone.

Half an hour after she had called to tell him what was happening, Sean had arrived at the 7-Eleven with trays of baked goods to hand out. The police wouldn't let him in and Malia had settled for waving at him.

'Your boss?' Ali had said.

'Yes, he's a lovely man.'

'Brilliant baker,' said Ali, finishing off a peanut butter brownie, and Malia felt her body fill with pride.

Now Ali is taking one call after another on her mobile

and each time she gets to the end of a call she shakes her head at the other detective, Mike, and Malia knows that means they have nothing. She watches Ali walk back over to her and can see the frustration on the woman's face. Malia knows that interviews are still being conducted but so far no one has told the police anything helpful.

Zach has simply disappeared. *Poof*, like a magic trick.

'I think it would be better if you took the children home,' says Ali.

'But …'

'We'll keep the 7-Eleven closed for now and I'm going to make sure that we have two officers here until we find Zach. The forensics people need to keep your car for now, just … just in case.'

'You think she had anything to do with this?' demands Ian, who has taken a seat near Aaron and Rhiannon. Malia watches him stand up and clench his hands into fists, shoulders back, teeth bared with aggression.

'Mr Ellis, in cases like this we never rule anything in or out.'

'Fucking ridiculous,' Ian growls, and he walks over to his car, grabbing his phone out of his pocket as it begins to ring. His parents and friends have been calling and, unlike her, he has been taking the calls. She doesn't know how he is able to talk to people.

'We need to take a look through the house,' explains Ali. 'Mike and I will follow you home and just do a quick inspection before you go in.'

'It's a mess,' says Malia, bewildered at feeling ashamed about her kitchen at a time like this.

'I have a child, Malia,' says Ali. 'I know how difficult it can be to keep things tidy and go to work. Forensics will be there soon as well. Also …'

'Also?'

'We're going to need to interview the children properly.'

'They were inside with me. They didn't see anything. They already told the first police officer who spoke to them everything they know.'

'I understand. But we need to do it formally. Kids notice the weirdest things. We have someone at the station trained to interview children and she's going to be with us soon.'

'They're just babies,' says Malia.

'I promise you we are not going to do anything to upset them. But if one of them did see something, however small, wouldn't you want us to know?'

Malia nods.

'Get the kids in your husband's car. We'll follow. It won't be long until we're done with everything and then at least you can get out of this heat.'

'What if he's in this heat?' says Malia. 'What if he's out in the sun? His skin is so new … He's not wearing a hat. He's … he's so … little.'

'We're going to find him. We won't stop until we do.'

Malia swallows and shakes her head. There is no point in crying anymore. She is drained. She wishes she could lie down and sleep until all of this is over. Her breasts are in agony. The wet patches on her T-shirt are getting bigger despite her efforts to stuff her bra with toilet paper from the ladies room.

'Let's go, guys,' she says to Aaron, who pulls his sister towards the car. She expects Rhiannon to protest but she doesn't. She never protests when Aaron tells her to do something.

They drive home in silence with the air-conditioning on full blast. Malia finds herself unable to look at Ian.

Ian has two car seats and a booster seat for Aaron in his car just like she has in hers. He hates them. 'They ruin the look of the car,' he had said when she told him he needed seats for the children in his car as well.

'If you have to drive the kids, you need seats. It's not something we're going to argue about.'

She knows that Ian frequently removes the seats because he drives the children so rarely. Today she is grateful he still has them from the weekend.

Now seated in the passenger seat, she can't help but keep looking back at the baby seat where Zach would ordinarily have been. *How could I not have checked? How could I have left him in the car? Why didn't I just go next door to Mrs Boulos and ask to borrow some milk? How could I have made such a stupid mistake? Where is he?*

The questions have been chasing each other around and around. She keeps re-imagining the events of the morning. She sees herself coming out of the store just in time to see the person who took him opening the car door. 'What are you doing?' she shouts, startling them and making them run away. 'You won't believe what happened today,' she hears herself tell Ian over dinner.

'I do it all the time,' she says to the silent car.

'What?' says Ian.

'I leave them in the car when I go in to pay for petrol. It's never very long, no more than five minutes, and there are always so many people around.'

'You shouldn't ever do it,' says Ian, and Malia feels her rage at him return.

'I shouldn't have had to do it today,' she says, swallowing the acid in her throat and sitting on her hands because she wants to hit him.

'I'm sorry, Malia, but you can't blame me for this. You were the one who made the choice to leave him in the unlocked car. What were you thinking? Were you even thinking?'

'Fuck you, just fuck you.' She spits the words out through clenched teeth.

'Mum, you sweared,' gasps Aaron.

'Mummy's sorry,' says Ian.

'Yes,' says Malia, swiping at her face as more tears arrive. 'Mummy's very sorry.'

Chapter Ten

I'd been walking for ages towards the large shopping centre past the blocks of units and the strip shops when he woke up. He was hot and sweaty and doing that squirmy thing babies do when they're getting hungry. My back was aching and my arms were sore, and the sun was beating down on me. I wanted to put him down so badly. I forgot how heavy a baby gets when you have to carry it for a long time, but when I looked around I saw I was standing in front of a supermarket.

It was a sign.

Marcus believes in signs. That's one of the first things he told me about himself.

We met in a beer garden one Sunday afternoon late in summer. I was sitting with some people from work. We'd been in the garden for a couple of hours already and at the time I remember thinking that the whole afternoon was beginning to feel a lot like being in the office, as I struggled to stop myself from saying something in response to some stupid comment. After a couple of drinks I have a tendency to say exactly what I'm thinking without a filter and I knew that I couldn't do that with colleagues. I had lost friends over saying things no one wanted to hear. By the time I met Marcus I rarely went out and then only with people from the office. My high school and university friends had drifted away from me or I'd drifted away from them, I'm not sure which. I was never very sociable. I never enjoyed getting ready for a night out, always finding the reflection in the mirror horrible and distorted. I used to think people were staring at me, making comments about how unattractive I was.

'Nonsense, you look just fine,' my mother said when I told her at sixteen that I felt ugly. 'You just need a bit more make-up. But if you lost ten kilos or so you'd have a lovely figure. Maybe straighten your hair.'

I wasn't even paying much attention to the conversation the day I met Marcus, just concentrating on holding my tongue.

I was only there because I didn't want to seem rude when Lacy asked me to join them. The journalists always thought they were being generous when they asked the researchers to come out with them, but I would have much rather been left alone. I was half-listening to Elliot tell the same old story about how he boarded a train without a ticket in the middle of a snowstorm in Chicago as I looked around at the other tables, wondering if everyone else was having as good a time as they seemed to be. That's when I saw Marcus with his curly black hair and green eyes and a smile that took up his entire face.

He looked like the kind of man everyone wanted as a friend. He looked like he knew how to relax in a group, how to enjoy being with other people. His laugh boomed across the garden and everyone at his table looked at him whenever they said something, as if seeking his approval. People are easily infatuated with Marcus, with his smile, with his laugh, with the way he touches them on the arm or the shoulder when he speaks to them.

I stared at him because even though he was looking in my direction I was sure he was looking at someone else. I am not the type of woman men notice. I fade into the background, disappearing into the walls and the furniture. 'Oh, I didn't see you there,' is something I've heard more times than I can count. Even before I lost so much weight I was never very interesting-looking. My hair is dull brown and frizzy and my eyes are dull brown and small. My skin is pale, but not pale enough to be different. I'm just average and ordinary. I'm just nothing.

Marcus made me feel less ordinary. Marcus made me feel special.

I thought he was looking at something else, but Marcus was in fact looking at me, and when I got up to go to the bathroom he followed me, not in a creepy way, just in a sweet puppy-dog kind of way. He was waiting for me when I walked back out.

'Can I buy you a drink?' he said.

He didn't say hello or anything else. Just, 'Can I buy you a drink?' Later, when we had been together for months, he told me that he had looked across the garden and seen me staring at him, and in that moment the sun had hit my hair in a certain way and for a few seconds it looked like I was wearing a veil. 'It was a sign,' he told me. 'A sign we were meant to be together, meant to be married, and I never ignore a sign from the universe.'

By then I knew how he felt about signs and I was warmed by the idea that he saw me as something so exceptional. 'That's what attracted you to me?' I asked.

'That, and how sad you looked. I wanted to comfort you.'

I wasn't sad, just bored, but I never told him that.

'Also, when you got up to go to the bathroom, I couldn't help noticing what a cute butt you had,' he said when I kissed him, making me laugh. He made me laugh all the time when we were dating. Marcus is Italian and all the women in his family are what the media politely calls 'curvy'. His mother has large breasts and rolls on her stomach and a huge behind and his sisters—all four of them—are overweight. Marcus liked the fact that my butt wasn't small, or that's what he told me. 'You are beautiful, *bella*, especially when you smile. I love your body. I love this dimple here and here,' he would say, kissing me on my back.

I didn't know why he had to look at other women then, I didn't understand it.

His whole family live in America. They never even got to meet our daughter. His parents had a visit planned for her first birthday but she never made it to that birthday. All they will ever have are pictures.

Marcus came to Australia to work in his early twenties and never wanted to go back. 'I love the lifestyle, love the beaches and the weather. I never want to have another winter in Boston again.'

I loved his accent, a mix of American and Italian, and his deep voice. I loved listening to him speak. I used to make him read newspaper articles to me just so I could lie next to him and listen to his voice.

It made him happy to see me happy and I'm not really sure when that changed. I felt like I was a better person when I was with Marcus, like I was more interesting, like I was prettier. I managed to get along with his friends, even to make jokes and make people laugh when I talked about the journalists I worked with. I thought being married to him would bring me nothing but happiness but then I started noticing how he looked at other women and I began to think about how he might like to touch those other women and when I looked in the mirror I could see why he would want another woman.

I decided not to ignore a sign from the universe either and took the baby inside the supermarket. The air-conditioning was turned up so high that goosebumps rose on my arms and my sweat dried instantly.

I felt the muscles in my neck seize and I wondered if it was possible that I'd made a mistake. I knew that it would be easy to take him back or to leave him somewhere. I could imagine how wonderful it would feel to be free of his weight and the heat from his little body. I could leave him outside a church or a shopping centre—someone would find him. In America there are places that you can leave a baby and know that they will be safe, but I don't know if we have them here.

I knew I should take him back, but the longer I held him the more I began to wonder if it is possible to love a baby not your own. Surely lots of people do it? People adopt children with a different skin colour from other countries and love them as much as they possibly can. This baby will be easy to love. He has a warm smell of sweet milk and baby powder and his body already feels as though it has moulded to mine.

I didn't know that babies do that until I had her. I used to hold friends' babies and feel like I would drop them. I had no idea how to position my arms or how to stand, but when she came along we just fused together. I could hold her and load a washing machine, make a cup of coffee, fry an egg or put on make-up if I needed to. It felt like after being inside me for all those months she easily became part of my body again.

I think I could love this baby, and if I can love him then

surely Marcus will love him too. Marcus loves children, in general. He's the one who gets down on the floor at family gatherings to play Lego with the children of friends. He listens to children and asks them questions so they will keep talking. I've always found other people's children boring, but not Marcus. He wanted to have lots of children—four or five, he said. This baby can be number one, I think. This baby can help us start again. I like the fact that he is a boy. I didn't enjoy hearing Marcus tell our daughter she was beautiful. I know she was only a baby but I used to look at her and feel resentful that she'd inherited his beautiful eyes and dark skin. I would imagine what she was going to look like when she grew up and I knew that she would always draw the attention in any room she walked into. From the moment she was born she was all anyone could look at. It didn't matter if I was with her or not. Everyone only had eyes for her.

My heart begins to race when I think about speaking to Marcus. I imagine telling him and I can see how his face will light up with joy, the same way it did when I told him I was pregnant. 'How wonderful, *bella*,' he will say, just like he did then. I loved that he called me beautiful, that he really thought I was beautiful.

I took the test without telling him. I didn't want him to be disappointed, at least that's what I told him, but the truth was I wanted to be alone when I found out. I wanted to be sure that I knew how to arrange my face when I told him. I wanted him to know that I was happy even though

I wasn't really sure what I felt. It wasn't supposed to happen so quickly. We'd only been married for a year and a half when I started talking about getting pregnant after Colin, playing his role as stepfather, said something at dinner.

'If it's what you want, *bella*,' Marcus said, 'then I'm happy to work on it.' He kissed my neck. 'Let's start right now.'

All the articles I read said to be prepared for it to take some time to fall pregnant. 'It may not happen right away,' I told Marcus.

'More fun for us,' he laughed. I felt like his focus was back on me. He wanted to have sex every night and afterwards we would lie together, speaking about the kind of child we thought we would have.

I wanted that time to go on forever, but one month was all it took and I felt cheated that I hadn't had more time to anticipate it all. I wanted to feel sadness at the arrival of my period, wanted to feel the desperate need for a baby that some women I knew talked about. I played out scenarios in my head where it took months and months, and then other scenarios where it didn't happen at all. But then it just happened and I couldn't articulate what I felt—which was terrified.

I feel like I'm more prepared now. I will do a better job this time around.

It's a pity that I won't get to experience being pregnant. Marcus was wonderful when I was pregnant. He went back to calling me a few times a day and he bought me gifts all the time, and he took over most of the housework.

He treated me like a princess. I was sad when it all ended, especially because of the pain and the blood and the mess. Once I had finally pushed her out, Marcus kissed me and then he had eyes only for her. 'What a miracle,' he kept repeating. 'Little Ella, my *bella* Ella,' he said as he kissed her.

'Women do it every day. The world is overpopulated with all of these miracles,' I snapped at him when I was tired of hearing him coo at her. I thought it was a miracle that I had survived the terrible ordeal of giving birth.

'Rest, *bella*,' he said. 'You've had a tough labour. You rest and I'll hold her.'

'Hold me,' I wanted to say, but his hands were busy holding her.

Standing in the supermarket I knew that I couldn't take this baby back. I couldn't do it to Marcus. Because I knew that once I told Marcus about him, my life would be wonderful again. I'm sure he's missed me. I know that even though I don't have a place for a baby where I live now I have to keep him. I won't be there long. Once I tell Marcus I know I will be moving. I don't know where he lives right now but anywhere has to be better than where I am now.

I don't think he liked the cold in the supermarket because he wriggled and squawked while I wandered around trying to find the baby aisle. It is also possible he just wanted to be fed. He's little enough to only really be awake for feeding time and a few minutes of play. He looks about four or five months old.

I used the fifty dollars I had in my purse to buy formula and nappies and bottles and dummies. It means I have nothing left for the rest of the week, but I don't care about that. *Something will come up.* Marcus has a great job and plenty of money. As I walked around the supermarket I thought about how it is possible Marcus and I could love this baby, and if that is possible then so is Marcus learning to really love me again, to love me the way he should love me. I know it can happen.

As I shopped I considered different ways to tell Marcus the good news. I'm sure his mobile number is still the same. 'Guess what I have for you?' I could say, or, 'Marcus, we're going to be a real family again.'

The baby let out a bleat and started to cry. I jiggled him. Another mother with a whiny toddler repeating, 'Mum, Mum, Mum,' smiled at me and rolled her eyes. I've missed that smile. *We're all in this together*, that smile says. I remember it from when I used to take Ella to the store. She was never quiet while I shopped. Even if I had just fed her she would cry up and down every aisle until I thought my head would explode. Sometimes I would leave the trolley and walk into the next aisle, pretending she wasn't mine until I heard someone trying to calm her down. Then I would run back and say, 'Oh, darling, Mummy's so sorry,' and the woman—it was always a woman—who'd been comforting Ella would smile at me and we would both roll our eyes like we understood each other and this wonderful club we were all members of. I didn't always get a smile—there were those mothers who shook their heads at me. 'You shouldn't leave a baby alone,' one woman with a toddler on a leash said to me—as if she had any real idea how to parent a child.

'Fuck off,' I replied, loudly and distinctly, shocking her into going away.

I was never a very good member of the club. I wasn't as good at acting out the part of the perfect mother as I should have been. I tried mother's groups a few times but I don't believe there is anything more boring on the planet. Who wants to sit and discuss baby poo while you fill your face with chocolate cake? I found it disgusting even though Marcus kept telling me that it would be good for me to meet other women with children the same age as Ella.

'You can't lock yourself away in the house. You need to get out and see people.'

'You're the only other person I need to see.'

'Oh *bella*,' he sighed, 'that's not the truth.'

Once I left the supermarket I walked over to a park nearby. I've been sitting here for ten minutes and I know he's not coping anymore. He's whiny and cross. The other children in the park distracted him at first, but now he's throwing his arms around and stuffing his fist into his mouth. His blue suit has some sort of stain on it. I hate it when babies look unkempt. She really should have changed him before she left the house.

His clothes will have to do for the moment because I don't have enough money to buy anything else. I can wash them and rewash them until I'm more settled. I imagine what it will be like to browse the aisles of a children's store looking for boys' clothes. I think Marcus will enjoy having a son. 'Shush, shush,' I say. I should call him something, not just *the baby*.

When I was pregnant with Ella we both decided we didn't want to know the sex of the baby. We had lots of names for boys, but only two for girls that we both liked. My favourite name for a boy was Xander. It's so different. I imagine that a child with a name like that will go on to do great things with his life. I bounce my legs up and down and imagine myself standing next to a tall young man dressed in his university hat and gown, and as a photographer clicks away he puts his arm around me and says, 'I owe it all to my mother.'

'Shush, shush, Xander,' I say, enjoying the way the name rolls off my tongue. It feels completely right.

I look around the park for something else to distract Xander and out of the corner of my eye I see her looking at me with her big green eyes. I turn away quickly, but of course there's nothing there. 'Go away,' I whisper. Since that day I see her all the time and all she does is stare. She was too young to speak, too young to call out to me, too young to call out to anyone.

Xander starts crying properly. I need to get home. I can't stay in the park any longer, even though it's cool in the shade of the trees.

It's strange how all crying babies sound the same. It's probably an evolutionary noise designed to terrify mothers into doing what the baby wants.

I sigh, feeling frustration building up inside of me. Babies are harder to take care of than anyone can imagine. This notion makes me laugh. I haven't had such a thought for five years. There's been no reason to think it.

I hope he doesn't cry as much as she cried.

She must have cried the day I left her.

I think she must have cried.

Chapter Eleven

Ali follows Mike's car as he trails behind the Ellises to their home. It's only a few minutes away from the petrol station but after two turns the streetscape alters and Ali can see a suburb in the middle of change. Small old houses on large blocks of land sit incongruously next door to giant McMansions with luxury cars outside. *Better than blocks of units*, she thinks. Her mother spends a lot of time at council meetings protesting the developments of endless blocks of units in her suburb. Ali smiles; her mother is always busy with something, with her friends or her bridge club or her meetings. It makes her an interesting woman to talk to but it means she doesn't see much of Charlie. Ali knows her father would have been more interested in Charlie had he been alive to meet him. Ali had always found him easier to talk to, easier to be around than her mother, who lives her life at a frenetic pace.

She risks a quick glance at her phone when she hears a text come in. 'Guess who loved his morning tea?' Kady has texted. Along with the text is a picture of Charlie with mashed banana on his face and his hands and his bib. He is grinning, showing off his six little teeth. Ali takes a deep breath in and lets it out. She hasn't worried about Charlie for nearly three hours. *I didn't worry about him and he's fine. I don't have to think about him every minute of every day. He's fine.*

She needs to concentrate on her case. Zach Ellis is five months old. Abigail was five months old. She couldn't save Abigail. 'Not this again,' she says, because she can't do this to herself now, can't replay that day in an unending loop as she attempts to pinpoint the exact moment of her failure. *It wasn't my fault. Think about the case.*

Handling this case will go a long way towards making everyone understand that she's ready to work again.

On any other day, she would pick up Charlie by 3 pm, but this is not any other day. Zach could be found in an hour, of course, but Ali has the feeling that this will not all be over by the end of the day. 'Always be prepared for it to go the wrong way,' Mike tells her. Still, she believes that this baby will be found, only she has no idea if he will be alive and, given they haven't any credible leads yet, wrapping up this case will take time. She knows the next step will be to talk to Ian, to really talk to Ian, but instinct tells Ali that

Ian is not involved. The children will be interviewed and forensics will go through the house but, again, Ali doesn't believe anything new will be found. She feels like someone took this baby because they saw this baby alone. The idea of it being a planned operation doesn't seem realistic but nothing can be ruled out without being examined. Police work doesn't rely on instinct alone.

She feels a physical tug in her gut as her need to get to Charlie grows, but she can't leave this family. Charlie is safe at day care, but Zach Ellis is out in the heat with a stranger. It is an unimaginable thing for a mother to have to go through. Ali can't leave until the baby is safely back in Malia's arms.

I wasn't going to do this, she thinks, and then she calls Reuben. Work was meant to fit in with her baby, not the other way around, but she reasons that Reuben has been married to a police officer for long enough to know that when he told her to go back to work he had to accept what came with that decision. A typical working day is a laughable idea when you're a detective.

'Ali?' he answers.

'Charlie's fine.' Since Charlie was born they don't say hello anymore when they call each other, not after the frantic, incoherent phone call she had made to Reuben the day Abigail died.

'Good,' says Reuben. 'So how's your day going?'

'I need you to get Charlie for me. I may not make it back tonight. This case I'm on is … it's going to take longer than

I thought. I know it's early still, but I wanted to let you know so that you can get prepared.'

'Ali, you're not on that missing baby case, are you?'

'You know about that?'

'It's all over the net, everyone in Australia knows about that. I have two reporters working on it right now.'

'Sorry, yes of course you know. Yes, I'm on that case.'

'Fuck, why did Oscar give you a case like this?'

'Calm down, Reuben. I asked for it, it was my choice. I have to get back to being the person I was. You know that.'

'What will happen if you can't find the baby?'

'You know I can't comment on a story that your website is working on.'

'Sorry, love, I wasn't looking for comment.'

Reuben is the editor of a news website that seems to be growing daily. When Abigail was born he had four employees, by the time Charlie was born he had fifteen. Every morning he wakes up to more subscribers. Ali has become used to beginning her morning with Reuben shouting 'Woo hoo!' and Charlie babbling his own version as he imitates his father.

He had begun the website with one other journalist and the two of them had run themselves ragged trying to keep up with national and international news. Now he has twenty-five employees who fly back and forth across the country and the globe in an attempt to be first to bring a new story to the twenty-four-hour news cycle.

Reuben had met Ali when he was a junior reporter for

a local newspaper, looking for information about a rash of bag snatchers across the suburbs. Ali had been the constable handling the case and regarded the serious-looking young man with trepidation, aware that journalists had a habit of dropping blame directly at the feet of the police. Her answers were monosyllabic and carefully constructed as she tried to concentrate on not saying anything that could get her into trouble.

Reuben says it was love at first sight. 'All I thought was, *Fuck, she's so pretty, she's so serious*—I wonder what would make her laugh.'

'So you've really given me nothing to write here,' Reuben said when the interview was over.

'As I said, Mr Greenberg, we are …'

'I know you're looking into everything, but I don't really have anything to write so you owe me.'

'Sorry, I *owe* you?'

'A drink.' Reuben had smiled. 'You owe me a drink, but I'll buy … I mean, please let me buy. Okay, that came out wrong. Do you want to meet me for a drink?' He smiled again and she had to admire his dimples and his long eyelashes. He ran a hand through his hair, messing it up and making curls appear where it had been smoothed down.

'I'm afraid not, no,' Ali had replied, ignoring her inability to look away from his brown eyes.

'Oh,' he had replied. 'Oh, okay.'

Ali had not imagined that she would see him ever again unless another case led to them crossing paths, but he turned up the next day, and the next, and asked her out again.

'You're a reporter, I'm a police officer,' she said. 'That doesn't work out, not ever.'

'Come on,' he said, 'you'll love me, I promise. My mother thinks I'm an amazing guy and I know you will as well.'

The next day he hadn't come into the station and Ali was surprised to find herself cranky and abrupt with her colleagues. But a week later he turned up, this time with his mother in tow. 'I want you to hear it directly from her,' he explained.

'He's worth it,' confirmed Joan, patting her short silver bob as she blushed; and then she and Ali had locked eyes and couldn't stop laughing.

'Okay,' said Ali. 'One drink.'

Ali wanted that one drink to turn into a lifetime, but pillow talk inevitably led to work discussions, and sometimes in the middle of a conversation winding down into sleep Ali would catch herself revealing something she shouldn't have.

'This is never going to work,' she told him. But then Reuben came up with the idea of the agreement. They formalised it and both signed. Anything she said was off the record and he never asked her about cases. He went to everyone else he knew on the police force except her.

'We'll give it a try,' said Ali.

Six months later they were married.

'I know you weren't asking for anything,' she says now.

'I'm sorry it's … Well, you know how it is. I have to believe that we will find him, so I'm going to stick with that thought. I need you to get Charlie so I can concentrate.'

'I have a meeting this afternoon, but I can cancel, unless you're okay with my mother fetching him?'

Ali takes a deep breath. *Too much, too soon.* But she knows she has to allow these steps to be taken. She feels her stomach churn and bites her lip against the urge to turn her car around and collect her son from day care right now.

Aside from Sarah and the other staff at the day care, no one except Ali and Reuben has ever looked after Charlie. Ali's mother has never been very interested in babies and never even babysat Abigail. On the other hand Joan loves babies. She was always delighted to be asked to babysit Abigail, and Ali knows it breaks her heart that Ali and Reuben are too afraid to leave her alone with Charlie. Ali knows that letting Joan fetch Charlie is another step she has to take. She and Reuben both have demanding jobs and one of them can't always be available to get Charlie in the afternoon.

'Any time, day or night. I never take the car seat out of my car,' Joan says to Ali every time they speak.

'I guess it had to happen sometime,' she says to Reuben.

'I'll reschedule if you're not comfortable, Ali.'

'No, I know she'll watch him as closely as we would. She can get him. Can you call Sarah and let her know?'

'I will, and I'll get home as soon as possible. And I'll call every twenty minutes to check on him.'

'I'm sure your mother thinks we're insane.'

'My mother understands why we're insane. It's getting better so don't even think about it. Do what you need to do, and Mum and I will take care of our little man.'

'Thanks, love you.'

'And you.'

The conversation has lasted the whole journey to the Ellis house. Ali parks behind Mike and they both get out and study the house as Malia shepherds her children inside. The property is an older-style home of fibro and brick with a large front yard filled with a swing set, empty paddling pool and patchy grass, browning in the relentless summer heat.

'Let's not give them any time,' says Mike.

'Right,' agrees Ali, and before Ian can close the front door they are standing on the step, waiting to be let in.

'I thought forensics would be here already,' mutters Ali.

'That's what I was told,' replies Mike. 'I'm sure we can go through, anyway. If there's something to find, they'll find it regardless of what we do now.'

Malia is in the kitchen, stacking the dishwasher with one hand and closing drawers and cupboards with the other.

'I'm sorry, it's such a mess,' she says when Ali and Mike enter the kitchen.

The house has polished wooden floorboards and white walls. The kitchen is big with a chipped laminate top and linoleum floor.

'We haven't really finished the renovation,' says Malia, and Ali can almost feel Malia's distress at the state of her house.

'It's a lovely house,' assures Ali. 'Please don't do any more. Forensics are only minutes away, I'm sure.'

'Oh sorry, I forgot … I mean I didn't think,' says Malia.

'It's okay. You can get the kids something to eat, just don't keep tidying.'

'We bought the house before prices went up and we were going to re-do everything but then …' Malia waves her hand to indicate Aaron and Rhiannon who are slumped in front of the television.

'Can you show me where Zach sleeps?' asks Ali.

'Yes, it's through here. Follow me.'

Ali follows Malia down a passageway, past the main bedroom and a bathroom with towels on the floor and toothpaste smeared on the mirror, to a small room at the end.

'It's really a study,' says Malia, 'but I wanted him to have his own room.' On the door is Zach's name in animal-shaped wooden letters. 'I show him his name every morning, even though he's too young to know what he's looking at.'

She stands at the door and absentmindedly runs her fingers over the letters.

Ali smiles. 'My son, Charlie, has the same letters on his door. I show him his name every day as well.'

'Oh, that's right, you have a son. How old is he?'

'He's thirteen months.'

'That's a gorgeous age. Aaron had a few words by then and he was into everything. I think Zach … oh … I'm sorry.'

Malia buries her head in her hands. Ali gives her a minute to compose herself. Ali knows that even though Malia is standing here with a police officer, she has, for a split second, forgotten that her baby is missing.

After Abigail died, Ali would get up in the middle of the night to check on her, and when she did walk into her room she was always freaked out by the empty cot, devastating her anew. Ali believes that surviving grief is a process of forgetting, first for a few minutes, then for a few hours, and then for a few days and so on. At first, those moments of forgetting lead to the terrible truth of remembering, but gradually it gets easier, and when you do remember you can still get through the day without curling into a ball and hoping the world just ends.

Ali doesn't want Malia to have to learn this. She wants to make sure Zach comes home.

'That's okay, Malia, I understand. I'm going to be as quick as I can and then we can leave you in peace until forensics gets here. They won't be long, but please don't touch anything else until they're done.'

'How can this help? He was taken at the petrol station.'

'I know, but we have to make sure we assess everything. I promise that the only thing we are all trying to do is get Zach back to you.'

'Why haven't we heard anything?'

'Malia,' says Ali as she glances around the room, noting the neatly stacked nappies and the folded Babygro's in the open cupboard, 'I know it feels like nothing is happening, but right now they are taking calls at every police station in the state and even some calls from out of state from people who think they may have seen or heard something. It's the way this works.' Ali knows it's not possible to convey the amount of work going into this investigation. There have been calls from places as far as Canberra—four hours' drive away—even though there is no way anyone could have taken Zach and made it that far in this timeframe. To explain this to Malia will not help because the only thing she wants to hear is—we have found your son and he's just fine.

Malia nods, turning to go. Ali is aware that she must be thinking that she has no real idea of what this feels like and she's right. Abigail was never missing, she was right there, but it's what people say: 'I know how hard this must be for you, I understand, I feel for you, my heart breaks for you, I'm so sorry for you.'

Ali heard those phrases over and over again at Abigail's funeral, and while she wanted to yell at everyone to shut up, she simply nodded and thanked everyone who tried to find a way to tell her they were sorry that her little girl had closed her eyes for an afternoon nap and never opened them again.

Afterwards, she kept wondering, *Did it happen as I was loading the washing in the machine? Or was it as I lay down on the couch for a twenty-minute nap? Was it when I woke up and stretched and listened to the monitor and finding it quiet, made myself a quick cup of tea?*

'It wasn't my fault,' Ali whispers as she looks around Zach's room. She keeps her hands behind her back, knowing that if she touches anything she will get into trouble from forensics, and eventually makes her way back down the passage. From what she can see, there is nothing out of the ordinary in Zach's room.

She peeks into Aaron's room where Minecraft figurines litter the floor, and then into Rhiannon's fairy princess room with its pink walls and butterfly decals. The children's rooms may have been decorated in different colours, but the kitchen, in need of renovation, has had to wait. That tells Ali something about Malia's priorities. There is nothing to indicate that the home is anything other than a typical one with three young children. There are toys all over the floor and a general feeling of chaos everywhere. Ali has no doubt that Malia would have found time during her day to tidy up and restore order, only to have everything turned upside down again when the children arrived home from school and day care.

At the petrol station Ali watched Malia deal with her children. She watched the way they became more fractious in the heat, watched how Malia reacted. Ali is not a psychologist, but she's taken a few courses as part of her training, and she knows what to look for when observing an interaction between a mother and her children. Malia has been mildly irritable with the children because she is under enormous stress but her mood has not changed quickly and she has not blamed the children for what has happened. 'This is very hard for them,' Malia had said once or twice in an attempt to explain Aaron and Rhiannon's behaviour, which is exactly what Ali had expected her to do.

So far all is as it should be. The kids seem to have no reason to be scared of her. They're whiny and frustrated just like any kids would be. Ali can see it's wearing Malia down and she's snapped a few times, but she hasn't said or done anything that causes Ali to be concerned about her capacity as a mother. It doesn't mean that she can rule out Malia's involvement in Zach's disappearance, but so far nothing is ringing any alarm bells.

'Trust your instincts,' Oscar always says when they discuss different approaches. 'Even if you weren't a cop you come equipped with natural human instincts and when you're faced with someone lying to you, you inevitably know.'

The front door bell goes and Ali moves to answer it, assuming it's forensics, but it's a reporter with a camera-man standing behind her. Ali can see that the camera is already recording. She lifts her hands up, 'Just move right back,' she says firmly. 'Who let you onto the property?'

'Georgia O'Malley from Channel 9,' says the reporter, holding out her hand.

'Move back and turn that off,' demands Ali.

'We were asked to come,' says the woman. 'We were given an exclusive by the media liaison unit. They said the mother wants to make an appeal.'

'Just wait here,' says Ali, closing the door on the reporter and her cameraman. 'Mike? Why are the media here?'

'Fuck, sorry,' says Mike, coming to stand next to her at the front door. 'Ossie called. He wants Malia to do an appeal. He wanted her to talk to the whole lot of them, but I suggested she only talk to one person and the media outlets share it around.'

'They all hate that.'

'Well, I don't think Malia can cope with a barrage of questions. At least Georgia will be gentle. Also Genevieve is here—she just texted to say she's parking her car—and you know she's a bit of a tiger when it comes to protecting people like Malia.'

Ali nods, happy that Genevieve, the media liaison officer, is here. She has the ability to comfort a victim and cut off a journalist in the middle of a hurtful question at the same time. She's sharp and funny and she never loses her cool. She's nearly six feet tall and she piles her dark hair in a beehive on top of her head to make her look even taller. There are very few journalists who will question a directive given by Genevieve.

'Georgia thinks she's got an exclusive,' says Ali.

'Bullshit,' says Mike, opening the door. 'Hello, Georgia … Please don't tell me you're stupid enough to think you don't have to share with every station and every news site in the country.'

'No,' says the bottle-blonde reporter, looking straight at Ali. 'I know it's not just for us.'

'Sorry, sorry!' calls Genevieve, sprinting up the front path in six-inch heels. 'Georgia, you weren't telling anyone that you had an exclusive were you? This is not some story. We need to get this information out to every single person in Australia right now. You know this is going to be shared, don't you?'

'Of course I do, Genevieve,' says Georgia, 'and we want to thank you for trusting us with this.'

Genevieve looks at Ali and rolls her eyes, and Ali responds with a rueful grin.

While the press need to be involved to get the message out about a missing child, Ali can't help but see them all as vultures, circling a tragedy, waiting to dive in to get the first bite of fresh meat.

'Just let me talk to Malia for a minute,' says Ali, wanting to prepare the distraught woman for the lights and the camera.

She finds Malia sitting on the floor in Zach's room. 'I'm not touching anything,' she says defensively.

'It's okay. Look, Malia, a reporter is here. We think you should do an appeal.'

'An appeal? I don't know how to do that. What would I say?'

'All you have to do is look into the camera and ask for anyone who has seen Zach to call the police. Describe what he looks like and what he was wearing so people can look out for him. Let them know he needs to be fed.'

'I can't talk to the press,' says Malia, dropping her head into her hands. 'I'm disgusting … my clothes …'

Ali crouches down next to Malia. 'You look like a mother

with a missing baby. It's better if people see the truth. It will only take a few minutes. I won't let the reporter ask you any questions. Just make the appeal and I'll get them out of the house.'

'I don't think I can …'

'I'll be there the whole time,' comforts Ali. She puts her hand under Malia's arm and encourages her up off the floor. 'I won't be more than a few metres away.'

Ian is already sitting on the couch in the living room. Aaron and Rhiannon are standing next to the couch, staring at the camera as the lighting is moved into place and Georgia finds a good place to stand: 'Remember my good side,' she barks at the cameraman.

'I don't want them on television,' says Malia.

'Where can they go? It will only be for a few minutes.' says Ali.

'Um … my room?'

'I wanna stay,' says Aaron.

'You can sit on my bed, Aaron, and you two can play a game on the iPad.'

Ali watches Aaron weigh up some time on the iPad against the novelty of the camera in the living room.

'You know,' says Mike, strolling into the room. 'I don't know how to use an iPad.'

'Really?' asks Aaron, disbelief written all over his face.

'Yeah, really. Maybe you and Rhiannon could show me.'

'I show you, I show you,' says Rhiannon jumping up and down.

'No,' says Aaron, 'I'm bigger, I'll show him.'

Aaron takes Mike's hand and drags him off to Malia's bedroom with Rhiannon following behind.

'Okay,' says Ali. 'Let's get started. You've got a few minutes.'

She looks hard at Georgia as she says this.

Genevieve holds up her hand to indicate that Georgia only has five minutes. Ali can see the firm expression on her face, leaving everyone in no doubt that she means business.

Reporters have to be controlled and Ali can almost see Georgia trying to figure out a way to get through the many questions already forming as she studies Malia and Ian, all the while knowing that if she says even one thing deemed unacceptable or potentially compromising to the investigation, Genevieve will cut her off and make sure she is never invited to do an interview like this again.

Malia sits beside Ian on the couch and the camera light goes on, startling both of them.

'Mr and Mrs Ellis, we want you to know that the whole country is hoping and praying that your son is found soon. Is there anything you want to say to the people of Australia who are thinking about your family right now?'

'I …' begins Malia. She and Ian look like rabbits caught in the headlights of a speeding car. 'I … I'm asking for your help,' she pleads. 'If anyone knows anything … anything at all … I'm asking … no I'm begging you to come forward. Please give him back. Leave him in front of a church or a hospital, in front of a store, anywhere. It doesn't matter why you took him, I don't care, just give him back. Leave him at a police station—anything please … please.'

Malia begins to cry. Ian puts his arm around her but he seems too stunned by the camera to say anything.

'That's it,' says Ali. 'You're done.' The appeal was a bad idea. Malia has not mentioned anything concrete about Zach but at least everyone watching will understand her distress. Malia and Ian have both looked directly at the camera, wide-eyed, trying to connect with the person who has Zach, looking straight at him or her through the lens of the camera. They haven't hidden their faces in any way. Two years ago Ali had a case where the mother made an appeal but did not look at the camera, she hid her face with a tissue she was ostensibly using to staunch her flow of tears. 'Give her back,' she pleaded in a muffled voice, never meeting anyone's eye. Ali knew right then that she was hiding the truth. Two weeks later, after yet another search of the property, they found her little girl buried under the cubby house.

'But …' says Georgia.

'Done,' says Genevieve, holding her hand up.

'Come on, Georgia, get it out there. Hopefully you can come back for the good part of the story,' she says.

'Mike!' calls Ali. 'They're ready to go.'

Mike comes in from the bedroom and bustles Georgia

and her cameraman out of the house before they can say anything more, nearly tripping the lighting guy in his haste.

'How's your little man?' asks Genevieve as she too gets ready to leave.

'Amazing, thanks,' says Ali, aware again that for the first time in thirteen months, Charlie has not been her only concern.

'Love you, let's catch up soon—call if you need to get me back if …' says Genevieve.

'I will.' Ali doesn't let Genevieve finish the thought. She will only need to come back and do another appeal if Zach is still missing tomorrow.

Malia gets up from the couch and runs to the bathroom, slamming the door behind her. Ali follows her, listening at the door to her crying, wishing she could say something else that would help. After a few minutes Malia re-emerges, blowing her nose.

'Did I do okay?' she asks.

'You were perfect.'

Ali heads back into the kitchen and sees Mike is still in the living room with Ian. The door to the living room is only partially closed, and Mike is talking quietly to Ian, obviously asking him about the night before the incident again, or at least he is attempting to ask him.

Ali can see from his folded arms and determined expression that Ian has no intention of telling Mike anything.

Ali joins them. She catches Malia watching what's going on from the kitchen and gives her what she hopes is a reassuring smile. 'We just need to check a few things.'

Malia doesn't say anything, although Ali can see she wants to ask what they have to check and why they have to speak to Ian. As discreetly as possible, Ali closes the door that separates the kitchen from the living room. 'Don't want to disturb the kids,' she says.

'Mr Ellis here,' says Mike as he hears her close the door, 'is concerned that if he tells us the truth about his pokies habit, we'll tell his wife.'

Mike's face is grim, and he stands with his legs far apart, taking up space. He looks threatening, but only mildly, which is what he wants. Ian needs to know he is talking to the police and he doesn't really have the option of staying silent at a time like this unless he gets himself a lawyer, and that would make all the bells ring. Everyone has the right to remain silent, but people only choose that right when they have something to hide. Ian should be falling over himself to answer their questions in the hope that he can somehow help bring his son home.

Mike really hates gamblers, having come from a family where the day after Melbourne Cup was either a celebration or a time to get out of the house and away from his father.

'Mr Ellis … Ian, can I call you Ian?' says Ali and she smiles, letting him know she's the good cop. 'I want to assure you that anything you say will only be used if it is necessary to help us get your son back, but we do need to know all the facts so that we can rule you out as having been involved in Zach's disappearance.'

'Why would I be involved? I was at work,' says Ian.

'How much money did you lose on the pokies last night?' asks Ali.

'Tell her,' says Mike, and he takes a step closer to Ian, invading his space.

'Just a hundred,' says Ian, staring at his shoes.

'Ian, you know that it won't take us long to contact the pub and get an idea of how long you were there and if you went to the ATM or not.'

'We know you were at the Gladstone Hotel last night,' says Mike. 'They have cameras everywhere so we can basically see everything you did while you were there. We can find out how much you withdrew and we can track the machines you were using and see how much you lost. You get that we can do that, right?'

Ali hopes Ian believes everything both she and Mike have just said, even though only part of it is true. The bank would eventually cooperate with the police, and the pub would be able to see which machines he was using but all of this would take time and a five-month-old baby who hasn't been fed doesn't have much time.

'I only ... I ... You can't tell Malia, okay, you can't tell her or she'll freak out.'

'Ian, mate, you're not in a position to be telling us what to do,' says Mike. 'Now Detective Greenberg has asked nicely, but I'm getting tired of waiting. How much did you lose?'

'Nine hundred, twelve hundred dollars,' mutters Ian. Ali watches his cheeks turn crimson.

'Fuck, mate,' sighs Mike. 'Where did you get that kind of money?'

'It's part of my commission. I haven't told her about it. I have a ... a separate account. She doesn't know about it. She'll freak out, totally freak out.'

'So you earned the money, did you?' asks Ali.

'It was my money,' states Ian.

'If you did get it from somewhere and you need to pay it back, you need to tell us, Ian. If you have old debts that people are harassing you about, you need to tell us. You have to help us so we can get your little boy back,' says Ali.

'I haven't,' whines Ian. 'I don't. I wouldn't do that. I just lost it all last night so I didn't have money for milk. Malia has lowered the limit on our joint ATM card ...'

'What's the limit?' demands Mike.

'Four hundred, but she must have paid some bills or something. She pays at the post office.'

'I'll check that with her,' says Ali, turning towards the kitchen door, but before she can move Ian stops her as she had known he would.

'Wait, don't do that, okay?'

'Why not?'

Ian chews on his lip and his cheeks colour again.

'I'm getting pretty fucking tired of this, mate,' says Mike.

'I lost fifteen hundred dollars.'

'What?'

'I fucking lost fifteen hundred, okay?' says Ian. 'I had eleven hundred in my account and I took four hundred from the joint account. I was going to get up early and get some milk, but I forgot. I just forgot this morning. I can't believe this has happened. He's only a little baby.'

Ian covers his face with his hands and sniffs. Ali tactfully turns away. Mike gives him a few slaps on the shoulder.

'It's okay, mate,' he says. 'We'll find him.'

Ali shrugs at Mike as his phone rings with another call from the station. Ian had lost his own money. The chances of someone taking his child to get him to pay back his debts were unlikely anyway. Bookies owed money tended to break arms and legs belonging to those who owed them the money. Kidnapping a five-month-old baby wouldn't really be part of their modus operandi.

Ian sniffs again as the door between the kitchen and the living room opens. Malia appears in the doorway. In one hand she is holding half an apple she was obviously in the process of cutting up for the children. She has a small fruit knife gripped in her other hand, her knuckles white. Her face is pale and Ali knows that she has heard the conversation. Her lips move, as though she is sounding something out to herself.

'Fifteen hundred dollars?' she finally says. 'Fifteen hundred dollars?'

Chapter Twelve

Edna dusts her room as she does every day, painstakingly wiping her figurines, making sure she gets dust out of every nook and cranny. Usually she likes to do this with the windows and door open to let the air flow through, but she is sure that she heard someone arrive home while she was in the bathroom after her breakfast and coffee and so she has kept the door locked because it may be Luis or Jackie. Even though neither of them have done anything that has actually bothered her, as her father always used to say, 'a leopard doesn't change its spots Edna—you be mindful of that when meeting new people.'

She is sure she heard the heavy front door slam even though Robbie tells everyone to close it gently because it's old, and then she heard footsteps up to her level of the house, but by the time she opened the bathroom door the hallway was empty and everything silent.

Edna would need to press her ear against Jackie's door to know if anyone was inside or not. Her hearing is not what it used to be. Besides, it's not something she would do since it's not her business if Jackie is home when she should be out looking for a job—although she decides that she may mention the fact to Robbie later on when he comes over for his daily check on the boarding house. Edna would like to know where Robbie actually lives and whether or not the paint at his place is peeling and the carpets dirty, but she would never have the courage to say such a thing.

Nate and William might though, especially after the two of them have had their daily dose of whiskey. Edna knows that Nate and William are more than just friends. They have breakfast together every morning and dinner together every night and by the end of each evening they're both the worse for wear because of their consumption of whiskey. Edna knows that her father would have seen men living together and loving each other as dreadfully wrong but she likes Nate and William. Neither of them is inclined to make noise or hog the kitchen or the television and, as far as Edna is concerned, that's good enough for her.

She will mention to Robbie when she sees him that she thinks Jackie came home before lunch. It's all very well for him to be earning money from criminals, but he should also be encouraging them to stop being a burden on society.

At least Luis got a job two days after he arrived. His old boss took him back because, as Luis said, 'I was the best electrician he had.'

Edna's not sure if she believes him, but she had nodded like she did. Luis seems to want her approval for some reason, though she's not easily fooled; he'll have to do more than fix a few things and be polite to get on her good side. Jackie doesn't seem interested in even having a conversation, but that's fine with Edna.

She replaces each figurine on the mantle of the unused fireplace when she's done and turns them to face different directions. Sometimes the ballerina is facing the clown, sometimes she is facing the little boy with his dog. The ballerina was a gift from her parents on her sixteenth birthday and the clown and the dog were both wedding presents: the dog from Harry's Aunt Judy who loved Harry like a son since she'd never had children of her own; and the clown from her father even though he told her the night before her big day that she 'could do better than this young man, Edna'. Even though he hadn't thought Harry the best choice for her, he had thrown them a lovely wedding, with a band and dancing and everything. They had prawn cocktails to start dinner and fifty guests—mostly friends of her parents. She thinks of Harry every time she dusts the figurines, of their wedding, of their life together.

Edna knows it's silly and a bit fanciful, but she pretends the figurines can see each other. By the time she is done straightening her bed and rinsing out a few things, the morning is over. She makes her way down the stairs and into the living room to turn on the television again. She can't stop thinking about the missing baby—poor little mite.

She's not the only one worried: all the channels are broadcasting the same thing. The number for Crime Stoppers scrolls across the screen over and over again and pictures of the baby in different outfits showing him laughing and looking serious constantly rotate.

'We're now going to take you live to the Ellis family home,' says the Channel 9 news reporter.

Edna knows that this reporter is never usually on this late in the day so the missing baby is a big story. The camera pans across the front of a house that reminds Edna of her own family home, although this one is much bigger. The garden is rather a mess and Edna thinks she would have had a quick tidy if she'd known her house was going to be on television.

The mother and father are sitting next to each other on a couch in what Edna assumes is their living room. They look quite young, but not as though they started having babies when they were teenagers. Edna disapproves of teenage mothers. She's seen them at the shopping centre and they always seem more interested in talking to each other rather than watching their babies.

'If anyone knows anything … anything at all,' says the mother. 'I'm asking … no I'm begging you to come forward …'

The mother begins to cry and Edna dabs at her eyes. The poor woman is beside herself and she looks such a mess. She's quite pretty with lovely dark hair and brown eyes, but she is wearing a terrible T-shirt and she has kept her arms crossed the whole time she's been talking.

The husband has said nothing; he doesn't even seem that bothered by the whole thing, but you never can tell with people.

Harry had been a bit like that. To the outside world it seemed that he never let anything upset him, but Edna knew when he was troubled.

The one time she'd managed to get pregnant he'd said, 'Well done, love.' But Edna had known how much it meant to him. When she lost the baby he said, 'What doesn't kill you, eh?' Edna remembers her mother being very upset about that. 'He could have at least bought you a bunch of flowers while you were in the hospital and said he was sorry,' she said.

'It's not his way, Mum,' Edna had replied. When she got home from the hospital the whole apartment was sparkling clean and there was a roast already in the oven. That's how Edna knew how sorry Harry was.

'Poor woman,' says Edna as the camera moves outside the house to where police and reporters are standing. The whole street is crowded with them and Edna can imagine that the neighbours are upset at the noise and the chaos.

A group of people are standing on the footpath, off to one side, dressed in wide-brimmed hats. They are all holding water bottles and Edna imagines that they are going to walk the streets looking for the baby. It's turned into a stinking day outside and Edna feels her heart race as she thinks of poor Zach in the sun.

She is so engrossed by the television that she doesn't hear Jackie come in behind her.

'What's going on?'

'Oh,' says Edna turning around, 'you startled me.' Jackie looks as though she's been out in the heat. Her hair is plastered against her head and her face is red and sweaty. Her eyes dart from the television to Edna and then around the room. Edna has no idea why the woman is so jumpy but it's very unsettling.

'I'm sorry. What are you watching?'

'A baby is missing,' says Edna. 'His name is Zach. He was taken from a petrol station this morning. It's been on the news for hours. Haven't you heard about it?'

'No, I just … I just came in.'

'Oh, I thought I heard you arrive home a while ago.'

'No,' says Jackie. 'I just came in.'

Edna hates it when people repeat themselves as though she's an idiot.

'Well, I'm going out to lunch in a bit,' she says. She feels uncomfortable in Jackie's presence, more uncomfortable than she feels with Luis, but because she can never help but be unfailingly polite, she says, 'Did you want to join me?'

Jackie stares at her for a moment as though she's lost her mind.

'No,' she says, and then she simply turns around and Edna hears her heading for the kitchen.

'Well, I never,' says Edna to the empty living room. 'Some people don't have the manners of a frog.'

She goes back upstairs and gets her handbag, checking twice to make sure her door is locked. No reason she can't get to the Rose a little early. William and Nate are probably already there, arguing with Paulo about whether or not Australia should become a republic. Paulo is a republican but both William and Nate love the Queen.

As she leaves the boarding house, Edna smiles in anticipation of a nice afternoon. There's a G&T with her name on it and right now she's very thirsty.

Chapter Thirteen

12.00 pm

Malia feels like she must be hearing things. It can't be possible that Ian has just confessed to Ali and Mike that he lost fifteen hundred dollars on the pokies last night; and also that he has a separate bank account she never knew existed.

'Did you ... did you actually just say you lost fifteen hundred dollars? Fifteen. Hundred. Dollars?'

Ian's face has paled. Malia can see his hands shaking a little. *How long does it take to lose that much money? How many times do you have to hit the button on the machine? How many times would you win ten or fifteen or twenty free games only to lose it all again? And if that was just last night, how much money has been lost over the years? How many thousands and thousands of dollars? Were there ever any bad months at the car yard?*

'No, I didn't … I …'

'No, you did … you really did,' says Malia, her voice rising. 'That's what you just said. I'm right, aren't I?' Malia turns to the detectives. 'That's exactly what he just said. Tell me I'm wrong. Tell me I misheard him … please?'

'Now look, Mrs Ellis,' says Mike. 'It won't do any good to get upset. We need to concentrate on finding Zach and then you can deal with everything else. If you could just give us a few more minutes we'll finish our questions and we'll give you some time alone.'

Malia feels her fists clench. She knows that if the police officers were not standing next to Ian she would fly at him, tearing his hair and biting his flesh.

'Malia, I know this is awful for you, but please let us finish. Everything can wait until we have Zach safely back in your arms. Think about that. Concentrate on that,' says Ali.

Her voice is gentle and smooth, designed to cut through the racing thoughts in Malia's brain. Malia steps back out of the room without saying anything more. She feels like she would like to take a walk, a long peaceful walk to be alone with this revelation. She needs to be outside in the open air where she can breathe, where she will be able to process what she's just heard.

She walks towards the front door without thinking. Some part of her feels that if she can just get outside and begin walking she can get away from this day and everything that's happened. That if she can get away from her house and her family, and stay away for a little while, when she returns they will all be here, safe and sound, and she would not have heard Ian say what he's said and everything will be exactly like it was yesterday and the day before that.

'Mum!' calls Aaron from his spot in front of the television. 'I'm hungry. Me and Ri Ri want lunch.'

Malia looks down at her hands and realises she is still clutching the apple and fruit knife. She puts both down on a small table by the front door.

'*Muuum!*' calls Aaron.

Coming, darling. But the words stick in her throat. All she can think about is being outside. She reaches for the door as the bell rings. When she opens it there are two people dressed in blue jumpsuits, holding plastic bags and a host of other things Malia can't identify.

'Forensics,' says one of them.

Malia stares into the man's green eyes for a moment, unsure of what's she's heard, rooted to her spot at the front door, her legs heavy.

Behind the two men standing on the doorstep Malia can see the street is crowded with people. She can't leave, can't go for a walk. She is stuck right here and it feels as though she will be stuck here for all of eternity.

'Come on through,' says Ali, who has appeared behind Malia.

'Malia, perhaps you and Ian and the children can go over to a neighbour's house for a bit so we can get this done as quickly as possible?'

She feels like she is hearing everything from a long way off, but her body is somehow moving back to where the children are. 'Come on, guys, we're going to Mrs Boulos's for a bit. She'll give you some lunch.'

She wants to pat herself on the back for managing to sound even vaguely normal. Aaron and Rhiannon get up to go with her. Mrs Boulos makes a chocolate fudge cake that both children love.

Malia steers them both towards the front door where Ali and Mike are both now standing. Malia hears Ian behind her.

'I think I might just go and check in with work quickly,' he says.

'You'll what?' says Malia swinging around to face her husband. 'You'll what?'

'Actually, we'd prefer it if the family stayed together,' suggests Mike, almost stepping in front of Malia to block her from Ian. 'Just until this is done. We won't be long.'

Malia shakes her head and takes Rhiannon's hand.

'You keep fucking saying that, but so far everything is taking a fucking long time and no one seems to be very interested in finding my kid,' says Ian, back on the offensive.

'Mr Ellis … Ian … is it still okay if I call you Ian?' asks Ali.

'No, you fucking may not,' says Ian.

There is a beat of silence and then Ali takes a deep breath.

'That's fine, Mr Ellis. But you need to stay with your family until we tell you that you can leave. I understand that this is a very distressing time for everyone, but it serves no purpose for you to get aggressive with us. You need to stay with your family until we tell you that it's okay for you to leave,' Ali's repeats, her voice low and tight.

Malia wishes they would have just let him leave, let him go where he loves to go and do the only thing he loves to do.

'Fine,' Ian sighs.

He follows Malia and the children outside and onto the pavement. They don't have to go too far to find Mrs Boulos because she is standing there, right in front of the house, shouting at a television reporter who is being herded back behind a line of police tape.

'You rude bugger! Who you think you are, saying such things? Get! Get away!'

The reporter is dressed in a suit and tie and Malia can see he's suffering in the heat, but he glares defiantly at Mrs Boulos who's only five feet tall and so thin that Malia worries Aaron might break one of her bones when he hugs her.

She may look fragile, but Mrs Boulos always assures Malia that she's 'like an ox!'. Malia and Ian moved in after her husband Bernard had died and were welcomed with her famous chocolate cake. She has five children and seventeen grandchildren so her house is rarely empty, but she has always made sure that Malia understands her door is always open for her and the children. Having her around made Malia miss her mother a little less and a little more at the same time. She doesn't want to think about what her day would have been like if she had just gone next door to ask for some milk, doesn't want to imagine where she would be now and what she would be doing.

'Calm down, ma'am,' says the police officer, but he's smiling. The idea of Mrs Boulos being a threat is comical.

'You do your job, you keep this … this rubbish away,' cries Mrs Boulos, shaking her finger at the officer.

'That's what I'm trying to do.'

'Oh, Malia,' Mrs Boulos says when she realises that the family have come outside. 'Go back in … don't talk to these bastards. They say such terrible things. Zach is a baby, our baby. No one would hurt him!' She shakes a fist at the reporter who is now standing behind the police tape. She is almost vibrating with rage.

'We can't,' says Malia. 'We need to let the police look through the house. Can we stay with you for an hour or so?'

'Of course, of course. Come children … come inside. I have cake.'

Mrs Boulos moves quickly up her own front path and into her house. Malia and the children follow her, breathing in the scent of jasmine that grows all along the fence. The garden is filled with summer flowers, lovingly tended by Mrs Boulos's oldest son, Con, who is a landscape gardener. The house is also freshly painted on the outside, as it is every year by one of her sons-in-law. Mrs Boulos lives her life surrounded by her family and friends, which is the way Malia had once imagined she would live her own life until she met Ian and he spirited her away to Sydney. *It was what you wanted. It was, but I had no idea, no idea what I was giving up.*

Malia is carrying her phone set to vibrate in her pocket, but she hasn't responded to any of the messages that have been coming in from her family and friends in Melbourne. At last count there were seventy messages and Malia fights the urge to tell them all to get on a plane and come here to be with her, to cry with her and to miss her baby with her.

The troops, her mother calls them, and Malia remembers being fifteen in Melbourne and being told about a devastating house fire at her Aunty Tabitha's house.

'Get changed out of your uniform, Malia,' her mother had said as she walked back into the house after school. 'Tabitha has called in the troops, we go now.'

Her mother's arms had been filled with food and blankets, as though she were a refugee running from her homeland.

'But I have homework,' Malia had said.

'And I have work,' her father had said coming in from the kitchen, 'but we have family first and so we go.'

She will let her mother update everyone when she arrives. Her parents' plane was supposed to be arriving at 1 pm, according to the first text Cassie sent her. 'They had to take an 11.30 flight because everything was booked up before that.

'Thanks, Cass,' she had texted back.

'Flight delayed, fucking airlines,' Cass had texted an hour later and now Malia has no idea when her mother will be here but she needs her. Oh how she needs her.

She doesn't have the energy to speak to anyone.

In the house the air-conditioning is turned on and all the curtains are closed so it's cool and dark and silent. Mrs Boulos takes Aaron and Rhiannon to the kitchen.

'Sit, sit,' she says to Ian and Malia. 'I bring tea. You poor people … the baby … oh my God, the baby. You must be so worried. They'll find him. I promise you they'll find him.'

Malia collapses into the worn leather couch but Ian remains standing. 'Malia, I …' he says.

'I don't want to hear it,' she cries, 'I can't hear it now. I need to get Zach back. He's the only thing I can think about.'

'I just want to explain.'

Malia sits forward and puts her head in her hands. 'I don't want to hear it,' she repeats, knowing there is nothing that Ian can say to make this better. She has finally reached a point in her marriage where she can't be persuaded to give him another chance. What do people call that? The tipping point, breaking point? Whatever it is she can feel a shift inside herself. It is large and small at the same time. Her body feels it, but only as a nudge, just a tiny nudge that has sent her into freefall. There is no going back from this. He has hidden money from her, money he earned for his family, money they needed. He has opened another account and instructed that his salary go into one account and who knows how many of his commissions into another. She wonders what he would have told them at work, how he would have explained his need to sometimes put his commissions into one account and sometimes into another. He has knowingly taken security away from his family to feed his habit. He has made it clear that no one and nothing matters as much as his gambling. She cannot stay with a man like that. She cannot let a man like that touch her ever again. She is ashamed to have trusted him.

She has always imagined that Ian would be the one to finally end things between them, if it ever came to that. He has the luxury of being able to walk away after all, but now Malia knows that *she* will walk away, despite having no money and no support in Sydney, despite not wanting to break up her family—she will walk away.

'What, Malia? What did you say?'

'I said I don't want to hear it!' she shouts. 'I don't want to hear it, I don't want to hear it, I don't want to hear it!'

Aaron comes running into the living room, followed by Mrs Boulos. 'Mum, stop shouting!' he yells.

'Just go back into the kitchen, Aaron,' says Ian.

'No, I'm staying with Mum.' He climbs onto the couch next to her and puts his small arm around her shoulders.

Malia can't help the tears that follow. Aaron is so small and his whole world has turned into a nightmare, and the worst part of it is that he doesn't know it yet but he can't even trust his own father. Ian is supposed to be a husband, father and protector, but he is none of these. He is a liar and a cheat—a man who takes money that should have been used to buy shoes and pay bills for his children and throws it away like worthless scraps of paper.

The idea of him having a secret bank account is almost too much for Malia to comprehend. She feels like a complete idiot. He earns a commission on each car he sells. She knows that. Some months there is more money and some months there is less, but Malia has just assumed that Ian has the same ups and downs that all car salesmen have. Some months she has worried about him losing his job when every sale falls through, despite all the work he claims he's doing.

'I'm on a bad streak, nothing is working. I can't seem to get anyone across the line,' he will say, and she will try to find something soothing, something positive and uplifting to say while she worries about losing the house if he finds himself unemployed.

Fifteen hundred dollars in one night seems like an impossibility. It is the electricity bill that's due two days from now and the gas bill that's already overdue and a trip to the grocery store. It's new underwear for her and new towels to replace the threadbare ones. Fifteen hundred dollars might as well be a million dollars.

What did I miss? What kind of a man did I marry? Who is he?

She feels her body grow warm in the cool room as a stray thought makes itself known. *If I have no idea who he is, how do I know what he's capable of? How do I know for sure that he isn't involved in Zach's disappearance? He's the one who didn't get the milk.*

Ian had to have known that she would need to get some for the children's breakfast. This morning wasn't the first time she'd made a quick trip to the 7-Eleven before breakfast. Did he have the whole thing planned out? Had he taken Zach to … to what? The thoughts make Malia feel like she's insane. Ian *can't* be involved.

Malia closes her eyes and leans back against the couch. 'Malia, please …' says Ian.

'Just go,' she says, feeling wearier than she's ever done. 'Just go.'

'Aaron,' says Mrs Boulos quietly, 'come and get the cake. Come and give Mummy a little rest.'

When he is gone Malia looks at Ian afresh and finds that she's not angry. She's not feeling anything. She is frozen inside because she knows if she gives in to her fear for Zach and her fury at Ian she will turn into a tornado and she will launch herself at him, striking him with her hands and feet until she has no energy left.

'Please go away,' she whispers.

'I can't, they want me to stay here,' says Ian. He sits down in a chair opposite the couch and wraps his arms around himself. 'I'm so sorry, Malia. I know I fucked up. I know it, but what happened to Zach is not my fault, it's not.' He sniffs and Malia feels herself relenting. His son is missing as well. They're in this together and does the money really matter that much, anyway? Zach is out there in the heat with some stranger, or all alone and he's crying and thirsty. Malia feels a streak of pain in her left breast. She needs to express more milk soon or she's going to get mastitis.

'I just want him back,' she whispers.

'We all want that,' says Ian.

'Really? Is it what you want?'

'Jesus, Malia, I can't have this fucking discussion again. He's my kid. I want him back. I'm sorry that I'm not fucking father of the year, okay?'

'You got that right. Father of the year wouldn't have gambled away the money needed to take care of his family.'

'It was one bad night, Malia, just one. I've never lost that much before.'

'I don't have the strength to believe you, I really don't.'

'Well, it's the truth. It hasn't exactly been easy for me since Zach was born, you know. I come home from a long day at work and everything is always such chaos. Zach is crying and Aaron's always whining about something and Rhiannon is drawing on the fucking walls. There's no peace in the house, Malia—what else was I supposed to do? Home should be a sanctuary, somewhere you recover from the day, not a madhouse. Some nights it's too hard to come home and I know that the minute I walk through the door you'll be on at me about helping you or money or talking and talking and talking about the kids. Believe me, I never wanted to say that to you. Sometimes I sit out in the car for twenty minutes so I can get my head right before

I come in. Some nights I need to unwind and where else was I supposed to go except the pub?'

Malia has heard these endless complaints from Ian before and she has always felt the need to apologise: for her lack of parenting skills, for her inability to keep things running in an orderly fashion, and for the fact that she can't give him the space and time he needs after a long day. But as she listens to Ian tell her once more that he only does what he does because he has to, she realises that she may as well be listening to Aaron justifying why he needs to bop his sister on the head with his Jedi sword. Ian may as well be five years old and stamping his foot in protest at his life.

'Perhaps you could try helping me when you come home?' she says. 'You could take the texta from Rhiannon and help Aaron with his homework, and maybe pick up a few things so I can get on with everything else I have to do. You could try being a father and a husband, Ian. You could do that.'

'I told you I didn't want kids. I told you right from the start.' Ian blurts out the words as though they have been sitting in his mouth for years, pushing to be let out.

Malia finds herself speechless. She feels her mouth open and close, but nothing comes out. The idea that her husband, her Ian, the father of her children, could say something so cruel, so self-serving, bewilders her. *This can't be my life*, she thinks. *I can't have allowed this to be my life.*

She leans her head back against the couch and closes her eyes.

She is not here.

This is not happening.

Her world has not imploded because she ran out of milk.

Chapter Fourteen

The four walls of this room look like they're getting closer together. I don't think I've been here for very long, but the feeling that I won't be able to stay here much longer is scratching at my skin. This room is starting to remind me of prison, of my cell. The noise he's making isn't helping.

At least my cell was quiet. I spent long hours there writing letters to Marcus, telling him that I was sorry and that I still loved him. I wrote about how wonderful it had been between the two of us at the beginning and about how much I wanted that again. I told him to wait for me and to hold me in his heart. Writing those letters kept me sane in those first few weeks I spent in prison.

It broke my heart when the letters came back unopened. I cried for hours, but I don't think I will tell Marcus that.

I know he was angry with me—and I understand it. I should have been more careful with her, but he's had time to put things into perspective now and it won't do any good to bring up the returned letters. It will be a clean start for both of us. For both of us, and Xander.

'Shhh,' I say now to Xander, but he ignores me and carries on crying. It's a pity he won't listen because it was all going so well.

After I left the park I lugged the bags back home—no, not home, back here. This is such a sad place to live that maybe prison is preferable. How anyone could regard it as home is beyond me. It smells of mould and piss.

I stood outside for a minute when I got here, feeling my heart rate increase and the muscles in my arms strain and pull because of the weight of the baby and the shopping. All I wanted to do was put everything down. I imagined the relief I would feel when I was finally free to move my arms again.

The baby wriggled and opened his mouth to cry. 'Shush, shush, shush,' I said and I bounced up and down the way I learned to do with her. He was quiet again as he studied me with his big blue eyes and I knew I had to get him inside, out of the heat and fed, or he would begin making a lot of noise.

I put the parcels down on the pavement and fished around in my bag for my keys. When I first moved in here the owner of the house, an odious, oily man named Robbie, handed me a key to the front door and a key to my room with a flourish, as though he were giving me the keys to a palace. He looked at me with a mixture of pity and suspicion. 'We all get along well in this house,' he told me, 'and we're all good Christians who believe that everyone deserves a chance to change their lives.'

'This place will not change my life,' I wanted to tell him. 'This place is the lowest point of my life.' The first week after my release I spent time in a cheap motel while I tried to find somewhere to live. My parole officer, Morgan, recommended this place.

'It's close to the city,' she said, 'so public transport won't be an issue and there are only six other residents there at the moment, most of whom are elderly.'

'Fine,' I said, interrupting Morgan as she started to explain exactly who lived in the house and where it was as she undid and redid her wispy brown ponytail.

'It will be fine, Jackie,' she said. 'You'll make a new start and your life will move forward.' She smiled at me, showing me a poppy seed caught in her teeth from lunch.

I have seen some of the residents at breakfast this week, hiding behind cereal boxes and newspapers so they can pretend they are anywhere but in the sad kitchen with its grey linoleum floor and yellow and white kitchen cabinets.

I nodded *hello* to all of them as I was introduced last week, but I could see that I would not have to indulge anyone in conversation anytime soon. I sensed, for the most part, that I was completely uninteresting to any of the residents here except for Edna, the old woman who looks at me like I'm filth. Morgan told me that no one knows that I was in jail, but she hasn't met the old bitch. She knows, so I'm sure they all know.

They don't look me in the eye and I've made sure that if I ever have to exchange a few words with them I look at my shoes when I talk. I look like an entirely different person now because I've lost so much weight, but you never know when someone is going to recognise you. My picture was in the paper a fair bit, and even though that was five years ago, everything lives forever on the internet.

Once I had the keys in my hand I picked up the parcels again. I needed to get to my room as quickly as I could. I knew that the worst thing would be if I ran into another resident.

I closed my eyes. If I am meant to have this baby I will get him to my room without anyone seeing me. I opened my eyes and felt a wonderful calm settle over me. Whatever happened would be a sign of what was to come.

The outside of the house is quite beautiful, with terraced balconies and an arched front door made of dark wood, but inside it reveals itself as a place where only the very lost or very alone come to live. The carpet is dark green and stained with what looks like urine and blood, even though it's probably been cleaned over and over again. The walls are covered in pale, embossed wallpaper, but I have no idea of the design since it's been worn thin over the decades and it's peeling everywhere. There are only three bathrooms, and the one I have to use looks like it was last renovated in the 1970s. There are brown tiles on the walls—the colour of shit.

As I entered the silent house I thought about how I was both lost and alone, and then I realised I had a way out of all that now, and I felt my heart lift a little. Once I got inside I felt instantly cooler. There's no air-conditioning, but it's an old house with thick walls and small curved windows, designed to withstand an Australian summer.

I listened carefully but couldn't hear anyone downstairs in the house.

I quickly walked up the steps to my room, rehearsing what I would say if I met anyone. 'It's my sister's baby, she had to work and her nanny was sick,' I could say. But then I thought, *What if they ask me why I'm not living with my sister?*

They won't ask, I decided, because no one asks anyone anything in places like these. It feels like prison, like we are all carrying our own terrible secrets and have no desire to deal with anyone else's.

I didn't meet anyone on the stairs and I quickly made my way down the passage to my room. As I turned the key and let myself in, I heard the toilet in the bathroom on my level flush and I knew that the old woman I share this floor with was home.

'Thank you, God,' I muttered even though I haven't ever really believed in God, because she could so easily have been in the hallway when I was. There are three levels to this house, with two bedrooms here on the top floor and three bedrooms on the next level and two on the ground floor, although I think the two bedrooms on the ground floor used to be one big bedroom.

As soon as I had locked the door to my room he started to cry again, but a few more desperate bounces and he was quiet. I put my hand gently over his mouth as I strained to hear the old woman walking to her room. Once I heard her door close I relaxed. He looked around the room, enjoying his new surroundings, no doubt.

'Good boy,' I told him as I put him down on the bed. He stared at me with those blue eyes and I could see him deciding that I was a good mother, that I would be a good mother for him. I stretched my arms and rubbed my back, grateful to be no longer carrying anything.

I knew I would have to be in the room for a long time and I was hungry. I needed to go downstairs but I didn't want him to start crying and alert the old woman to his presence.

'What am I going to do with you?' I asked him.

He started waving his legs and arms and making sounds and I knew he wanted to cry again. I picked him up and put him on the floor on the other side of the bed and then I opened one of the dummies I had bought and shoved it in his mouth. I didn't know if he had used a dummy before but he began to suck furiously. I left him on the floor and lay down on the bed next to him, just watching him suck his dummy as though he thought he could get something to come out of it. I don't know how long I was there for but eventually I realised I was actually starving. 'You must be hungry too, little one,' I said, 'but mothers need to take care of themselves first.'

I was afraid to leave him, especially when he spat the dummy out. I put it back in his mouth. 'You keep that in there if you want to get fed,' I said and he obediently held on. 'Good boy,' I said. I knew I was taking a big risk but I had to get to the kitchen.

When I got downstairs I heard the television was on and I looked into the small room with brown velvet couches to find Edna staring at the television. She was watching a story about a kidnapped baby named Zach. I felt my heart race as pictures of the baby flashed up on the television screen. I knew I needed to get back to Xander quickly. I didn't want him to start crying. I was so relieved when she said she was going out.

Xander behaved very well and stayed quiet while I was downstairs.

He's only become difficult in these last few minutes. I'm sure I'm the only one in the house now, but I can't take the chance that someone may hear him cry so I've had to put my plan into place.

I knew what to do if he cried as soon as I opened the door to my room.

The last person who lived here left an old radio behind, so I've turned it on and it's blasting some ridiculous song about dancing that I would never normally listen to, but it's drowning out his noise. Unfortunately, his crying and the noise of the radio are giving me a headache. I breathe deeply and remind myself to remain calm. People have no idea how hard it is to be a good mother.

I used to turn on the radio when Ella wouldn't stop crying. In court, they interviewed the idiot gym-bunny from next door, and she went on and on about how often I would turn up the music to drown out Ella's cries. People have no idea how the sound of a child crying affects their bodies until they have one. My stomach would clench and my breasts would leak and my back muscles went into spasm. I hated it.

Ella was a crier. Not all babies are criers. Some of them only cry when they're hungry or tired or sick, but Ella cried all the time for no reason. I was a good mother, despite that. She was always dressed beautifully, smelling of baby powder. I didn't let her cry for long, even though all the books I read said that sometimes it is okay to give the baby a few minutes to settle themselves. I couldn't bear the sound. It went straight through my head and I felt like I couldn't breathe properly, so it became easier to pick her up and bounce her or sing to her or take her for a walk in the pram. If none of that worked I used the radio for a while—not for long, never for very long. I don't care what was said at my trial—I never let her cry for hours at a time. Never.

Some days Marcus would get home and I would shove her into his arms and lock myself in the bedroom where I would cover my head with a pillow. That was only when

I'd had a really bad day. I think she liked Marcus more than she liked me. She always calmed down whenever he held her—maybe it was just because he was a new person who wasn't wound up from trying to settle her all day. Still, I couldn't help thinking that sometimes she knew what she was doing, even though she was a baby.

'You're not serious, are you?' Marcus said when I told him that I thought Ella liked him better.

'She's always so calm with you.'

'That's because I'm calm with her. You have to relax, *bella*. She's not going to explode if you let her cry for a bit. She can feel you tense up and that makes her tense.'

'Just wait until she can talk. She'll be Daddy's girl for the rest of her life.'

Marcus loved that idea. 'Who's Daddy's girl?' he would say every time he picked her up and she would smile at him and gurgle for him like she was in love.

'For God's sake, just shut up,' I say to Xander. I put my mouth right up against his ear so that he can hear that he's making me angry. But he's in a mood and doesn't listen.

The walls are moving in and I feel myself begin to panic. His voice is loud and intrusive. My head begins to pound the way it did when Ella wouldn't stop crying. 'Don't panic,' I tell myself. He has to stop crying!

I turn the radio up some more and take out the rest of the things I have bought and quickly mix up a bottle of formula with some bottled water. I follow the instructions carefully. I pick him up off the floor and put him on the bed and push the teat into his mouth, but he doesn't like it. He makes a vague effort to suck at the bottle then he spits out what he has in his mouth and screams.

'That's not nice, Xander.'

I can feel myself getting anxious, my hands sweat and my head pounds, and I know that's never a good thing. Luckily I have two bottles. I feel bad that I haven't been able to wash them but I'm sure he'll be fine. Germs help build a baby's immune system. I fill the second bottle with water and when I give it to him he seems to like it better. He sucks for a few minutes but then he starts crying again.

'Shush, shush, shush,' I say as he lies on the bed and thrashes his little legs. He is really cranky now. Ella had a temper, too. Even when she was only a few months old I could see that she would grow up full of fire. She would have been a terrifying teenager. I would have preferred a quiet baby, but Ella clearly emerged from my womb with Marcus's personality.

'Just listen to those lungs,' he would say proudly when she was in the middle of another one of her fits.

'You don't have to listen to it all day,' I told him but he didn't understand.

'She's just a baby. Babies cry all the time. Don't take it so personally.'

Marcus wouldn't say a word against Ella. He wouldn't hear anything bad about her either. People think babies are just trying to communicate their needs, but they're human beings as well. They are born capable of more than simple needs. I believe that sometimes babies get angry and they set out just to piss you off. I never told Marcus that. He would have thought I was unhinged.

I believed this baby would be quiet like me. I try the water again and thankfully he takes it and sucks long and hard and then, even though he's had no real food, he falls asleep again. I feel almost weightless with relief as I turn down the radio and admire his beauty. His head is covered in soft blonde curls and his cheeks are perfect peaches. I feel a rush of love for him and I know that I can love him forever. I know Marcus is going to absolutely adore him as well.

I'm supposed to be at a job interview right now, but working in a clothing store is beneath me and, anyway, being a parent is the best job in the world. I may not have known that once, but I know it now. Right before they led me away to a prison van Marcus came up to me, grabbed my hand and said, 'You didn't deserve to be a mother.' He whispered it so the guard didn't hear. His words were sharper than any knife could be. Marcus always knew how to wound me.

His words pale in comparison to the things that were said to me in prison. In my cell at night I thought a lot about why there was so much vitriol directed towards me. I think it has to do with fear. The first reaction most people have on hearing my story is, 'Oh, that could never happen to me. I wouldn't do that.' But if they are patient enough to listen to the whole story they start to look scared because, if they are honest with themselves, they can see how easy it would be to make the same mistake.

They can picture themselves in the car on the way to work, humming along to the radio, enjoying those few moments when you have nothing to do but sit in traffic, and they can imagine themselves arriving at work and making a cup of hot coffee and really enjoying it because it's the first cup they've had time to drink all morning. Marcus used to laugh about how many cold cups of coffee he found when he came home at night. He used to laugh, but it made me want to cry as I looked at all those cups, poured with the hope of a few minutes to myself.

If they listen to me for long enough they can imagine getting lost in the day as they get through their work and answer calls and daydream about the weekend. They can see themselves at lunch, laughing over a quick pasta with a work colleague about how hard it is to be a working mum and then they can feel the little flip of despair that I know all working mothers feel at the end of the day as they're going home to work all night as well. And then, because they've managed to be with me that far, they recognise that it's possible for it to happen to them. They recognise that it has nothing to do with how clever you are or how much you love your baby or what kind of a mother you are. It's just something that happens because you're a human being—and that is terrifying to most people. That's why they wrote terrible comments on the internet and tweeted that I should have died. It's not that they hated me. It was just fear.

This baby will change everything. I'll be a mother again and no one will look at me with hatred or disgust. I'll join a playgroup and go to music class and make organic baby food. I will be the best mother in the world.

I sit back on the bed and kick off my shoes. I can't wait to tell Marcus. He'll be so excited that we're going to be a family again.

Marcus wouldn't recognise me now.

I think he will like me better now that I am so thin.

Before my life became such a hideous mess I was one of those women who always complained about her weight. I was always trying to lose ten kilos and then, of course, after Ella was born I kind of hung onto the baby weight. Some days, when she finally stopped crying and went to sleep, I would eat my way through a whole tub of ice-cream. And then I would look in the mirror at my rolls of fat and stretch marks and I would know that I was ugly, ugly, ugly. I was too tired to get my hair or my nails done and I couldn't fit into any of my beautiful clothes. Oh how I hated what I had become.

I was permanently exhausted. I dreamt about sleep when I was asleep.

I went into prison twenty kilos heavier than I am now.

My first day in prison was a Tuesday in the middle of July. It was cold in my cell, cold and lonely, and I was feeling violated and degraded from the strip search. I remember being stunned that I was there, sentenced to four years in hell for making a mistake. I thought the nine months I waited for the trial to begin and then the three months I waited to be sentenced were the worst periods of my life. I missed her every day and I was living with Colin and my mother who subjected me to silent dinners and sly looks; but then I was given four years in prison and I learned that there were worse things than living with my mother.

In prison I kept thinking that if I could just get hold of the right person I could explain the situation and they would send me home.

That first day I was sitting on my unmade bed when the siren for lunch sounded. I didn't want to leave, but one of the guards told me I had no choice. I wasn't hungry, but I had to eat. It was an astonishing idea to me and I felt that I was, once again, a child subject to adult rules.

I followed the other inmates to the canteen where the smells reminded me of school-camp dinners of boiled vegetables and greasy chicken schnitzel. I shuffled along, letting them put everything on my tray. I wasn't concentrating—I didn't care. Once I had my food I picked a half-empty table and went to sit down, but when I got there I realised that I had forgotten to get myself cutlery.

I left my plate on the table. No one had told me not to do that in prison. I hadn't done the research on what it would be like to be incarcerated. I didn't have the facts I needed to survive.

By the time I came back to the table it was full. I slipped

onto the bench seat as quietly as I could without looking at anyone, and started to eat. I just shovelled the food into my mouth, needing to get the whole experience over with as soon as possible.

I was halfway through when I realised that the other women at the table were all smiling. Some were hiding giggles behind their hands.

'Enjoying that big wad of gob, are you?' said the woman opposite me, and I looked at her properly for the first time. She had long grey hair tied back into a ponytail, but she didn't appear much older than me. The other women at the table couldn't help themselves once she'd said this: they all began laughing hysterically.

'Settle down!' shouted one of the guards.

'Baby killer,' whispered the grey-haired woman. I had to run for the bathroom with my hand over my mouth, catching vomit as I went.

I couldn't eat the food after that first day. I could only eat the stuff that came in packages I could open myself or fruit that I could peel. I ate a lot of bananas.

I couldn't sit still in the exercise yard, either. I had to keep moving because if I stopped even once there was always someone around to saunter over to me and say, 'Hey, baby killer', or 'It's the murdering mother'. If I kept moving around and around the perimeter with my head down, they didn't bother me.

I was never a very social person so I didn't care about having no one to talk to. I think only children are either outgoing or introverted. I'm an introvert. I prefer my own company to the company of a friend.

By the time my mother and Colin were married, both of Colin's sons had already moved out of home. They only came over for dinner once a month, which I hated because my mother would go into overdrive with her sweet voice, giggling at everything they said and complimenting them all the time. *I have no idea who this woman is*, I wanted to tell them, but I buried myself in books instead, carrying one to the dinner table and the kitchen table and anywhere else I might encounter my mother or Colin or his sons.

'She's just shy,' my mother told everyone.

I couldn't wait to move out, to be alone.

I thought I would happily be alone my whole life until I met Marcus, then I preferred his company over anything.

Chapter Fifteen

'Anything?' says Ali to Liam from forensics.

'Nothing obvious,' he replies. 'I mean, the carpets are stained, and we've taken swabs from everything in his room, but it's a house with three young kids. My place looks the same.'

'Yeah, I thought so,' says Ali.

'We'll be back if we find anything worth looking into after we've analysed the samples. We've got the family computer and the husband's laptop, some clothes from the laundry hamper, a dummy and a used nappy. I'll let you know once we've had the IT people go through the computers.'

'So I can let them back in?'

'Yeah, no reason not to.'

'Do you want me to go and get them?' asks Mike.

'No,' says Ali. 'I'll do it.'

They have been sitting at the kitchen table surrounded by pencils and colouring books, waiting for forensics to finish. The house feels frozen in time, as though the last time air moved through it was this morning and now nothing will move again until the family is restored. On the floor of the family room is a baby gym where Ali knows that Zach lies watching the black and white shapes designed to stimulate his brain.

Ali doesn't want to think about what will happen if they do not find Zach or if they find him but someone has ended his life. *What kind of a person?* is a question that gets thrown about a lot when it comes to criminal cases involving children. Human beings are biologically designed to protect the young to ensure the survival of the species— someone who will take the life of a child is an anathema, a freak of nature that can never be truly understood.

Ali can imagine that if the worst happens and Zach never comes home, Malia will close the door to his room and leave everything the way it is right now for years and years.

When Abigail died, Ali had felt the need to get rid of everything as quickly as she could. The pain was so intense that she thought she would only be able to survive if she erased all evidence of her child's existence.

She's glad that Reuben stopped her; that he made her wait until she could go through Abi's room slowly and hold onto a few things that smelled of her daughter or that held some memory of the little person she was becoming. At the top of the linen closet in her house she has a collection of Abigail's things. There is the jumpsuit she wore home from the hospital and the divinely soft fluffy pink dog that her mother-in-law Joan gave her to keep in her cot, and a copy of *Guess How Much I Love You* along with two albums filled with photographs.

She and Reuben had documented every moment they had with her, and even though her friends with more than one child had laughed at how many pictures she took of Abigail, she's grateful that she did now. A month after she died and everyone else had gone back to their lives, Ali would look through the albums and reassure herself that her daughter had existed and that there was a reason why she woke up in tears every morning.

It has been a few months since Ali has felt the need to take down the small collection and go through it, touching and holding things that Abigail touched and held.

It's one in the afternoon and Ali can feel her hunger headache coming on.

'Do you think we can leave them to get something to eat?' she asks Mike.

'Sure, I'll call Ossie, make sure that we can get another team here for an hour.'

Mike has been twirling one of the pencils and dropping it over and over as he takes calls from the station about possible leads. The sound is starting to drive Ali insane, another indication that she needs to eat.

She stands up and stretches. She suspected forensics wouldn't find anything, but everything had to be done by the book.

She walks next door and knocks. Mrs Boulos, the neighbour, opens the door, and Ali can see Malia standing behind her. The woman looks pale and haunted. Ali knows she's probably had nothing to eat all day and her blood-sugar level is low.

'You can bring everyone home now,' says Ali when Malia steps outside.

Malia looks at her for a moment. 'Not everyone,' she says.

'I'm sorry …'

'I know,' says Malia. 'You're doing everything you can. I can't actually bear to hear those words again.'

She turns and goes back into the house and Ali hears her calling the children. Soon the whole family is outside. Malia starts to walk down the front path and then she turns and goes back to hug Mrs Boulos.

'They find him, they find him,' says the older woman.

Back in their own house the children return to their station in front of the television.

'You should try and eat something,' says Ali to Malia.

'I don't think I could swallow. Mrs Boulos gave me some tea. I'll be fine.'

'Are you sure? Mike and I are going to step out for an hour or so just to get something to eat and check in with everything happening at the station. It would obviously be best if you stayed here in case we need you. Another team will be along soon, keeping an eye on things while we're at lunch.'

'If they find him, you have to come and get me. He needs to be fed. It's been hours.'

Malia gestures to her chest where, once again, milk is staining her T-shirt.

'Of course I will. There is no way I wouldn't do that. I know he needs to be fed.'

'I feel like I'm going mad,' says Malia.

Ali touches her shoulder and nods. She remembers the feeling well. Once Abigail had officially been declared dead, she kept thinking she was imagining the whole thing. When they told her that an autopsy would have to be performed she said, 'But you'll put her to sleep, won't you—so it doesn't hurt?' That was when Reuben had asked her to take something to help her sleep.

'Ali, sweetheart, please, I'm begging you,' he said, and so she had taken the pill and curled herself around a pillow and drifted off to sleep. When she woke up the truth of what had happened had hit her and she had screamed into the pillow until she was hoarse.

'Malia, can I say something?' says Ali.

Malia doesn't answer, but Ali takes her silence for acquiescence. 'This is the worst situation possible for a mother to find herself in. If you go over and over what happened you'll drive yourself crazy and you won't be able to help your kids or deal with Zach when we find him. Think in small steps. Do one thing at a time and only think about what you're going to do next. Take a shower and only think about that, and have a cup of tea—and only think about that. It will make it easier to get through this time.'

'How would you know that?' says Malia. She crosses her arms and her lips thin, locking Ali out of her situation, believing, Ali is sure, that she has no idea what Malia's suffering.

Ali opens her mouth to reply but then she shuts it again and takes a deep breath, pushing down the confession. This is not about her.

'I've been doing this a long time,' she says. 'Trust me on this: sometimes when you stop going around in circles you remember something new. If you can rest you should. When Zach comes home he's going to be unsettled and you're going to be up all night.'

'Please God,' pleads Malia.

'Ready to go,' says Mike as he walks past them.

Ali gives Malia's shoulder another squeeze and she follows Mike to his car.

Outside the house the press throw a few questions at them—'Do you know where the baby is? Do you suspect the parents? Do you have any leads?'—hoping that something will provoke a response from one of them, but

Ali and Mike know better than to catch a reporter's eye. Cameras flash, so at least there will be pictures of the detectives looking serious. Ali nods at the constable whose job consists of keeping the reporters behind the police tape.

'You drive, okay?' says Mike. 'I'm starving.'

'Me too,' Ali says when they have pulled out onto the main road. 'And I could drink an entire bottle of wine.'

'You and me both, but I don't think we're heading home anytime soon. Burgers okay with you?'

'Yeah, great. When do you think Olivia will be ready to interview the kids?'

'Ossie says she'll head over there in an hour. She's finishing up with a six-year-old who was molested by her stepfather.'

'Do you think the kids know anything more than they've said?' asks Ali.

'Probably not, they were inside the whole time and if either of them had seen anything they would have said so I'm sure, but Olivia does have a way of getting kids to remember small details.'

'Yes, she's really good,' agrees Ali, thinking of the petite Olivia who wears her hair in pigtails and seems to know what kids of every age are into. 'I don't know how she does what she does, how she spends all her time talking to traumatised kids.'

Olivia was a child psychologist before she joined the police force, but sometimes Ali looks at her and can't imagine how her small frame doesn't buckle under the weight of all the broken children she interviews and the terrible things they tell her.

'So … gut feel?' asks Mike.

'I don't know, Mike, it's like the kid has disappeared into thin air and usually that would mean that the parents had something to do with it, but I'm not getting that feeling from these people. How about you?'

'Nah, I have to agree. She loves the kids. He's a dickhead, but I don't think he'd ever do anything to hurt them.'

'Did you get hold of the manager at the pub?'

'Yeah. He told me he was there from around six and that he was using a one-dollar machine and chewing through twenty bucks at a time. He only left just before he closed up at two. The manager said it was almost like he wanted to lose. Apparently he comes in regularly, sometimes only one night a week, sometimes two or three. He's never with anyone and he doesn't really make conversation with the other habitual gamblers.'

'Why does he do it? Why throw away all that money?'

'Beats me. I never understood why my father needed to do it. The risk was so much greater than the reward.'

'Maybe because sometimes there's a big payoff,' suggests Ali.

'I suppose, but I don't think that's why addicts get so hooked.'

'Why then?'

Ali parks the car in front of a gourmet burger restaurant they both love. Mike gets out without answering, but

Ali knows that he's heard the question. He'll answer when he's ready. Mike may not like having to deal with gamblers because of his father, but it would be hard to find a member of the force who never came across a case that brought up their own baggage. Mike came from an unstable home where some days there was not enough money for food. There were constables who found themselves on domestic violence calls that reminded them of their own lives and those who arrived at car accidents that gave them flashbacks of their own experiences.

Inside the restaurant Mike waves at the chef standing at the counter.

'Hey, guys,' calls the young man, smiling. 'The usual?'

'Yeah, mate,' says Mike and they take their seats at a small round table. It's past the lunchtime rush and the place is quiet. Mike twirls the salt and pepper shakers on the table while they wait.

Only when they both have their burgers in front of them does he answer Ali's question.

'I once went to one of those meetings—you know, for the families of addicts?'

'Yeah.'

'It wasn't specifically targeted at gambling, but there were a few people there who talked about it. I think it's a way of relieving stress—a legal way. One guy said his mother told him that when she was in front of the pokies she didn't have to think about anything else except the wheels going round. Her bad marriage and shitty kids just disappeared. It's like any other addiction, except it's legal and it doesn't fuck up your body or brain. It's about not having to think.'

'So what is Ian trying not to think about?'

'Okay, this is just a theory,' says Mike as he takes a large bite of his burger and then washes it down with some Diet Coke. 'But …' He finishes chewing. 'I was watching him with the kids—you know, when he arrived—and he seems to get tired of them really quickly. He lets them climb on him for five minutes and then he gets pissed off and tells them to leave him alone. It may just be today but the kids don't seem to be finding his behaviour that strange. They just get off him and go back to sitting next to Malia or back to the television. He seems to have a low tolerance for them. Like he only wants to play with them for a few minutes and then he's done. I could be wrong about this, but I don't think Ian is finding fatherhood all it's cracked up to be. I think he spends his nights in the pub so when he gets home the kids are asleep and he can pretend it's just him and Malia.'

Ali picks up one of her fries, breaks it in half and then puts it down again.

'I'd eat all those carbs,' says Mike. 'You don't know when we're going to eat again.'

Ali obediently finishes what's left on her plate. 'But do you think he may have actually had something to do with this?'

'I toyed with the idea. I mean, a third kid throws things into chaos. If you have two kids you have two parents going in two different directions, but a third one makes it more difficult, especially financially. It's possible that Zach was a surprise.'

'It's hard enough with just one child and two working parents,' says Ali.

'Right, but when you think about it logically a whole number of things would have had to go right for him to be able to snatch his own kid. What if Malia hadn't gone to get milk? What if she and the kids had pulled into Maccas on the way to school instead? What if she had gone next door to the neighbour for milk? It would have been too difficult to make the whole thing work. This crime is most likely opportunistic. Someone was walking past and saw the baby in the car.'

'They had to open the car door to see the baby,' says Ali. 'Whoever took him actually thought about it.'

'Yeah, but I don't think he or she woke up this morning and decided to steal a baby.'

'So where does that leave us? I know they're getting calls back at the station, but Ossie says it's just the usual crackpots who see aliens every Tuesday. It's not getting us anywhere. He's a breastfed baby and he won't take formula unless he really has to and he may dehydrate before that in this heat.'

Ali feels her eyes fill as she thinks about Charlie. She should not be away from him. Malia would give anything to have her baby in her arms right now and here Ali is, wasting this precious time by being at work.

Mike leans forward and covers her hand with his. 'Don't question yourself, Ali, don't do that to yourself. Linda drove herself mad when we first put River in day care. She used to stay up all night worrying about how he was pining for her during the day. I don't know why you women question yourselves so much. If Linda hadn't gone back to work we would have lost the house—simple as that. And both my kids are fine. They're going through the dickhead teenage years now, but mostly they're fine.'

Ali laughs. 'I don't know how someone like you ends up with two sons called River and Stone.'

'I don't know either. I married a hippie and I thought I could change her—never a good idea. Come on, let's get back to it.'

'Bathroom first,' says Ali. As she moves to the back of the restaurant to the ladies Ali pulls out her phone and calls Reuben.

'Mum is counting down the minutes until she can pick him up. I told her she could get him early if she wanted to. I think she's just sitting on her couch watching the clock. She says she'll feed him grilled cheese on toast and fruit for dinner, and she wanted me to check that it was okay with you?'

'Hello to you, too,' says Ali. 'Don't worry, I'll text her.'

'I have to go, babe, the meeting is starting. I promise I will keep you updated. Breathe and get on with your job. Get that baby home to his mother.'

Once Ali has used the bathroom, checked her appearance and decided that there's nothing she can do about how pale she looks because it's just what happens on a day that is so emotionally draining, she texts Joan.

Charlie will love toasted cheese.

But do you want me to try something else? comes the immediate reply.

Whatever works. I trust you. Reuben is six feet tall ☺, she texts back and is answered with a smiley face from Joan.

Back at the car she finds Mike in the passenger seat, the phone glued to his ear, nodding.

'Okay,' he says. 'I know, okay. We'll check it out first before we say anything.' He hangs up.

'What?' says Ali.

'They have a woman down at the Willow Street station,' says Mike, stumbling over words in his urgency to get the information out. 'She came into the station alone and she's going ... she's going on and on about how she didn't mean to hurt the baby. She told one of the constables there that she only wanted to help him, to save him and now she can't wake him up.'

'Willow Street is only two suburbs away,' says Ali, and she feels a draught of cold air in the sealed car.

'She won't tell them where the baby is. She's refusing to tell anyone except the mother. She says she wants to speak to the mother.'

'Fuck,' whispers Ali.

'Yeah,' says Mike. 'Fuck.'

Chapter Sixteen

'Never speak too soon,' Edna's father used to say, and she has always believed that to be the truth. She thought she and Jackie were going to get along just fine despite what the woman had or had not done, but then the music started.

Vincent used to play the radio when he lived in the room Jackie now lives in, but he loved classical music so even when he turned it up a bit, Edna didn't mind. Vincent was a bit of an odd lad. Robbie said that he suffered from autism. Edna had never heard of autism before she met Vincent. In her day Vincent would have been declared strange or retarded, which is an evil-sounding word, but it was a different world then. Vincent was all right at the beginning, but then he went a bit funny, started getting angry over nothing and banging his head against the wall and his social worker said it would be better for him to be somewhere with more carers.

Robbie said he had no idea where he'd been sent, which made Edna cross. She would have liked to visit the boy, although he was hardly a boy. Robbie said Vincent was twenty-seven when he arrived to stay in the house. He used to take off all his clothes and run around the place, and sometimes he would open the door and sprint up the street and Robbie had to run after him if his carer wasn't around to stop him. The carer only came for a few hours a day because Vincent had been declared 'self-sufficient', according to Robbie.

Vincent wasn't a bad boy, just different. He liked to hug and Edna never minded if he was dressed. Truth was, it was quite nice to have a hug every now and again. People never really grew out of the need to be touched.

Harry liked to hug. Edna tries not to think about Harry too much because it always makes her sad that they never got to live out their last years together, but he crosses her mind two or three times a day even though he's been gone for nearly twenty-five years.

He would have been a good dad too, but when they were trying for kids there wasn't anything to be done if you couldn't have a baby. Harry hadn't liked the idea of adopting, but Edna would have loved any baby—black, brown or white, it wouldn't have mattered. All she had wanted was a baby.

Edna gives herself a shake so she stops thinking about

Harry and remembers what is bothering her. *The music.* She hadn't seen Jackie when she got back from her pub lunch, which had been excellent. She'd been going to have a steak sandwich, but Paulo had convinced her to give the fish and chips a try and she's glad she did. The batter on the fish was light and crispy and seasoned perfectly, and the chef always makes the best chips. Paulo made sure she got two great big wedges of lemon on the side as well. Edna can't remember the last time she had a meal that good.

Paulo told Edna that Gunther, the chef, trained in Europe, but she's not sure she believes him. Sometimes Paulo likes to pull her leg a bit and she doesn't know why a chef trained in Europe would be working at the Rose Hotel which is, after all, quite run down with its shabby furniture and stains on the bar. She had two G&Ts instead of her usual one, and then she played her five dollars on the pokies. She hadn't won anything, but that's why she restricts herself to five dollars a week. The pension doesn't stretch very far but Paulo had given her two for one on the drinks. 'Senior's discount,' he'd said, but she knows that it's not really the case. Paulo likes to give the regulars a free drink every so often. Paulo had also been watching the news about the baby but he didn't know anything more than what Edna had seen earlier. 'I've never heard of something like that before,' he said. 'If I was the dad I'd be ready to kill whoever had done that.'

'And you'd be right,' Edna had said.

All in all, it had been a lovely way to pass the time and she'd come home this afternoon ready for a good long nap. But she hadn't been asleep for more than five minutes before the music started—so loud it made the walls shake.

'This isn't on,' she says resolutely and heaves herself off the bed. She takes her dressing gown off the back of her bedroom door and ties the belt tightly around her waist. 'Even young Robbie would have a problem with this,' she grumbles and opens the door, only to be blasted by noise. She makes her way along the passage until she comes to Jackie's room where she bangs as hard as she can, hurting her hand in the process. She stands there for a good five minutes, resting in between thumps, but no one opens the door. Finally she gives up and goes back to her room.

Her nap has been ruined and she gets dressed again, determined to go and find young Robbie and make him get the woman to turn it down. He's usually about at this time of the day.

As she makes her way to the stairs that lead her to the main part of the house, one song on the radio ends and there are a few seconds of blissful silence during which Edna is almost sure she hears a baby cry. She stops walking for a moment and holds her breath while she listens, but another song starts up and all she can hear is someone screaming about wanting to … something, something.

Her head starts to pound. She'd really needed that nap. 'Rude, so bloody rude,' she mutters to herself. She'd warned Robbie about letting in the riffraff, oh yes she had, and now look what's happened. Even Vincent was a quiet member of the house when he wasn't taking off his clothes and shrieking around the place. Edna is sure that Jackie has come to them straight from prison where she was probably jailed for killing her neighbours after they complained about the amount of noise she made.

She thinks she hears the sound of a baby crying again, but she knows it's only her ears playing tricks on her. She'll have to get herself checked next time the audiologist visits the senior centre. 'She'll make us all mad,' she says as she enters the kitchen and puts the kettle on to boil.

With tea and a chocolate biscuit in front of her, Edna sits down at the kitchen table to wait for young Robbie, who's not sitting in the little alcove where he has a desk and a chair so he can pay bills for the house and whatever else it is that he does when he's here—not get in the carpet cleaners, that's for sure. She intends to sit there until he comes in—that is, if she can stand the bloody awful music.

Chapter Seventeen

2.00 pm

Malia stands under the hot water with her eyes clenched shut. It's such a relief to be under the warm water, letting her breast milk flow down her body and disappear down the drain. The terrible swollen feeling has subsided, but she is still afraid of a blocked duct if she doesn't feed soon.

It's after two. Zach has not had her milk for seven hours. He would have been fed with his bottle by Sylvie or one of the other carers at around ten-thirty, and she knows he would have been fretful for an immediate feed when she picked him up at two. She often feeds Zach before she leaves to pick up Rhiannon and Aaron from preschool and school. Sylvie has looked after all three of her children and although she deals more with the older children she always makes sure to check on Zach and sometimes feed him and give him a cuddle. Malia and Sylvie have been friends since high school and Malia was overjoyed when her friend moved up to Sydney with her partner soon after she did and opened a day care centre.

'Very fortuitous for you,' Sylvie had said when she came to visit Malia in the hospital after she gave birth to Aaron.

'Oh, I think I'll keep him home with me forever,' Malia had laughed, but she put Aaron's name down on the list to get in anyway. Sylvie has called three times and Malia knows that her other friends from mother's group and Gymbaroo have called as well. She has stopped looking at her phone. There have been hundreds of calls from friends and relatives.

Maybe Zach hasn't had any milk at all. She thinks about how thirsty he must be, how afraid and confused he must be now that everything he has known for his five months of life has disappeared. He's basically an animal at this age, motivated only by his need to be warm and fed and feel safe. When she picks him up from his cot each morning he snuffles at her neck like a puppy would, smelling his mother. She imagines him crying and lifting his arms, looking for comfort from her and finding no one—or, worse, finding someone who wants to hurt him.

'Oh God,' she says aloud as her tears mingle with the water and disappear down the drain with her milk. She simply can't accept any of this.

Ian comes into the bathroom and stands watching her until she turns her back on him. She doesn't want him to look at her because she can't stand to look at him. She finds it difficult to believe that she let him touch her this morning; that she let him inside her. She doesn't think she could ever let him touch her again.

She wants to hurt him, wants him to feel some of this slicing pain because even though he looks devastated she knows that he can't be feeling the same. Ian doesn't like babies and he'd always had little to do with the children when they were small. He made a bit of an effort with Aaron—changing nappies and feeding him an expressed bottle if she pushed him into it so she could sleep a little—but when Rhiannon arrived he concentrated on being with Aaron when the two-year-old was funny and delightful company and then handed him back when he was hard work. Malia doesn't think he's even changed Zach's nappy yet. He prefers the children when they are old enough to communicate their needs. Caring for the babies is her job.

When Aaron was born Ian had seemed, at first, to relish his role as a father. Malia's parents had come to stay. Her mother had cooked and cleaned and done the washing, and even managed to get up at night to take Aaron after he'd fed so Malia could go back to sleep. Ian and her father had baby-proofed the house together, and Ian had seemed excited about being a father, about having a son. He used to sit next to Malia when she fed Aaron and they would talk about what kind of boy they were going to raise.

In those first few weeks Malia would often find Ian in Aaron's room, just staring down at his sleeping son. 'Amazing, isn't he?' Ian would say, and she would nod, and they would stand together and marvel at the beautiful boy they had created. It seemed too good to be true—and, of course, it was.

The reality of the huge life change set in soon enough. When Malia's parents left to go back to Melbourne Malia had asked Ian for more and more help. Without her mother there she had to keep the house clean and do the washing and make dinner and get up at night and settle the baby. On days when Aaron was fussy all day and had slept little, Malia would hand him to Ian as he walked through the door at night only to have him passed straight back.

'I'm exhausted, Ian. Please just give me half an hour.'

'I'm tired too, Malia. I've been at work all day. I need to unwind.'

'And I'm still in my pyjamas. You need to hold your son so I can do something else.'

Sometimes Malia would put Aaron on a blanket on the floor next to Ian and simply walk away, locking herself in the bathroom and turning on the shower so she couldn't hear anything. She congratulated herself on the strategy until the one time she emerged from the shower to find Aaron on the floor, crying, covered in vomit and Ian nowhere to be seen.

'I couldn't stand listening to him cry,' Ian told her when

he returned home from the pub to find Malia waiting up for him. 'I told you I'm no good with babies.'

'But … but …' Malia had spluttered, aghast at his ability to ignore his child when he was clearly in need.

Malia thought about leaving him that night. She slept on the floor in Aaron's room, ashamed of leaving her child to someone who didn't care as much as she did. She barely closed her eyes, instead contemplating what she would do the next morning and how long it would take to pack. Only when her plan was in place had she managed to drift off. She had woken late in the morning to find the cot empty and Ian giving Aaron an expressed bottle of breast milk in the family room.

'Sorry I was such a dick last night,' he said, smiling at her, disarming her, pulling her back to him again.

By then she was part of a mother's group and all the women who came each week complained about how little their husbands did, how little they understood about what it was like to be home all day with a baby. Malia convinced herself that she was overreacting but she never left Aaron alone with Ian unless he expressly agreed to babysit him, something he seldom did.

When Rhiannon was born Ian had seemed enamoured with the idea of having a daughter—until, once more, her parents returned to Melbourne and he became Malia's only support. Standing in the shower now, she wonders at herself and her inability to simply walk away from Ian. She recognises she had no idea how bad his gambling problem is, of just how much money he has wasted, but even the little she did know should have been enough. He had told her he didn't want children. He had said it over and over again when they were dating and she'd still stayed with him and tried to make him fit her idea of the perfect family man and now she is standing under a hot shower and all she feels is stupid and humiliated for having ever trusted him. Ian is a boy and she should have married a man.

A man would have made sure he brought home the milk, she thinks and finds herself choking on her anger.

'He's probably dead,' she says to Ian, wanting to shock, wanting to wound him.

'God, Malia, why would you say that?'

Malia turns off the shower and grabs a towel.

'What are you saying? Why are you talking like this?'

'I'm sure it doesn't bother you, Ian. One less kid to worry about is not a bad thing.'

'You sound fucking insane, Malia.'

'I sound insane?' Malia laughs. 'You literally took food out of your children's mouths last night. Do you understand that? You lost so much money that you couldn't get them milk for breakfast. Aren't you ashamed of yourself, Ian? Aren't you ashamed of the man you've become?'

'Yes, all right, fucking yes!' shouts Ian. 'Don't you think I know this is my fault?' He sinks onto the bed in their bedroom and drops his head. 'It's all I can think about, Malia. I'm so scared for him, for us.'

Malia opens her cupboard and pulls out a dress she can

wear with her nursing bra. She gets dressed with her back to Ian.

'Bullshit, Ian,' she says as she stuffs more nursing pads in her bra. 'The only person you're really scared for is yourself. You've never worked out how to be part of a family. For the past five years I've been hoping that your priorities would change, that you would find yourself looking at your beautiful, perfect kids and know that you should be thanking God for them every day, but it's not going to happen. It's never going to happen and I know that now.'

'I'm sorry. You have no idea how sorry I am, and I promise you that once this is over and we get him back it's going to be different. I won't let you down again, I promise. I won't go back to the pokies. I'll be home for dinner every night, we'll go on holiday, we'll do things other families do. Please, Malia, you have to believe me when I say I'm sorry. I can't lose you. I can't lose the kids.'

Ian is crying now. Malia has never seen him like this. She knows that she should feel it's a breakthrough, but she finds herself feeling nothing at all.

'How long have you had a separate account?' she asks.

'Not long,' says Ian.

'Please don't lie to me, not again, not anymore.'

'I opened it after Aaron was born. I just wanted to have a little bit for myself. I was working so hard, and you were home with him, and I just needed some money so I could go to the pub and not worry about you watching every dollar I spent.'

Malia can't allow herself to calculate how much money Ian has lost. When Aaron was six months old and Malia's savings could no longer be a buffer between what Ian was making and how much money they needed to live, she had gone to the bank and lowered the amount that could be withdrawn from their joint bank account. Ian had only protested a little but seemed to accept why it needed to be done. 'I'm just like my grandfather,' he would say. 'Can't keep away from pretty women and gambling.'

'You need to stop,' she'd told him once, twice, two hundred, a thousand times.

'I need this to preserve my sanity. I don't lose much. The most I ever put in is about a hundred. It's not a lot over the course of a month.'

Malia feels like an idiot now that she knows the truth. How many bills could his secret bank account have paid? How many sleepless nights could have been avoided? How many fights about money? A sad truth has become apparent about Ian—his own happiness is more important than his family's wellbeing. He is willing to sacrifice their needs in order to satisfy his own and Malia can't live with a man like that, not anymore.

'I think you need to leave,' she says to Ian.

'Okay, I'll wait for you in the living room and then we can talk.'

'No, Ian, I mean you need to leave this house, this marriage. I can't deal with this anymore.'

'Malia, don't,' says Ian. 'Don't say things you're going to

regret. You're wound up about Zach. When they find him we'll work this out. I'll see a counsellor and I'll get it under control. We can start again and I'll do better.'

'I don't think so.'

She picks up her hairbrush and begins to brush her hair. The movement is soothing. She doesn't say anything else because she doesn't want to hear anything else from Ian.

'Malia, listen,' says Ian, but he is interrupted by the sound of the doorbell. 'Fuck.'

He leaves the room to answer the door. Malia pulls her hair into a ponytail. It's the right decision; she knows it's the right decision. In the mirror she sees a woman who's had enough. There is no going back now.

'Malia,' says Ian returning to the bedroom.

'Ian, I don't want to discuss this now …'

'The police are here. Mike and Ali, they're here again. They want you to go with them.'

Ian's face is pale and he is breathing fast. Malia feels her hands grow cold and she forces her mind to still and think of nothing but movement. She must find shoes. She must put shoes on her feet. She must walk to the door. She must look at the detectives when they speak.

It's over now.

She knows it's over.

Chapter Eighteen

He's gone back to sleep again. When he woke up and started screaming I felt acid rise in my throat. I thought he would sleep for hours. I fumbled for the radio and turned it back on, filling the room with music. I shoved the bottle in his mouth, holding it there until he drank some more water. In the middle of everything someone pounded on the door, just hitting it again and again, and I knew it was that old bitch back from her lunch. He pushed the bottle out of his mouth and I grabbed the dummy, ignoring the witch outside my door, and held it in his mouth until he finally started sucking and went back to sleep. She must have left after a minute or two because she's not there now. I'm keeping the music on in case he wakes up again, just not as loud. Babies need to learn to sleep with noise.

I don't know why he wouldn't drink some of the formula earlier; he must be very hungry. He's probably just being stubborn. He'll eat soon enough.

I thought I would have a heart attack when she thumped on my door. It seems almost funny now.

Maybe she would have known how to get Xander to take his formula? She probably had a houseful of kids when she was younger, although I haven't seen anyone visit her in the week I've been here. I imagine she was a real bitch of a mother and her kids hate her.

I don't think I will let my mother be in Xander's life. She hasn't earned the right to be a grandmother to another child of mine. When I was in prison she visited me once a month for a whole year before I asked her to stop coming. She would sit across from me with her sad eyes filling with tears and talk on and on about Ella. God, it was boring.

Her whole phone was filled up with pictures from when she used to babysit and she kept making me look at them. Ella smiling and Ella laughing and Ella looking surprised and Ella looking upset and Ella tasting some minced pear and Ella sleeping. Ella, Ella, Ella. It was all she could talk about. She kept telling me how much she missed her and how terrible she felt when she walked past the room in her house where she stored all her Ella things.

I don't know what she was trying to do, but there was no way I was going to join her in her wallowing. It was taking everything I had in me to survive being in prison and I wanted her to ask about me, to talk about me.

'Either stop saying her name or don't come back here again,' I said to her the last time I saw her.

'Surely you want to discuss your child?' she said. 'Surely you want to be able to remember her with someone else who loved her?'

'No,' I said, 'and if you want to keep talking about her, I'd prefer it if you didn't come back.'

The next time she was supposed to come I was told no one was waiting for me in the visitors' lounge. I knew then that I'd made the right decision.

I don't miss her at all. My mother had no interest in me beyond my ability to produce a grandchild for her to love and adore the way she never loved and adored me. Bad mothers don't get to be grandmothers, no matter how much they claim to have changed.

I breathe in the wonderful silence, luxuriating in the peace and contentment I feel. It's so easy to love your children when they're asleep. Marcus is really going to have to help with this baby. He's very difficult. Not as difficult as Ella was, but still a man needs to be involved in raising his child. I don't approve of women at home and men out in the workforce.

The worst time of the day for me was when my mother was home. It was better when she was at work. After she married my stepfather she gave up her work and tried to go back to mothering me, but I was over her by then and sceptical of everything she said and did. There is nothing wrong with children spending the bulk of their days with nannies and in day care until they can behave like adults and take care of themselves. Marcus didn't believe in that, but I'm sure he'll be ready to see things my way now. He wasn't happy when I went back to work.

'But she's so little, *bella*. How can anyone love her like you can?' he said.

'I can't stay home anymore, Marcus. You told me to stop calling you and to find something to do so that's exactly what I did.'

'But won't you miss her?' he asked. 'I miss her like crazy when I'm at work. It would be much harder for a mother.' He asked me the question quietly and then he stared at me with that intense look he sometimes got on his face when he was trying to understand me, as though I was someone he didn't know very well.

'The day care I've found for her is very good. She'll be happy there, you'll see. It's good for women to go to back to work, Marcus. It's necessary. My mother worked when I was little.'

'Not six months old,' he said.

'Marcus, if you want to you can stay home and take care of her. I'm going back to work and we'll all be much happier because of it.' I thought that if I went back to work I would find a way to reclaim the person I had been when we were first married, that I would be able to engage him again because I would have something more interesting to tell him when he came home at night than just what she had eaten or how much she had slept. I wanted to be interesting to him again but it didn't work. I sat at work and thought about him surrounded by all the women at his office who hadn't had children, just like I'd sat at home and thought about them and their perfect bodies and pretty faces, and then I had to call him over and over again.

My room is getting a bit smelly because he's pooped and there's no way I'm going to change him because I'll have to go downstairs to throw out the dirty nappy, and I can't face any questions. Even over the music I've heard the front door slam a few times so I assume there are more people in the house now.

I've already changed his wet nappy once. I haven't changed a nappy for five years and I couldn't believe that my hands could remember what to do. I think he pooped about five minutes after I changed this nappy, which is exactly what Ella used to do, but it's something he needs to know won't be acceptable in my house. I swear I saw Ella smile at me once while she did it. It went all up her back as well, and it took me twenty minutes to clean her up and change her. I was late for work in the end and had to deal with all the sly glances from everyone in the office who didn't have children.

The quicker he knows who's in charge, the better. He can sit in his stinky nappy for a few hours.

I hope he manages to keep himself quiet. It's going to be difficult to ignore one of the men or the fat owner banging on the door. He thinks he's so fucking superior because he has rented a room to an ex-convict. He thinks he deserves some sort of reward for letting me stay but he and his sanctimonious smile can go fuck themselves. I take a deep breath because I can feel my body heating up with rage. I need to calm down.

'You stay quiet,' I tell Xander, even though he's sleeping peacefully. He's sweating a lot, but so am I. It's hideously hot in my room now. He must be tired from all the screaming he did. Babies should come with an 'off' button. The next time he wakes up I might have to give him a shake, just to let him know that screaming will not be tolerated. I used to give Ella a shake every now and again when she wouldn't stop crying. I didn't hurt her, it was just to give her a bit of a fright and make her take a deep breath. It worked sometimes and she would stop crying, but one day Marcus saw me do it and lectured me about damaging her brain.

'I'm not stupid,' I told him. 'I would never shake her hard enough to do any real harm.'

'You don't know that,' he said. 'You have no idea how little it takes to damage a baby's brain. She's very fragile.'

Marcus used to go on and on about how fragile Ella was, while I was the one who'd read all the books and spent all day taking care of her. I knew that she was tougher than she looked.

'People dump their babies in garbage bins and they still survive,' I said and he gave me this look; I hated that look. It was a look that said, *I have no idea who you are.*

I used to fantasise about going back to the beginning of our relationship. I wish I knew how quickly that time would pass so I could have savoured it. I think we'll begin again now. It will be a new beginning, except we'll already have the baby. Xander looks like he's in a deep sleep. His breathing has slowed. He must really be tired.

I take out my mobile phone. It's nearly three o'clock and I wonder where Marcus will be. He may be onsite dealing with clients. I should wait until he's home and he's unwound from the day to speak to him, but I can't help myself. I feel all fidgety, just as I used to when I would wait for his calls after we started dating.

At work they told me that I wasn't concentrating. I got a few things wrong and the journalists were upset when people wrote in to complain.

'I'm sure you're aware that because of the internet, researchers like you are no longer as vital to a magazine as they once were,' my boss Amanda said after they'd picked up the third mistake I'd made in one issue.

'As long as the writers are too lazy to do their own googling, I'll always have a job,' I said.

Amanda was shocked. I could see that she had no idea what to say to me. I'd always been such a mouse. I never challenged anyone or bothered anyone. I'd learned to be quiet from my mother.

'She's such a well behaved young lady,' my stepfather told my mother the first time he met me, and she smiled and blushed as though he was complimenting her parenting skills. I smiled too because I knew what would happen if I explained to Colin exactly how my mother taught me to be so well behaved.

After I'd been sent to prison my mother was interviewed by a journalist for a major newspaper and she told them she was *deeply ashamed* of me. The media loved that. There were pictures of her all over the internet with the words *deeply ashamed* over her head as though it was all she had ever thought of me and all she would ever think of me.

'I didn't say it like that,' she wailed when I quizzed her on the article. 'I was misquoted. They asked me how I felt and I said I was deeply ashamed, but I meant because I didn't call you that day to check on Ella.'

I didn't believe her. Besides, she did call me. I told her Ella was fine. I thought she was fine, after all. I didn't know about the mistake.

The jury at my trial was instructed to disregard anything they may have seen or read about the case, but that was impossible to do. Some facts are hard to forget. One article on the internet said that Ella had died in pain as one organ after another shut down in the broiling heat. I'm sure that's an exaggeration and that she simply went to sleep and didn't wake up again. I keep seeing her crying and lifting her arms as she waits for someone to pick her up. She was my baby and I failed her, but I'm going to do better this time. I know I am.

I take a deep breath. It's time. I can't wait any longer.

I punch in Marcus's number on my mobile phone. It's

the first time I've used this new phone—it's cheap and crappy but all I could afford. I thought about calling my mother and stepfather, but what for? I'm sure my mother has spent the last few years trying to forget that she ever made the mistake of having a child. I feel a bubble of excitement in my stomach. I can't wait to hear Marcus's voice again; I can't wait to hear him call me *bella*.

Marcus's phone rings for a long time and for a moment I think that I will have to leave a message, and I start to compose one in my head. I won't tell him about the baby now, I'll just let him know I'm free.

'Hello.'

'Marcus?'

'Yeah.'

'It's me.'

My heart is racing and my hand holding the phone is hot as I wait for him to speak. He is silent for at least a minute. I begin to think that perhaps the call has been dropped and I look at my phone, getting ready to dial again.

'Why are you calling me?' he says at last.

'I'm home. Well, I mean, not home, but I'm … I'm out.'

'I heard.'

I don't know how he heard, but I feel a sharp pain in my chest. He should have called me. A good, loving husband would have called.

'I wanted to get together,' I say. 'I have something to tell you. Well, I have something to show you, really.'

'What's that noise? Where are you?' asks Marcus abruptly.

'I'm just . . . it's just some music . . .' I reply.

'Why are you calling me?' he asks again. 'I thought I made myself clear when I returned your letters. I don't want to hear from you. I don't want to see you ever again.'

His voice is hard and I know that the green of his eyes will be darker than normal. He's angry, but as soon as I tell him what I have for us he'll stop being angry.

'I know, Marcus, but I have a wonderful surprise. We can be a family again. We can be together. It's all going to be just the way you wanted it to be. I promise I'll be a wonderful mother this time. I won't make any mistakes.'

'What?'

'We can be a family again, Marcus,' I say patiently. I have no idea why he doesn't understand what I'm saying. 'We're going to be together again.'

'Fuck, you're truly insane.' It sounds like he's spitting the words at me.

'That's not a nice way for you to talk to your wife, Marcus. I'm trying to tell you that we can start our lives again. I have a wonderful surprise.'

'I don't want to hear it. I don't want to speak to you. I never want to have to see you or hear from you again. Why can't you understand that?'

'What are you talking about?'

His words don't make any sense. I know he was angry at me, but he's had time to get over Ella now. He should be really happy to hear from me.

'Why don't you want to talk to me, Marcus?' I make sure I don't shout. He hates it when people yell at him.

'Why on earth would you think I could even stand to be in the same room as you? You killed her. You're a murderer. Ella's death wasn't a mistake. I know that. You should have been put in prison for the rest of your life, not just a few years. I didn't want to be with you before she died and I don't want to be with you now. Why can't you get that through your thick skull?' His voice is tight with fury now. Marcus has a temper although he rarely loses it, but when he does he shouts and screams and sometimes even throws things. When the police found the search I did on my computer he threw a silver candlestick holder at my head. It missed me but it was scary. We were standing in the dining room and I sank onto my knees and cried and cried while I waited for him to put his arms around me and tell me he was sorry, but he didn't. He just packed a bag and left and then he refused to pay the rent on our flat anymore and I couldn't go to work because I was a grief-stricken mother so I had to move in with my mother.

'Marcus, *please*,' I say, knowing that he's just lashing out. He doesn't mean these awful things. I open my mouth to say something else and then I hear a baby cry. I turn quickly to look at Xander lying in the middle of the bed, but he's still fast asleep. Then I realise that I am hearing the baby cry through the phone.

Before I can speak again I hear a woman's voice in the background.

'Babe, can you get him? I think he needs a feed.'

Chapter Nineteen

Ali feels like her whole body is vibrating as she and Mike drive to the Willow Street station. They cannot get there fast enough. 'We should have brought Malia with us,' she says.

'Ali, you know that this is unlikely to be anything, don't you?' says Mike. 'It's probably some crackpot who's seen the news and wants some attention.'

'Then how come they've called us in? There must be something to it. They've obviously interviewed her and decided it's important enough to involve us. Malia needs to feed Zach.'

'Ali,' says Mike gently, 'the woman has said she can't wake the baby up. We don't want this to be Zach.'

'Maybe if it is he's just … just sleeping really deeply,' says

Ali, and then she bites down on her fist to keep the tears at bay and looks out the window.

'Are you going to be okay?' asks Mike. 'If this is hitting too close to home ...'

'I'm fine,' snaps Ali.

Mike is quiet.

'Sorry, I'm sorry,' she says.

'Don't even think about it.'

'It's probably some nutcase,' she says, nodding her head, convincing herself that this is the truth, 'and I bet we'll know that in five minutes.'

'I have no idea why they couldn't figure it out themselves. You would think they would have learned how to conduct a half decent interview,' says Mike. 'What a waste of time.'

Ali nods. She needs to calm down, to think like a detective. She's too desperate to find Zach and it's starting to affect her judgement. It will be better if this is a hoax because if it's not ... if it's not ...

Ali watches the houses fly past, thinking about all the mothers getting ready to fetch their children from school, all the mothers groaning a little because the baby has woken up from his or her afternoon nap. Motherhood can be so boring, so repetitive, so filled with endless minutiae, often forcing women to wonder what has happened to their lives. But she knows that if something happens to your child, the boring, repetitive elements of the day are what you remember most and what you wish back with every fibre of your being. Her heart breaks for Malia, who would have picked up her child from day care and be on her way to get Aaron and Rhiannon by now if this had been any other day. Maybe she would have been tired and maybe she would be dreading the dinnertime routine but her children would be there. All her children would be there.

She was going to take Abigail to the park after her nap on the day she died. She had tried to get one of her friends from mother's group to come with her but everyone was busy. She hated going to the park alone because it was really boring having no one to talk to and, anyway, Abigail couldn't do much except look at the ducks. She had cursed herself for having that thought later, berated herself for not knowing how much joy that afternoon could have given her. Abigail always giggled when she saw the ducks and Ali would never hear her little laugh again.

Mike has the siren on so cars are pulling over to the side of the road to get out of their way.

Ali shakes her head and concentrates on where they're going and what needs to be done. She repeats the phrase, *what a waste of our time*, over and over to herself.

The woman is sitting in one of the interview rooms eating a sandwich. When she sees Ali and Mike walk in she quickly pulls another plate of sandwiches towards her.

It is immediately apparent that she lives on the streets. Ali has learned to identify the particular odour of an unwashed body. The woman's hands are grimy with dirt and her fingernails long and ragged. Beside her, on the floor, are four rubbish bags.

'She wouldn't sit down to be interviewed unless we let her bring her bags in,' says the constable who'd been waiting for them.

'Have you had a look through?' asks Mike.

'We did,' says the young woman. 'Nothing to worry about.' She wrinkles her nose. 'Except the smell.'

'Probationary constable, are you?' Ali says, taking in her perfectly pressed uniform and general air of helpfulness.

'Yes, how did you know?'

Ali feels like it's the first time she's really smiled all day.

She joins Mike in sitting down opposite the woman, who is eating as fast as she can. There are also two chocolate bars on the table that she keeps looking at, her eyes darting from the sandwiches to the chocolate.

'They said those were for me,' she mumbles.

'They are,' says Mike. 'We've already had our lunch.'

The woman nods. She slumps a little in her chair, relieved that she does not have to fight the detectives for the food.

'We're not going to stop you eating, but we do need to talk to you for a few minutes. Can you concentrate for a bit so we can ask you some questions?' asks Ali.

The woman takes her eyes off the sandwich and looks at Ali. Her grey hair is wound up into a thick bun and her face is weathered by the sun. She has given her age to the constables as seventy-five, eighty and ninety. She has no ID but her prints are in the database so Ali knows she's seventy-two and her name is Garnet Bently. According to the file the constable has given Ali, she was in prison for a year on a break and enter charge.

How can this be the woman who took Zach? thinks Ali. *She doesn't look capable.*

'Are you ready for some questions?' Ali asks slowly.

'I'm not a fucking idiot,' says the woman. Ali sits back in her chair, a little startled by this aggressive tone from someone who had seemed quite pathetic a moment ago.

'I didn't mean to suggest you were,' says Ali.

'Ask away,' says the woman, giving Ali a big smile.

'We wanted to talk about the baby.'

'I took him to keep him safe,' says the woman. 'I used to be a nanny. I worked for all the best families, you know, I even worked for royalty. I raised Prince William. No one believes me, but I did. He loved me, used to call me Nanny Gan. My name's Garnet. It's a stupid name, but my parents liked it.'

'You took the baby to keep him safe?' questions Mike, steering her back onto the right track.

'Yes, it was hot and he was alone in the car. Mothers shouldn't leave their children alone in cars. I've read newspaper articles about that. It's wrong.'

'So where did you take him from?' Ali asks.

'The Fairmont Street petrol station, just like it said on the television.'

'You saw it on television?'

'I stayed at that women's hostel on William Street last night. Too many insects around now. I never get any sleep. They have a television and I saw the news before I left today.'

'So you saw the news of the baby after it had happened,' says Ali, thinking, *crackpot*.

'No,' replies Garnet, patiently, as though Ali is stupid. 'I saw it on the news after I took the baby out of the car. I brought him back to the hostel with me. I hid him under my clothes. He was very good, and then after I had seen the news I left and took him with me.'

'Where did you take him?' asks Mike casually, as though he doesn't care about the answer.

'Me to know and you to find out,' says Garnet, giggling.

'He needs to be fed,' says Ali. 'You need to tell us where you took him so we can help him. You said he wouldn't wake up.'

The woman frowns. 'I did try to take care of him. I gave him some water, but he still won't wake up.'

Ali leans forward, 'Can you tell us what kind of car the baby was in?'

'It was a Toyota, and it was red.'

'And do you remember the colour of the baby seat that the baby was in?'

'It was blue. He's a lovely little boy. He and I were going to be together forever, but now he won't wake up.'

'Could be a guess,' says Mike under his breath.

'Why were you at the 7-Eleven so early in the morning?'

'They give away their stale donuts. I didn't get one, but I got a baby instead.'

'I'll check,' says Mike, standing up. 'Fucking forgot to ask that, didn't they?' he whispers as he leans down towards Ali. She knows that he will have some things to say to the constables who conducted the initial interview.

'You ask Ash at the station. He knows me, he'll tell you I'm always there.'

'Okay,' says Mike, and leaves the room.

'Maybe he's just really tired.' Garnet stuffs the last bit of bread in her mouth.

'You know if something has happened to that baby, Garnet, you could be in a lot of trouble,' says Ali.

'Suits me. If I go to prison, at least I'll have somewhere to be. I've been before, it doesn't bother me. You know I didn't mean to hurt him. I really wanted to take care of him. I don't have any family. He was going to be my family.'

Mike comes back into the room and nods at Ali. *Fuck,* she thinks. *She might be telling the truth.*

'Tell us where the baby is,' she says.

'I won't tell you, but I'll tell the mother. I want to give her a piece of my mind. Women shouldn't forget their babies in cars. It's dangerous.'

'You need to tell us and then we can let you talk to Malia. You've really hurt her and her family, and taking someone else's child is a crime. Tell us where the baby is.'

'Or what?' says the woman. 'I told you I'll tell the mother, but no one else. Throw me in jail. See if I care.'

Ali stands up abruptly, knocking over the chair she was sitting on.

'Not worth it,' says Mike firmly, putting his hand on her arm. Ali steps back and allows him to usher her out of the room.

'The attendant at the 7-Eleven says she comes down there every day for the donuts. He says she was there this morning at the exact time it was happening. He knows because he stopped serving the queue to tell her to leave because he'd already given away his stale donuts.'

'Fuck, fuck, fuck,' says Ali. 'Why didn't he tell us that before? Why wouldn't he have said something?'

'He says he didn't think it was important since she's there often.'

'Just fuck it,' says Ali.

'Calm down, Ali.'

She opens the door of the interview room. 'Garnet, we can let you talk to the mother, but only if you tell us where the baby is.'

'No,' says Garnet. 'You bring her here to me and then I'll tell her.'

'Is the baby far from here, Garnet?' asks Mike.

'It's a bit of a walk, to tell the truth. But I've got the baby. I just need my husband back.'

'Where's your husband?'

'Oh,' says Garnet, and then she waves her arm around. 'He's somewhere. We're going to be a family.'

'If you tell me where the baby is, Garnet, I can find your husband and tell him,' says Mike softly.

Garnet seems to consider this for a moment but then she reaches forward and grabs a chocolate bar off the table, opening it quickly and stuffing most of it in her mouth.

'I told you I'm not a fucking idiot,' she spits as she chews and swallows, giving Ali and Mike a look at her chocolate-coated teeth and tongue. 'I can take you somewhere close to where he is, but I'll only tell his mother exactly where I'm hiding him.'

'Okay,' snaps Ali, 'where?'

'Do you know the park that's on the block after the petrol station?'

'Yes.'

'You bring her there and I'll show you where he is. He's having a lovely sleep.'

After Mike has stepped out of the room Ali can hear him issuing an instruction for all available officers to make their way to the park and begin searching the grounds. The sounds of sirens start to fill the air as police cars leave the Willow Street station car park.

'They won't find him,' says Garnet. 'He's very well hidden. The cops come to that park all the time and they never, ever find me.' She smiles at Ali, a big wide grin as though this is a wonderful joke. Ali feels her hand stray to her gun just as her mobile phone goes off.

I'll be home in about an hour. Mum has picked up Charlie and says he's doing great ☺.

You need to calm down, Ali tells herself.

'Come on,' she says to Garnet, 'we'll have someone take you to the park and we'll meet you there with his mother.'

In the car on the way over to the Ellis house Ali rehearses how she's going to explain the situation to Malia so that she doesn't either get her hopes up or send her spiralling into despair.

'It's unlikely that it's anything except a hoax, Malia,' she begins when Malia comes to the front door, 'but there is a woman who says she was at the service station and that she took Zach.'

'Oh, oh,' whispers Malia. Her knees buckle a little and Ian reaches out to grab her but she quickly swats his hand away and stands up straight again.

'She won't talk to anyone but you.'

'The children …' says Malia.

'I'll stay with them,' says Ian and Ali can almost feel the heat coming off the look that Malia gives him. She wonders if she is actually watching Malia's marriage disintegrate right before her eyes.

Mike uses the siren again as they make their way to the park to meet what Ali hopes is a crazy woman who has never even seen little Zach Ellis. The park is a large one, with two artificial lakes filled with ducks for children to feed, bike tracks, walking paths and a restaurant. In summer they have a growers' market on the grounds.

Ali and Reuben often bring Charlie here on a Sunday afternoon so he can feed the ducks, which mostly means him tossing the bread into the water and then crying when the overfed birds don't eat it. She hasn't been able to go back to the park she used to go to with Abigail. Not yet.

Ali knows that even a hundred uniformed police won't be able to cover every nook and cranny of the place.

She feels sick. Her stomach churns and she regrets the burger and fries. She's afraid she's going to throw up.

The park is swarming with uniformed police when they pull up. Ali can see groups of the public pointing at the police, trying to figure out what's going on. Quite a few people are getting into their cars and leaving, deciding that, whatever is happening, they would rather be far away from it.

Ali can't believe this may be the park where a baby is dying or has died. She is momentarily enraged that the attendant at the 7-Eleven never mentioned Garnet. If he had they would have been looking for her since this morning and maybe they would have found her, or at least found someone who knew she lived in the park.

Malia makes a small sound in the back seat.

'Are you okay?' asks Ali, but Malia just shakes her head.

They all get out of the car. Ali goes to stand next to Malia, who has her hand over her mouth. Mike takes a call on his mobile, squints into the distance, and then waves his arm at a group of uniformed police standing with Garnet.

'They're over there,' he says.

'Let's go quickly. We'll take you to the woman who says she has Zach,' Ali explains to Malia, touching her arm and encouraging her to walk because Malia seems unable to move.

'It's too big,' says Malia. 'They'll never find him. It's too big.'

We'll find him, Ali wants to say, but she doesn't open her mouth. She has no idea what will happen. Silence is better than platitudes right now.

She remembers being on a missing child case five years ago. She had refused to go home to sleep because she'd convinced herself that if she stayed awake then they'd still be in the first day of the investigation, and if they were in the first day they were more likely to find the child. It had been ridiculous on her part; anyway, the little boy had been found stuffed into a box in the attic—courtesy of his stepfather.

Her body feels heavy, tired and defeated, as she nudges Malia along, the defeated leading the destroyed.

Chapter Twenty

Edna gives up waiting for Robbie.

She'd been rehearsing the speech she was going to give him, but after half an hour she realises he probably won't be in until much later, remembering that today is the day he usually goes straight from work to practice with the church choir. He'll only be in after dinner.

The idea of Robbie enjoying his singing while she sits here suffering through the awful noise grates on Edna, but quite suddenly the music stops, and what a blessed relief it is. She takes her cup of tea into the living room, enjoying the usual silence of the house.

She heard Albert come in from his work in the charity shop but he didn't stop in to say hello. When everyone is back she'll have to share the television room with whoever else wants to sit there. Robbie keeps saying he's going to get cable television for the whole house, and then she'll be able to buy her own TV and watch it in peace, but he's been talking about it for years and never done anything and Edna thinks she'll probably be dead long before it happens.

'I watch television on my computer, Edna,' he said to her when she complained about him not getting cable television. 'You should get one for yourself. You and William and Nate and even Solomon could go to classes together—it would be good for you.'

Edna hadn't replied to that comment. She knows when she's being made fun of. They're all too old to learn how to use computers.

She should have bought a computer when she was younger and learned to use it then, but it had always seemed quite a frightening machine to figure out.

'No use crying over spilt milk, Edna,' she hears her father say.

'No use at all,' she agrees and, anyway, it's time for her favourite game show. She gets all the answers right. Most people are fairly stupid. Edna believes it's because of the internet, so computers have their faults as well. People don't have to think for themselves anymore. They just press a button and *poof!* There's the answer.

The newsreader reports that the baby is still missing. More pictures of the poor little thing appear on the screen and then the number for Crime Stoppers. Edna can't get the number out of her mind she's seen it so many times today.

She doesn't like to point fingers but really that young mother should never have left her baby alone in the car. If Edna had been allowed to have a baby she wouldn't have let it out of her sight for even one minute. She feels an ache in her heart. She would still love a baby even if she is too old to take care of one now. It would have been lovely to have a daughter. Edna can imagine some beautiful girl who would call her up and say, 'What about going out to tea, Mum?'

'No use crying over spilt milk,' Edna tells the television, but she's not sure if she's talking to herself or the newsreader.

As the news ends the music starts again, loud and disturbing. It's not as bad in the sitting room as it is on her floor but sound carries through this old house, and it irritates Edna that Jackie hasn't thought about other people. It means she can't go upstairs to her room even if she wants to. She hates modern music. It's just drums and shouting.

'Oh, for goodness sake!' Edna cries.

She doesn't know how much more of this she can take, she really doesn't. She slips her shoes back on just as Nate comes into the room.

'Where's William?' asks Edna.

'His daughter has taken him out to tea. She prefers it if I don't come.'

'Rude so and so,' says Edna.

'What's that noise?' he asks.

'It's Jackie. She's been playing that off and on all afternoon. I tried to knock on her door and get her to turn it down, but she won't open the door. Go upstairs and ask her to shut it off.'

'Not likely,' says Nate. 'Last week I had a fight with Albert because he left a cereal bowl in the sink. I loathe fighting with people. Robbie will sort her out.'

'Robbie won't be here until much later.'

'Well, I suppose we can all put up with it until then.'

Edna sips her tea and nods. *Typical*, she thinks. *No one wants to put themselves out.*

She turns up the television so she can hear what the reporter is saying about the missing baby. She is standing in a park and the camera sweeps across to show policemen everywhere.

'I've been there,' says Edna to the empty room. 'I know that park.'

She feels like she's in the middle of a crime thriller of her own. She's never been able to recognise the places crimes have been committed before.

'Sources have informed us that Zach Ellis may, in fact, have been taken by someone who is currently homeless and living in this park. Right now, as you can see, police are combing the area, searching for any sign of a baby. Malia Ellis has just been escorted to the back of the park by police officers. As yet we do not know if the baby has been found. We will keep you updated on details as they come to hand.'

Edna shakes her head. 'Terrible,' she mutters, 'just terrible.'

Upstairs there is a gap in the music and Edna hears the sound of a baby crying once more. She puts her fingers into her ears, jiggling a bit, and then listens again, but the music has restarted and she can hear nothing but the sound of drums beating through the house.

Chapter Twenty-One

3.30 pm

Ali keeps her hand under Malia's elbow and gently guides her towards the group of police surrounding an old woman dressed in so many layers of clothing it might have been winter rather than the afternoon of a scorching summer's day.

Malia doesn't look at Ali, knowing that if she does she will see the truth that her child is dead. She is veering wildly between forcing herself to accept that Zach is gone and refusing to believe that he will not be home in his bed tonight.

She has heard the things Ali has said in the car and knows that Ali doesn't want to believe that Zach is gone either. But there was something in her voice that Malia caught—sadness tinged with defeat, perhaps. Even if Ali is a detective, Malia knows that she's a mother first because once you have children you're always a mother first, and Malia imagines she's also thinking about her own child, safe at home. The defencelessness of a child should allow a mother to feel protectively in control, but all it really does is expose her own terrible vulnerability. It often amazes Malia that just as she was starting to feel in charge of her life after moving away from her parents' protective gaze, Aaron came along and catapulted her back to the power-lessness of childhood.

She smells the woman Ali is taking her to meet from a few feet away. *Mama, I need you*, she thinks as Ali keeps pushing her forward. She thinks about turning away, about running back to the car.

'I was here for mother's group last week,' she tells Ali. 'There's a small section for babies and toddlers over near the restaurant. I put Zach on the ground and he waved his arms and legs—you know the way they do?'

Malia demonstrates with her own arms and then feels herself colour with humiliation. She has no idea what she's doing.

'Malia,' says Ali, 'this is Garnet.'

The woman seems to be smiling, although Malia can't believe this to be the case.

'Hello,' she says softly.

'So, you're the mother,' says Garnet.

Malia nods and clasps her hands together. She would like to scratch the woman's eyes out. 'Don't speak any more than you have to,' Ali has told her in the car. 'She may try to draw you into a discussion, but just keep saying that you want to see the baby.'

Malia wonders what it would take to kill the woman. She is small and clearly very thin under all those layers. Her hands are bent and bony, covered in liver spots and her skin is burned by the sun and sagging on her cheeks. She has every appearance of being a witch, and Malia thinks about her grandmother who once taught her a curse to spit at a boy who was bullying her at school. She can't think of the Greek words now but she wishes she could retrieve them to hurl at this woman. English would not do her fury justice.

She feels like she has split into two people. One Malia is standing in silence waiting for the woman to speak, while the other Malia is raging, screaming and demanding blood. Behind her she hears the continuous arrival of vehicles and the shouts of police to 'Stay back, please!' and 'Turn that camera off!'

'Fuck,' says Mike. 'How do those vultures know?'

'When do they ever not know?' mutters Ali.

'Please,' says Malia to the woman.

I would like to rip your head off.

'Please tell me where he is.'

I will break every bone in your body.

'Please.'

275

She imagines her hand reaching into the woman's chest and pulling out her still-beating heart. It's a violent image from some horror movie she's seen. She needs violence and blood now; she needs to inflict pain and suffering on this woman. She holds her hands tightly together, feeling rage speed up her heartbeat.

'Please tell me where my baby is,' she says slowly. The effort it is taking to control herself is giving her a headache. She thinks about Zach's blue eyes and her rage dissipates, swiftly replaced with absolute despair.

She can't think of anything else to say. She and the woman—Garnet—she and Garnet have only been looking at each other for a few moments but Malia feels as though a whole lifetime has passed. Part of her would like to stand here forever because until she is holding her child's body he's still alive.

'I bet you really want to see your baby, don't you?' asks the woman.

Malia nods. 'Very much.' Her voice is hoarse.

'You really shouldn't have left him alone. You know that, don't you?'

'I do,' says Malia, and she can feel that her cheeks are wet.

'Don't cry, don't cry,' says Garnet, pulling a soiled tissue from her sleeve and offering it to Malia.

Malia shakes her head and manages to croak the words. 'No, thank you. Can I please see my baby now?'

Garnet stuffs the tissue back into her sleeve. 'Of course you can. Where are my manners? I'll show you your baby. Follow me.'

She crooks her finger at Malia and grins as though she is leading her on a secret adventure. Malia thinks of the story of Hansel and Gretel. Rhiannon loves the old fairytale, delighting in Malia's imitation of the cackling old witch inviting the children into her house made of candy. *Once I know he's gone*, she thinks, *I will kill her. No one will stop me. I will tear her apart.*

Garnet marches to a section of the park where the bush has been allowed to grow freely. Malia knows, suddenly and without reason, that this is where Aaron's kindy class is due to come for a nature walk in a couple of weeks. Behind her the police are directing everyone to move back as one reporter after another attempts to get close enough to film or take a picture.

'Just back the fuck off!' shouts a policeman.

Malia saw them trying to cordon off where the woman was standing but the park is too large and there are too many ways to get around the police tape.

Even though Malia knows the park is filled with people watching the police with interest, and reporters trying to be the first to get the story, inside her head it's quiet. She can't seem to hear anything except the slight crunch of her footsteps as she walks over the grass.

Garnet walks, muttering to herself about a 'good mother', followed by Malia, Ali, Mike and all the other police. In the silence, the sounds of footsteps over fallen leaves and small bushes fills up the air.

Malia feels the sun's heat on her face and she glances up into a perfect blue sky. The whole thing is surreal and she can't help thinking that this is a joke. She can't be on her way to see her child's lifeless body.

Garnet walks around the edge of some dense growth until she finds what appears to be an opening.

'This way, this way,' she says to Malia, as she begins to squeeze between two overgrown plants. *Native broom?* thinks Malia, realising she knows the name of the plant with its yellow flowers.

Garnet moves through, and for a moment she seems to disappear, but then she sticks her hand out. Garnet clicks her fingers, and without considering it Malia grabs hold of her outstretched hand and is pulled through. The leaves and branches scratch against her arms and legs, but the small stinging pain she feels has an oddly calming effect on her.

'Not far now,' Garnet giggles. She pulls Malia along behind her and only turns to look back as Ali and everyone else crash through after them.

I'm going mad, thinks Malia. *I must be going mad.*

The woman leads Malia along a trodden path until they come to what appears to be a makeshift camp. A piece of blue tarpaulin hangs over a branch, offering some shade to a collection of blankets. There is a tin pot and a dirty spoon on the floor, along with at least a hundred paperbacks with their covers ripped off. Piles of linen and clothing are scattered everywhere.

'Welcome to my humble abode,' says Garnet. 'The police have never found me here. Sometimes I hear the children coming for class, but no one ever comes here. You never would have found the baby if I hadn't shown you.'

'My baby,' says Malia. She pulls her hand away, hating Garnet's rough skin and dirt-encrusted nails. Her hands are too filthy to touch a baby.

'You won't make that mistake again, will you?' asks Garnet.

'No, I won't. But please, show me my baby.'

'Children are a blessing, you know. I think when you're young you forget that, but I know that children are a blessing. I wish I had children. I was going to have your baby to be my own sweet little boy, but now he won't wake up, you see.'

Garnet looks down at her shoes as she speaks.

'I'm begging you,' whispers Malia. 'Where is he?'

'Oh, he's here,' says Garnet. 'He's having a lovely nap.'

'Where is he?' Malia yells.

Garnet looks up and then she reaches forward and strokes Malia's face.

'Relax, my dear, he's in there. Go on in, have a look.'

Malia looks to where she is pointing, but can only see a pile of old clothes.

'Where?'

'In there, underneath,' says Garnet, nodding her head encouragingly.

'Oh God,' says Malia.

'Malia, wait!' cries Ali.

But Malia has already dived for the pile and starts to fling clothes aside. Everything feels slimy with mould and stinks of sweat and urine. Garnet laughs before coming forward to reach underneath the pile. She begins to pull.

Malia leans forward to look at what Garnet has in her grasp. Garnet tugs and grunts, and then a small foot appears, followed by a chubby leg.

Malia feels her breathing speed up. Her bones turn to liquid and then, mercifully, everything turns black.

Chapter Twenty-Two

'Who's that, Marcus?' I ask and my voice is strained.

'Why have you called me?' he asks again, and I experience the scratch of irritation. I hate it when people don't answer my questions. It's very rude.

For a moment I think about just hanging up to teach him a lesson, but then I realise he's only made a mistake. He's made a mistake by being with another woman, but I made a mistake with Ella, and the best thing both of us can do is forgive each other and move on with our lives.

'Who is that?' I ask again and I harden myself for the truth.

I knew all along that he was having an affair. Oh, he denied it, told me I was paranoid and that he hadn't touched another woman since we'd been together, but

I knew he wasn't telling the truth. He wanted me to stop calling him, to leave him alone. Why would he want that if he didn't have someone to replace me?

It could be his secretary, Elise, who always giggled when she answered the phone, making me want to hit her. It could also be the barista at the coffee shop he used to go to. I saw the way she looked at him when she took his order, I saw the way she smiled and pushed out her chest so his eyes were forced to stray to her breasts. Or it might be that woman who lived next door to us and spent every day in the gym, toning her arse. 'You've got a good one there,' she used to say to me when she saw Marcus and me together, making him laugh.

She hated me as much as I hated her, otherwise she wouldn't have lied about me to the jury; she wouldn't have said that I was a bad mother who let her baby scream. Such rubbish.

If I don't know her, I imagine that the woman he's fucking is beautiful with wavy blonde hair and giant breasts. I know that she will be younger than me, that her body will be beautiful and her laugh will come easily. I'm sure that she's never called Marcus at work. I'm sure she's very secure in his love. I imagine my hands around her slim white throat. I will not allow this woman, whoever she is, to get in the way of Marcus and I being together.

Whoever it is I'm sure she has a shaved vagina. I was right to keep checking up on him back then, and the only reason I didn't catch him is because he's clever and sneaky. I know I'll have to watch him extra carefully this time.

'Who is she?' I ask again.

'My wife,' he says.

'Your what?'

'My wife,' he repeats.

There is a ringing in my ears. 'But … but I'm your wife. You can't be married to two people at once. It's illegal.'

Marcus starts to laugh. 'Illegal? You're a fucking joke, you know that?'

His laughter strengthens me. I never like it when people laugh at me. I'm many things, but I'm not funny, and I know when people laugh at me it's because they think I'm stupid or pathetic. I'm neither.

'Marcus, don't be rude.'

'Are you actually hearing yourself? I swear, you should have gone with the insanity defence: you are fucking insane. We got divorced when you were in prison.'

'We didn't,' I say. 'I would have known if that had happened.'

'You did know. You said you wouldn't sign the papers, but I didn't need you for that. You're a murderer. Murderers don't get to hold up a divorce. You killed my child—how on earth could you believe that I'd want to stay married to you?'

'I didn't kill her.' I remember the papers, but I thought he wasn't serious. He needed time to calm down. I believed if I didn't sign them we couldn't get divorced.

'The whole world knows you killed her. You left her there on purpose. You left her in that car to die. You're a fucking monster.' His voice is thick with unshed tears. I hope he's not going to cry. Getting hysterical never achieves anything.

'Marcus, calm down. I didn't do it on purpose. I made a mistake. Lots of people thought I made a mistake.'

'I can't speak to you. I can't bear the sound of your voice.'

Now he's crying on the other end of the phone and I don't know why he's become so dramatic.

'I see her in my dreams, you know. I hear her crying and I see her reaching out for me. I hear her calling "Daddy", begging me to help her. How could you have done that? What kind of an evil human being are you?'

'Listen to me,' I say firmly, hating the way he's so weak right now. 'Ella couldn't speak yet so there's no way she would have called for you.'

I can't stand it when people get the facts wrong.

'That's what you have to say to me? Who are you? Who the fuck are you?'

'Look,' I say over the noises he's making, 'I didn't do anything on purpose. I miss Ella too, I think about her, but I have a way to make things better now. I love you, Marcus, I've always loved you. I made a mistake with Ella, but that won't happen again. I have another baby, a baby who's going to make us a family again. He's such a beautiful little boy—I know you're going to love him. He's sleeping now, so peacefully. I think he's going to be an easier baby than Ella was, and I want you to know that I will be a better mother this time. I've made up my mind to do a really good job.'

'What the fuck are you on about? You've been in prison. You can't have a baby.'

'But I do, Marcus, and he's got the most beautiful blue eyes.'

'Marcus, what's going on?' I hear the woman in the background call. The baby is silent now and I wonder how she managed to get it to keep quiet.

'I need to go,' he says. He has stopped crying, but his juddering sighs are annoying.

'But you can't go!' I yell. 'I'm sorry,' I say quickly. 'I just wanted to let you know that you can come and get me now, get us. We can go away together until things sort themselves out. We can go to that resort we visited for our honeymoon. I know they have babysitting there. We can just relax by the pool and enjoy being together again. Xander will be well taken care of.'

'Xander?'

'He's our little boy,' I say patiently, 'and I promise you that I will be the best mother in the world this time. I won't ever make a mistake again. Just give me one more chance. Please, Marcus.' I have no idea why I need to keep explaining this to him. It's making me feel like there's something wrong with him or maybe there's something wrong with me. Am I not making myself clear? Why doesn't he get it?

'My God, this is ... this is insane. Don't you understand? I have a wife. I'm married with a child. You tried to ruin my life, to ruin me, but it didn't work. I don't know how you could ever have expected forgiveness for what you did. I'm going now. Don't ever, ever call me again. I have a restraining order against you and if you dare, if you so much as dare to contact me again, I will have you thrown back in jail where you belong.'

He hangs up the phone, but I keep it pressed to my ear, hoping that he isn't really gone.

I am stunned. Marcus can't be married to anyone else, he is married to me. Marcus has a new baby? Marcus has a new wife? That wasn't supposed to happen.

I replay the conversation in my head and try to figure out where it went wrong. I dial his number again. I have to speak to him, but it goes straight to voicemail. I will give him a chance to calm down and call again. No, I won't call again. He was a bad husband; he cheated on me.

I won't call again. I will go to his house. No, I don't know where he lives now. I must call him again. I don't know what to do, there are too many thoughts running through my head. I try his number but it goes to voicemail once more. I don't leave a message. How can he have a wife and a baby? It's absurd. I'm sure if I can just talk to him he will understand that he needs to leave his wife and come with me. Marcus loves me and only me. It's what he said every time I asked him. Why would he say that he doesn't love me now?

I stand up, needing to go to him, to run through the streets until I find him. But then I remember the baby. You can't leave a baby alone. Well, you can, but you shouldn't. Terrible things happen to a baby if you leave it alone. Terrible things.

How can Marcus have a new baby? And if he already has a baby, what am I going to do with this one?

What am I going to do with Xander?

Chapter Twenty-Three

'Catch her!' shouts Mike, and Ali holds out her arms as Malia's legs collapse.

At the same time Garnet yanks the small leg she has been pulling on out of the pile and triumphantly holds aloft a life-size baby doll, which is grimy and naked.

'See,' she crows. 'He's just having a sleep. Wake up, baby boy, wake up.' She pushes at the plastic eyelids. 'I can't seem to wake him up.'

'Give me that,' says Mike, and grabs the doll from Garnet roughly, causing her to stumble.

'Don't hurt him … he's sleeping,' she says. Then, bizarrely: 'Who took my chocolate bar?'

'What the fuck?' says Mike to the uniformed police officers, holding the doll up to them. 'How could you have let this happen? Search this whole place. Leave no fucking pebble unturned, *now!*'

Ali knows he's talking to himself more than to them. They couldn't have known, just as she and Mike couldn't have either. Garnet could have been telling the truth. Everything pointed to that possibility and they had to do whatever it took to get Zach back. The uniformed police fan out around the area and start pulling apart the piles of clothing and blankets, throwing things aside.

'What a mess,' says Garnet mildly. 'Why won't she hold her little boy? He's a lovely little boy. Doesn't she love him? She should love him. I love him.'

Ali looks at the doll Mike is holding by one leg and something about its stiff limbs draws Ali back to the day she found Abigail in her cot, so still, her eyes shut tight, never to open again.

She tries to stop the memory of that day from overwhelming her but it fills her head, brilliant and detailed, as though it is happening at this moment.

She remembers being on the couch and opening her eyes from her nap, stretching luxuriously and looking at the quiet monitor. 'Bonus,' she had said.

That word has haunted her for years. She had imagined that Abigail was just having a particularly long afternoon sleep, and Ali felt rested and ready for the rest of the day. She'd thought about going into her daughter's room just to check on her, but knew that the instant she entered the room Abigail would open her eyes. Her child could smell her, could smell the milk, and so she made herself some crackers and cheese and flipped on the television, put her feet up on the coffee table and breathed in the peace.

Fifteen minutes of a reality show about housewives had taken her away from her living room and into a world she couldn't believe existed. It made her laugh, but as soon as she had finished eating she had stood up to go and check on her daughter. The baby monitor was still silent, but she made the decision that she would wake her anyway or the night ahead would be difficult.

Ali had friends with babies. She knew that a lot of them didn't believe in breathing monitors, but she'd been given one as a baby gift so she'd used it. It went off whenever Reuben picked Abigail up because he always forgot to turn it off in advance, but they'd kept it in the cot until Abigail started moving around all the time, making it go off in the middle of the night, waking everyone.

'Just take it out,' said Reuben. 'She's fine.'

Ali knew that he'd gone over and over that decision afterwards, condemning his judgement, hating himself for his supposed stupidity.

She remembers tiptoeing into Abigail's room, wanting to watch her daughter asleep for a moment so she could enjoy the peaceful sight of her, so she could drink in her baby's beauty, maybe even snap a quick picture with her phone. But she had looked down into the cot and known instantly that something was wrong.

Abigail was lying on her back, loosely wrapped in her soft pink cotton wrap. Usually her arms would have worked their way free and would be above her head, her body sprawled across the cot sideways, but she was in exactly the same position as when Ali had put her down. Her cupids' bow lips were blue, her skin pale.

Ali had reached in and grabbed her roughly, hoping to startle her awake, but Abigail's body was limp and unresponsive. Lying her on the change table, Ali's training as a police officer had kicked in as she began CPR. She only needed one hand to push on her daughter's chest and with the other she dialled emergency services on her mobile.

'Baby not breathing,' she said before any questions could be asked, and then she barked her address twice before dropping the phone to concentrate on her daughter.

Five minutes later she heard the sirens and ran downstairs with Abigail in her arms to open the door. Only when the paramedics were working on her did Ali call Reuben and then her training failed her and she became hysterical. One of the paramedics had taken the phone from her and explained to Reuben what had happened and which hospital to go to.

The lights and sirens hadn't been necessary. Ali had known that, but the paramedics had raced her daughter to the hospital anyway.

'I shouldn't have removed the monitor,' Ali had said over and over again during those first few terrible days after Abigail died.

'I shouldn't have told you to do it,' Reuben had said and they both competed for blame because it had to be someone's fault. How could it not be someone's fault?

'It wouldn't have helped,' the coroner told Ali after the autopsy. 'These monitors don't prevent sudden infant death syndrome. At best the noise it makes could have startled her out of an episode of sleep apnoea, but it could never have prevented this from happening. Maybe you would have gotten to her sooner, but maybe it would already have been too late. We don't have all the answers yet. As you said, she was always moving off the thing. It's not a reason to blame yourself.'

'So why did it happen?' Reuben had said and the coroner had rubbed his eyes.

'We don't know, Reuben. We're getting better at putting stuff into place to try and stop it happening, but sometimes it just happens for no rhyme or reason.'

'That's unacceptable,' Ali had said.

'I know,' the coroner had replied.

'Ali? Ali? Alexandra?'

Ali is startled back to where she is, with Malia's body slack in her arms, her face pale.

'What do I do?' says Ali, feeling panicked, feeling lost and unprepared for where she is right now.

'Slap her,' says Garnet.

Ali does, just a light slap, but it's enough.

'Is he … is he dead?' says Malia opening her eyes.

'It's a doll, Malia,' says Ali, 'just a doll.'

'Just a doll?'

'Just a doll.'

'He's a lovely boy,' says Garnet. 'I must have his clothes around here somewhere.'

She shuffles around the campsite, picking things up and putting them down. Most of the uniformed police have moved away now to search the rest of the park.

'I think you need to take her away,' says Mike to the policewoman standing next to Garnet.

'Let's go and get you another chocolate bar,' the constable says softly, and Ali is grateful for her presence. If it had just been Ali and Mike, she knows that both of them would have had trouble keeping calm.

Garnet is led away and Ali hears someone telling the press to move back.

'I'm sorry, Malia,' says Ali. 'We should have checked first, but she refused to show us the baby without you.'

'How do you know she doesn't have him, that she hasn't hidden him somewhere else?' says Malia, standing up.

'She seemed upset that you didn't want to hold the doll. She's clearly deranged. She thinks the doll is real. We have everyone searching the whole area and they'll keep looking until they're sure there's nothing here.'

'Then where is he?'

'Everyone is looking. We're doing everything we can.'

'Stop saying that!' shouts Malia. 'I'm so sick of hearing

that. You drag me out into the fucking bush to find a baby doll and you think you're doing everything you can?'

She looks at the doll in Mike's grip and then tangles her hands in her hair, pulling out strands.

'My baby is out there in the heat, starving and crying for me. It's been a whole day. I don't know how long he can go without anything to drink. He could be dead already and the only place you people have been interested in looking is in my house. I didn't hurt him, Ian didn't hurt him—he was stolen from my car. Why won't you find him? Why? Tell me why, I need to know why.'

Malia has begun crying. Ali can see the front of her dress is wet and knows that her breasts are leaking again. She wants to put her arms around Malia and protect her from the eyes of others, but it is Mike who steps forward and puts his arms around her.

'Shhh,' he says. 'It's okay, it's going to be okay.'

Malia buries her head in Mike's shoulder. 'You don't know that,' she says, her voice muffled. She pushes herself away from Mike and rubs her nose with her arm. Her hair is a mess and her face dirty. She looks as wild as Garnet did, and Ali wonders if perhaps a long time ago Garnet, herself, may have lost a child. She's heard about cases where women substitute dolls for babies. Something must have set Garnet off on her spiral into madness and Ali knows that the loss of a child can do this.

'We want him home as much as you do, Malia,' she says. 'Believe me, we do.'

'Just take me home, please. I need to be with my children.'

*

Back at the Ellis house the front door stands wide open. Ali sees a woman standing in the doorway. This must be Malia's mother: they have the same heart-shaped face and the same build.

When the woman sees Malia she doesn't say anything, just opens her arms. Mike has barely pulled the car to a stop before Malia jumps out and runs towards her.

'Oh Mama,' Ali hears her say as the woman's arms surround her. 'Oh Mama, oh Mama, oh Mama.'

Chapter Twenty-Four

Edna slides onto the barstool and waves at Paulo.

'Hello, love, twice in one day? It must be my new aftershave.'

'Don't flatter yourself, Paulo. I just couldn't stay in that house for even one moment longer and now I'm going to miss my five o'clock game show and I just knew I was going to get all the answers right today.'

'What's up? Is Robbie being a dick to you? 'Cause you know I can come round and have a chat with him.'

'No, no … It's the new resident.'

'The woman?'

'Yes. Today she's been blasting music all through the house, really blasting it, and I can't get her to turn it down.'

'Rude. Did you ask her to turn it down?' says Paulo,

pouring two tots of gin into the drink he's making for Edna.

'I tried. Believe me, I tried. I knocked on her door until my hands were sore, but she didn't open it. I think she's probably enjoying winding me up. She's just a little slip of a thing who didn't even look me in the eye, so I thought she'd be a nice quiet addition to the house whatever she's done, but then she's been playing her music and it's just dreadful. I wanted to have a word with Robbie about it, but he's at his rehearsal and who knows what time he'll be by the house tonight.'

Edna watches Paulo slice lemon. She doesn't usually drink this much in a day, but she believes it's fine to over-indulge once in a while, and today has been a particularly difficult day. She has a headache that Panadol can't seem to take care of. Some more gin might just do the trick. She wishes she could ask Paulo to let her lie down in one of the rooms above the pub, but she doubts he's allowed to do that.

'Well, my love, you can hang out here until later,' says Paulo, sliding her drink in front of her. 'You can stay here as long as you like; no one will bother you. Have some dinner and then by the time you get back someone else will be home and you can get help dealing with her.'

'Nate was there, but he's never one for an argument. I will stay here. It's my only option, I suppose. The bloody music is so loud I can't even hear the television and I'm waiting for them to find that baby. I've been waiting all day.'

The drama of the missing baby is beginning to obsess Edna. She would like to call the police and shout, 'Hurry up and find him!' but that would be silly and she's sure they would lock her up for being crazy.

Maybe that's why Jackie was in jail—for being crazy. You would have to be a little nuts to play music that loudly. Edna doesn't like the idea of having an insane person in the house. Jackie might just be the kind of person to murder you in your bed. She resolves to take one of the kitchen knives to bed with her tonight. Then she'll be ready for anything.

'Yeah,' says Paulo, drawing Edna away from her contemplation of kitchen knives. 'It's a bloody shame for that family. I hope they find the little bloke soon.'

Edna nods and takes a big sip of her drink. 'Lovely,' she says to Paulo.

'I'm telling you, Paulo,' she continues, 'I don't know what my house is coming to. I told Robbie not to let common criminals in, but would he listen to me? No. Mary used to listen to me. We used to have some lovely chats in the kitchen. "What do you think I should do, Edna?" she would say when we talked about letting in a new boarder or painting the house or something like that. I really miss Mary.' She sighs.

'I know, love,' says Paulo. 'We all do, she was lovely. Hang on a tick, let me just serve this bloke.'

Paulo moves off and Edna stares into her drink. She feels very down. She hasn't felt this way since Harry died. Maybe it's because Solomon is leaving and everything's changing. She's willing to bet that they won't have loud music at the old-age home. Maybe she should think about giving it a try.

'I'm sure Robbie will sort it all out when he gets home, Edna,' says Paulo returning to pat her hand. 'He won't let her play her music all night. Don't let it get you down, love.'

'It's not just getting me down, Paulo, it's making me a little mad as well.'

'What do you mean?'

'I mean that sometimes a song ends and I swear I can hear a baby cry, but then the music starts up again and it's all just noise. I'm obviously hearing things, but I have no idea why it would be a baby crying. I better not say anything to Robbie, or he'll have me shifted off to a home in no time.'

'Robbie's a good bloke, Edna. He wouldn't do that. Maybe you need your hearing checked. Don't they have people to do that for you down at the community centre?'

'Maybe she has got a baby in there,' comes a voice from down the bar, and Edna nearly falls off her chair, but recovers herself just in time.

'I didn't see you there, Luis,' she says, trying to remember if she's said anything to upset him. 'Sometimes your mouth runs away with you, Edna,' her father used to say, making her feel ashamed of herself. Luis is riffraff, but he's not bad riffraff, although that could just be the strong gin talking.

'Yeah, just having a knock-off drink. Bloody hot day. Thought I would treat myself to a beer.'

Edna nods. 'I didn't mean—' she starts.

'Don't worry about it,' says Luis. 'If I were you, I would be worried about who was living in my house as well. I know I've done wrong, Edna, but I'm doing my best to get back on the right path.'

'Yes, you are,' Edna acknowledges. 'Why do you think she has got a baby in her room? Is the noise making you hear things as well?'

'I don't think so. I stopped in at the house to change my shirt and I swear I heard a baby crying over the music.'

'We must both be going mad,' says Edna.

'Or she does have a baby in there,' says Paulo. 'Maybe it's her kid.'

'Robbie has a strict *no children* policy. He wouldn't have allowed her in with a baby. Besides, I'm sure she's been in prison. How can she have a baby? And why haven't we heard it before?'

'If she went in pregnant, she could have a child,' says Luis.

'Wouldn't they have taken it into foster care?'

'Maybe they gave it back and she's keeping it a secret because she doesn't want to get kicked out of the house?' says Paulo.

Edna glances over at the television on the wall. A reporter is now standing outside the 7-Eleven where the baby was taken. She looks very smart in a red dress and her hair is neatly styled.

'What if it's not her baby,' says Edna, almost to herself.

Luis looks up at the television. 'Jesus, you don't think she stole that baby, do you?'

301

Edna starts shaking her head and smiles. She doesn't need Luis to think she's crazy, but if Jackie has a baby in her room, where did it come from? She just knew no good would come from letting those types into the house.

'Do you think we should tell someone?' she says.

'I'm not saying anything,' says Luis. 'I just need to keep my head down.'

'Keep yourself to yourself, Edna,' she hears her father say.

But what would you know about it? she thinks bitterly.

'We'll wait till Robbie gets back,' says Luis. 'He can sort it out.'

'I don't think so,' says Edna. 'If she has got that baby someone needs to know.'

She pulls out her mobile phone. She never has much cause to use it, but today seems like a good time to put all her dialling practice to use. She keys in the Crime Stoppers number that is still scrolling across the bottom of the television screen.

'At the very least, a visit from the police will get her to turn the music down. You have to open your door for the police,' she says to Luis and Paulo.

Luis shrugs his shoulders. 'Do what you have to do.'

'I will,' says Edna. 'I will.'

Chapter Twenty-Five

5.00 pm

Malia is on her bed with her eyes closed. 'Sleep,' her mother had said, but there is no way that's going to happen. Her mother is making moussaka, having stopped off at the supermarket on the way to Malia's house from the airport. Malia would usually have laughed at her, but the rich smell she knows so well from her childhood fills the house and seems to wrap itself around her. *How can it not be okay*, the smell seems to say.

She can hear her father talking to Aaron about a game he is playing on the iPad. Aaron is speaking quickly and her father has to keep telling him to slow down so he can understand. Malia is sure that Rhiannon will be standing in the kitchen, playing with the dough her mother makes for all her grandchildren.

What will become of Aaron and Rhiannon if Zach is never found? She tries to picture a future without Zach, tries to see how she will be able to function as a mother to her two children, but she can't make the image work. Zach needs to come home. He must come home.

Malia feels a stab of pain in her breast and touches the sore spot. Her breast is pulsing with heat and she can feel she's on the way to getting mastitis. She knows she should express more milk, but when they find Zach he will need to feed.

She opens her eyes and stares at the ceiling. The house is cool because her parents have switched on the air-conditioning, something she rarely does because of the cost. Ian always turns it on when he gets home as he's used to being cool after a day in his office at the car yard.

Why did I never just turn it on for us?

It's a sacrifice she regrets making now. Perhaps if she had, and their electricity bill had been too high for her to pay, then Ian would have revealed his secret account to her. She wishes she could stop thinking about the money, but the lack of it has clouded her life for years. Who knows how much Ian has lost? Maybe they could all have gone on a holiday or she could have taken the kids to visit her parents more than once in five years?

She doesn't know how he could have done it, how he could have watched her struggle with the bills every month and said nothing. He had been part of discussions about where they could cut back and how many more hours Malia could get at the bakery. He had sat next to her at their small kitchen table and lamented their lack of money, and told her over and over again that it was all going to get better, while all the time he'd had money in a separate account.

When Aaron started school she'd spent a lot of money on his shoes, reasoning that he would wear them for at least a year, and she can remember Ian's face when Aaron proudly showed off the new purchase.

'I'm not a fucking millionaire, Malia,' he'd whispered to her when Aaron left the room, and Malia had quickly regretted spending the money. Aaron's happiness had no effect on Ian; her unhappiness had no effect on Ian. Nothing made any difference to Ian except the next spin of the wheel on the pokie machine.

Malia finds it unbelievable and then she's furious, and then she's simply exhausted again.

She's never fainted before, but as that woman—that awful woman—pulled at that little foot, all she could think was *No*, and then everything went black. She was sure that it was Zach, certain that he could only have been abducted by an insane person. She feels bad for yelling at the detectives now. They're only doing their job, and she hopes they won't decide to give up and go home without finding her baby.

'We're not leaving until we find him,' Ali had told her in the car just before they had turned into Malia's street.

Before her mother guided Malia to her bed and told her to rest, she explained that Ali and Mike had gone to make calls from their car, maybe to give Malia and her parents some time to talk, but who knew if they were coming back. If she were Ali she would gratefully hand the case over to another set of detectives and go home to her own family.

Ian had left as she walked in the door. He was carrying a small suitcase, still wearing his suit from this morning. His tie was straight and his hair neatly brushed. He looked as well put together as he did every other day, while she, in contrast, was a sweaty, milk-stained mess with red eyes and wild hair.

'Where are you going, Ian?' her father had asked, incredulous.

'I'm just … ask Malia,' Ian had said, his voice strangled with grief. *Is it really how you feel?*

Malia had put her head on her mother's shoulder and thought about stopping him, about getting him to come back inside so they could face the night as a family, but she realised she still didn't want him in her home and near her children. If Aaron asked she would say that he had to work. The children were used to being without him at night.

Malia is not surprised Ian has chosen to run away. He is aware, perhaps, that she will tell her parents everything, that the bond between them that has led her to keep his gambling a secret has been broken. Ian's need for self-preservation, not his shame at his actions, has led him to pack a suitcase. He makes Malia sick.

Ian was stopped by Mike as he walked to his car and questioned so Malia presumes he has told the police where he is going. She feels a momentary flash of humiliation that she is married to a man who would leave her at a time like this. *What must they think of us?*

Malia's mother had folded her arms across her body and raised her eyebrows at her husband before pulling Malia inside the house and closing the door. Then she had held her, stroking her back in circles and clicking her tongue. Malia's father had ushered the children into Aaron's room to play. 'The family is coming,' he said as he left the room.

Yes, Malia thought, *I need them. I need the troops.*

The idea of her aunties, uncles and cousins arriving helped stop the tears. Surely together they would find Zach?

'Now, Malia,' said her mother, 'now you calm down and we talk. Theo,' she called, 'leave the children. Malia needs you.'

She followed her mother to the kitchen and sat down at the table, quickly stacking colouring books and putting crayons and pencils back in their boxes. Her hands worked without her thinking.

'Why has that boy gone now?' said her father as he came into the kitchen. 'This is not the time for Ian to leave. What has happened? Why would he go at a time like this? Where could he be going? How can he walk away from his family? He is the father—the father should be here.'

'Let her talk, Theo, give her time.' Her mother placed a cup of hot sweet tea in front of Malia.

Malia had wanted to say, 'It's nothing,' or, 'It's just a fight,' but she didn't have the energy to lie to her parents anymore, so she had told the truth instead.

She had whispered the whole story to her parents so that the children wouldn't hear, and with each truth she told she had felt a little stronger. She had been hiding the shame of Ian's gambling from everyone, but as she explained it to her parents it became clear that the only person the shame belonged to was Ian. His gambling was not her fault, regardless of what he told her, and she was no longer willing to hide it for him.

'Why didn't you call us?' her mother had said. 'We would have come to help, we would have given you money. You could have come to us … anything.'

'I know, Mum, but I wanted to … protect him, I guess. I thought that if I just let him have some time to himself when he needed it that he would eventually realise that he was happy being a family man and settle down.'

Malia didn't say that part of the reason she had kept the secret of Ian's behaviour from her parents was because she did not want to hear that they had known she was making a mistake from the very beginning, that they had asked her to consider again and that they had seen something in Ian that she didn't want to see. She was embarrassed to think what her stubbornness had cost her—her parents' help and support and now—possibly, horribly, unbelievably—it may have cost her Zach.

'And how long have you been waiting for that to happen? For him to grow up and realise how to be a husband and a father, how to be a man?' her mother had said quietly.

'Forever,' said Malia.

'You will come home with us,' her father had said.

'But Daddy ...'

'No, Malia. There is no conversation. When Zach is home you and the children will come to us. You pack up your things and you rent out the house. You need to rest, to get strong again, and then you will see what you will do about this husband of yours.'

Malia felt that as an adult with three children of her own she should protest, but she had simply nodded. She was so tired of carrying the load of being a wife and a mother without any help. Even today, on the darkest of days, Ian had chosen to leave instead of stay with his family. She had asked him to go, but she couldn't help feeling that he should have demanded to stay until his son was home safe and sound. She thought it likely that he would head straight for the pub and his beloved pokies where the whole world would soon disappear.

Now she is lying on her bed with her eyes closed, picturing Zach's face, picturing him in his cot, smiling at her. She doesn't know how she can get through another five minutes without holding him.

The sun is still high in the sky, but it's time for the children to have dinner. The relief of having her mother here washes over Malia. She can just lie here and think about Zach, surround him with her thoughts, keep him safe in her mind. For the first time in years there is nothing else required of her. She knows that if the worst happens, if they never find him—or they find him dead—she may never be able to get up off this bed again.

How do you go on? she wonders. *How do you go on if you lose a child—especially if it's your fault that he is lost?*

Chapter Twenty-Six

He opens his eyes and looks at me as though he knows that I'm thinking about him.

I hate the way babies look at you like they can see inside your soul. He doesn't like me. I can tell he doesn't like me. When he starts crying I pick up the cold bottle of formula and try to shove it into his mouth, but he pushes the teat away with his strong tongue.

I raise my hand to give him a slap for being naughty but hesitate. I slapped her once and it didn't do any good. It certainly didn't stop her crying and I felt terrible afterwards. The skin on her face turned ruby red and I had to pretend I hadn't seen it when Marcus asked about it. 'A rash?' I suggested. I'm not sure if he believed me because he told me to have a rest and he would take care of her until she needed to be fed again.

He's such a good father, people used to say to me when they saw the two of them together, when they saw the way he looked at her and spoke to her and held her; and I would nod and smile and act like it was the only thing I wanted, but some days I wanted to shake her and say, 'He was mine first, mine!'

I'm tired now. Too tired to deal with this noise and this baby. I turn the radio on loud and put him on the floor. I lie down on my bed and try to relax, but it only takes him a minute to go from crying to screaming and his screaming drills a hole in my head. I have the radio up as loud as it will go and soon there will be other people knocking on this door, not just the old bat, and still I can hear him screaming.

I wish I could stick him outside my room and let that silly old woman take care of him. I could leave him on someone's doorstep, I suppose. I could leave him in the street for someone to find. I could drop him out of my window and that would be that.

I'm sure his mother must be looking for him. I'm sure she's sorry about forgetting him. She should be sorry.

I need a break, just a little break.

'Keep quiet,' I say to him, but he keeps on crying. His face is red and he is no longer beautiful. He looks like she used to look when she was angry with me.

Sometimes I used to think she was a demon. A demon sent to destroy me. Her cries would wake me from my sleep at night and I would lie listening to her, imagining her in her cot with a smile on her face, waiting to see how angry she could make me. I would only get up when Marcus started to move around. I didn't want him to wake up—the baby was my job, my fucking horrible job.

I never told Marcus I thought she was a demon. He always thought she was perfect, an angel. It was only me he would criticise.

I look around the small, disgusting room where I have ended up, trying to find a place to put him.

There is a chest of drawers but the drawers are not deep enough to hold a baby. My eyes fall on the cupboard. It's an old wooden one, and as I look at it, it creaks, expanding in the heat.

It's a sign.

I get up and open the door. Stale, hot air rushes out at me, smelling of mothballs and damp at the same time. I don't have much in the cupboard, just two pairs of shoes, a dress, a pair of jeans and a pair of black pants. Most of my stuff fitted into the chest of drawers. I used to have lots of beautiful things, but my life has been reduced to nothing. I don't know if Marcus has kept all our wedding presents or if he has thrown them away. I'm sure he received a whole lot of new things when he married his ... his wife.

He has everything and I have nothing. Marcus and Ella reduced my life to nothing. I'm not going to let this baby take anything more away from me.

I lift up the squalling creature and place him gently in the cupboard. I hope he's comfortable there. I stroke his head and he cries harder. He definitely doesn't like me. At the very least, a little time in the cupboard will teach him to keep quiet.

His nappy reeks now and his body is damp with sweat. He needs to be fed and changed and bathed and ... and ... and. Taking care of a baby is so mind-numbingly boring. It's just one set of tasks repeated over and over again until you're driven to despair. Feed, change, scream, pat, feed, change, scream, bounce, feed, change, scream, scream, scream, scream, scream, scream.

The stinky creature will just have to survive his own revolting smell. I close the cupboard door and his cries grow softer, weaker. Maybe he will be happier in the dark?

I wish he would shut up already. I lie on the bed and close my eyes. I'll keep the music on until he's learned how to be quiet, but it doesn't need to be as loud now. Ella never learned how to be quiet, how to behave—not until it was too late.

I didn't mean for her to die. I needed her to know that I was in charge, that she couldn't keep pushing and pushing me. She already had Marcus wrapped around her finger, but I could see that wasn't enough. She wanted me to devote myself to her completely. I don't know why she thought she deserved that from me. There was nothing special about her. She was just an ordinary baby even though everyone said she was pretty. She had Marcus's beautiful eyes, but she had my mouth and my thin lips. 'You'd be prettier if you smiled every now and again,' my mother used to say. Ella smiled all the time, at my mother, at Marcus, at strangers, even at me; but I wasn't fooled by her smiles. I knew they were only moments away from her screams.

I wanted Ella to know that I wasn't going to simply fall at her feet and adore her, but I didn't mean for her to die. I think I didn't mean for her to die.

I was prepared for it when I got back to my car at the end of that day—it is five years ago now. In fact next week it will be exactly five years.

She had screamed the whole way to day care, just screamed and screamed for no reason at all. She'd been fed and she was wearing a clean nappy. I'd given her a little pinch when I was putting on that nappy because she'd kicked out at me and caught me on the chin, but that wasn't a reason for her to scream.

I was trying to think on that drive, trying to concentrate on the road and find something to say to Marcus that would make him come home again. He had left the night before, just walked out of the house without even his toothbrush, and then called me from his friend Rob's house to tell me he would be staying there for a few nights.

'But you haven't got any clothes,' I said.

'I'll pick up something tomorrow when you're at work. Please don't be there. Just take Ella to day care and I'll get her on my way home. She can stay with me. Rob doesn't mind having her here for a few days while I sort out somewhere to live.'

'Don't be ridiculous, Marcus, she needs too much stuff. You don't know how much she needs.'

'I do know. I've been taking care of her a lot lately. I know that you're finding it hard to deal with Ella at the moment. I think I should have her for a few days so you can sort yourself out, get a lawyer and whatever else you need to do.'

'I'll be able to deal with her perfectly well if you come home.'

'I can't come home. I can't do this anymore. You called one of my clients and accused her of having an affair with me. She said it was like speaking to a mad woman. You really frightened her.'

'All I did was ask a question. I'm entitled to ask questions about my husband.'

'You told her you would kill her. Don't you remember screaming that? She said you were crying and screaming and threatening her and her kids. I have no idea what kind of a person does something like that.'

'Oh please, Marcus. She's just being dramatic. I never said any of those things, and if she said I did then she's lying. I'm sure she has a crush on you and she's embarrassed that I know about it. She's trying to get you to hate me so you'll sleep with her.'

'I can't even begin to explain how ridiculous that sounds. Portia is a happily married woman. She has no interest in me and now she's worried about the safety of her children.'

Marcus didn't want to admit that he knew Portia liked him. She texted him all the time. When he was home

I would check his phone and there were endless texts from the woman, asking questions about the bathroom and the size of the living room and how much cupboard space she would have. I knew she was sending Marcus all those questions just so she could stay in touch with him, so she could speak to him. And he answered all her texts, within minutes. He replied with answers to her silly questions and a smiley face and all the while he was ignoring my texts, ignoring my questions, refusing to take my calls.

I found her picture on Facebook. Her account was private but her cover photo showed her in a bikini with a flat, tan stomach, giant breasts and tumbling blonde hair. I knew he was fucking her.

'Why do you believe her instead of me? I'm your wife, the mother of your child. There should be no one you trust more than me.'

'Jesus, Jesus, Jesus,' said Marcus. 'Can you hear yourself? Do you realise how much damage you did? Her husband freaked out and they cancelled the contract. I can't live with you any longer. I don't want to be married to you anymore. I don't know how I can make myself any clearer. Find a lawyer. I'll make sure that Ella has everything she needs. I'm happy to have custody if you want me to, but our marriage is over.'

It was nearly the end of summer. It was a Tuesday, and the weather man had called the day *a scorcher*. After it happened, her day care instituted a policy of calling parents if their child had not turned up for the day, but back then if the child didn't arrive they assumed they were sick.

I was taking her to day care, I was, but somehow … somehow I didn't make it. I took my usual route with the radio turned up as high as it would go so that I couldn't hear her screaming, and I went over everything Marcus had said the night before.

'I can't come home.'

'I can't do this anymore.'

'I can't live with you any longer.'

'I don't want to be married to you anymore.'

'I can't, I can't, I can't, I don't. I can't, I can't, I can't, I don't. I can't, I can't, I can't, I don't.'

Eventually the words ran into each other and I started breathing really fast, shallow breaths in and out. I couldn't stop myself. My heart rate sped up and I understood that I was having a panic attack.

I pulled over to the side of the road and switched off the music and tried to calm down, but oh my God the noise she was making, the dreadful, awful screeching that was coming from her mouth. My heart rate just kept going up and I was drenched in sweat. I could smell myself—a thick, dark odour. I wanted to tear my clothes off. My skin was itchy all over and still she didn't give me any peace.

I moved my seat back and turned around to see her. 'Shut up!' I shouted. 'Just shut up!' But she wouldn't be quiet. I leaned towards her and grabbed her dummy and shoved it into her mouth. She tried to push it out again but I clamped my hand across her mouth and held it there until eventually she gave up fighting me and started to suck it. I held it there as I tried to breathe, as I concentrated on calming down, and I knew that I hated her. I absolutely hated her for what she had done to my body, for what she had done to my life and for the love she had stolen from me. I hated her.

When I knew she would keep sucking her dummy I took my hand away and moved the seat forwards again. It was quiet in the car, finally blissfully, perfectly quiet. I was able to breathe in and out slowly, and then I opened the window for some air, even though all that blew in was heat.

When I started the car again and pulled back onto the road I left the radio off. I didn't need the music anymore, because her dummy was keeping her quiet. I enjoyed the silence. I felt my heart rate slow right back down and I managed to get some air into my lungs before continuing on my way to work and I thought, *This is how it should be all the time.*

I think it was because I wasn't used to her being quiet that, when I saw the day care, I didn't stop. I just kept driving until I got to work. I parked in the outside parking lot and when I got up to my sad work cubicle I made a really big deal of it to Katya, another researcher.

'I drove around for almost ten minutes to try and find a spot in the indoor parking lot,' I said, 'but eventually I had to park outside.' I wanted her to know that I had tried to park inside where it would be cooler. She may have stood a chance if I'd found a space inside but what could I do? I had to park where I could find a spot.

'It sucks if you don't get here early enough to get one of the underground spots,' Katya said. 'How's Ella?'

'Oh, she's wonderful,' I told her. 'Her daddy is dropping her off at day care today. This is the only day he drops her off and he loves doing it so much.'

It was a Tuesday and Marcus only dropped Ella off at day care on a Wednesday, but Katya didn't know that. She also didn't know that Marcus had moved out, that he had left me.

On Wednesdays Marcus would meet clients on site and since none of them liked to be there too early he had more time in the morning. He should have dropped her off every day and given me time to get myself ready without having to feed her and change her and listen to her scream over nothing. That's what he should have done.

'It's not hard to confuse one day with another,' my lawyer explained to the jury when he told them I had thought it was Wednesday.

'It's possible that because of the state she was in she assumed that it was Wednesday instead of Tuesday. How many of us have to stop and think, "What day is it today?" How many of us?'

'Didn't you see the day and date on your computer? On a calendar? On your phone?' the prosecutor asked. She was such a bitch, so smug in her suit with her hair in perfect curls.

'I may have seen the date but not the day, and I was so tired and so worried about the divorce I couldn't think straight,' I said before bursting into tears. I was very good at bursting into tears by then. I had practised.

There's a name for what happened to me on that dreadful day. It's called Forgotten Baby Syndrome.

I saw a story about it on some news program when Ella was about five months old. It was two o'clock in the morning and I happened to turn on the television while I was walking back and forth across the lounge room floor with Ella, trying to get her to go back to sleep.

I turned on the television right at the moment a psychologist was explaining what Forgotten Baby Syndrome is. It was fascinating and I sat right up close to the television so I could hear as I tried to get Ella to take her dummy and stop crying. Just as the psychologist started her explanation Ella's little mouth grabbed onto the dummy and she sucked herself quiet.

'What people need to understand is that Forgotten Baby Syndrome or, as it is sometimes known, Fatal Distraction, can happen to anyone. This type of tragedy is not confined to a single social group. It has happened to people from all walks of life.' A band across the bottom of the television screen identified her as Dr Lisa Page PhD Psych.

'I have been researching this phenomenon for many years and I have come across many stories of wonderful, loving parents who have fallen victim to this syndrome,' she said, looking at the camera with absolute authority, and I knew that no one would ever question this woman on anything. I listened to every word the doctor said while I stroked Ella's back. She was so lovely when she was asleep.

'I think that if people have a clearer understanding of what happens in situations like these they may be less inclined to judge those who make this mistake.'

'Goodness,' I whispered when Dr Page had finished speaking. I had never heard of such a thing, but after listening to the doctor I understood exactly how something like that could occur.

I turned off the television and took Ella back to her room feeling better than I had in months.

I felt like I needed to know more about Forgotten Baby Syndrome after that. I read everything I could find on the subject. According to the prosecution I had read over two hundred articles about it.

'What rubbish,' I told my lawyer, but he couldn't dispute my search history.

I read one article where the writer explained exactly how it happened, how tasks that are performed every day, like making dinner or dropping your child off at day care, become part of your routine and you are able to do them without conscious thought.

'I'm sure everyone has found themselves at a regular stop and thought, "How did I get here?" and that's because your motor cortex took care of getting you to your destination so the rest of your brain was free to think about something else, like a problem at work.' I read and I thought, *That's right, that happens to me all the time.*

'If the child is asleep or too young to alert you to his or her presence in the back seat of the car then it's possible for you, the parent, to get out of the car and go on with your day and assume that your child is at day care,' the article said.

By the time I got to work that morning I assumed that the silence in my car was because it was a Wednesday and Marcus had Ella. I was distracted by the breakdown of my marriage. I was thinking only of how I could get Marcus to give us another chance. I forgot she was in the car.

'It's a little slip, a small mistake. But it's a slip that can be fatal for a young child, especially on a hot day in the middle of summer,' another article stated.

It would be so easy, I thought as I read those words, *so easy to make such a mistake.*

My lawyer found a doctor to testify for me, to explain exactly what I had suffered from. It wasn't Dr Lisa Page—I'm assuming she was too important or too expensive—but Dr Smith was the next best thing. He told the jury it was possible that I had suffered from Forgotten Baby Syndrome.

He didn't want to say he was absolutely certain, not after he'd spoken to me.

I had to have two sessions with him before he would testify on my behalf. He asked me so many questions I didn't want to answer. He asked about my mother and my father and what my childhood had been like. He wanted to know if I'd been sexually abused, if I'd wanted to have a baby, if I loved Marcus, if I was angry with Marcus, and on and on. I spent most of the hours I was with him in tears. It seemed the easiest way to go.

In the end it may have been a mistake to let him testify because after he'd explained about Forgotten Baby Syndrome the prosecutor got up and straightened her tight little skirt and said, 'How would you explain the fact that the defendant had searched topics online, such as what happens to a child left in a hot car and how quickly a car heats up depending on the outside temperature? And that she had researched this very syndrome, reading hundreds of articles on the subject?'

'It could have been an innocent precaution,' Dr Smith said, 'or she may have simply been interested in the subject.'

'How would you explain her constant checking of the weather on the days leading up to her child's death?'

'She is a very literal individual. It could merely have been a case of her needing to know so she would know how to dress the baby,' answered Dr Smith, but he didn't sound terribly convinced.

It's funny to think that on the day she died I actually had a good day at work. I only called Marcus once, though he'd stopped taking any of my calls. If I had spoken to him, maybe he would have mentioned her—of course he would have, he couldn't talk about anything else but her—and I would have remembered. It wasn't my fault

I was distracted and stressed and upset. He should have taken my call that day, he really should have.

At work one of the journalists complimented me on catching a mistake he'd made before his article went online, and Katya and I had a lovely lunch. I allowed myself a glass of wine because I knew I wasn't going to have to feed again until that evening and I had penne with carbonara sauce. There is a cafe downstairs from the office and they do a very good carbonara.

'I don't know how you do it,' Katya said. 'I can't imagine going back to work with such a young baby.'

'It's hard some days,' I said. 'I can't even remember what I'm supposed to be doing half the time.'

Katya was a good witness for me. She said that she admired me for trying to do it all.

You can't have it all. That's the problem with being a woman today. You're expected to work and raise the children and do the cooking and the cleaning and the shopping and keep track of birthdays and social events—and sometimes it's just too much.

I walked slowly back to my car at the end of that day. I waited in the foyer, looking at my phone until a few other people started making their way to their cars, and then I went too. I suppose I just wanted the company.

She could have just been asleep, except for the smell. The hideous, hideous smell. She'd soiled herself. *Poor thing*, I thought, but then I pulled myself together and began screaming, 'My baby, my baby!' People came running and

I kept repeating, 'I didn't know she was in there, I didn't know.'

By the time the ambulance arrived I was so hysterical I needed to be sedated and I drifted off to sleep. It was the best sleep I'd had in months. I didn't have to listen for her cries or worry about when she would wake up.

Marcus was so kind to me—at least, until they found those searches on my computer. He lay next to me in bed and held me while I cried. He didn't go back to Rob's house.

'I need you now,' I told him.

'I'm here,' he said. We even managed to make love after a few days, although he felt guilty about that.

'I don't think I can ever have another child,' I told him.

'Shhh, don't think about that now, Jackie. Just rest, rest.'

It was supposed to be the start of a new chapter for us. Her death was supposed to bring us closer together, but I underestimated everything. I underestimated the police and their sneaky ways, and I underestimated how little Marcus loved me, because he couldn't have loved me very much at all.

His lack of feeling for me is crystal clear now. I can see the truth. My mother was right about him. It wasn't me he loved or wanted. My mother was right about everything. He didn't even give me time to get out of prison before moving on. I am sure his new wife is very beautiful and she never gets tired of taking care of his baby. I'm sure she doesn't call him at work or check his phone to see who he's texting. I'm sure she's perfect in a way I could never be.

'Sometimes you're impossible to love, Jackie,' my mother told me once, twice, a million times.

Impossible to love.

I would have been a good mother this time around, I know I would have been. But I'm not going to get the chance to show that to Marcus because he already has a baby, a baby and a wife he truly loves, and now I have no use for this blue-eyed baby.

No use at all.

Chapter Twenty-Seven

'Maybe you should call it a night,' suggests Mike.

'No, I'm not going home until this is over, one way or another,' says Ali.

They are sitting in Mike's car outside the Ellis house with their windows open, waiting to be updated by the station on any new information. The day's heat is not going anywhere, but at least there is a slight breeze blowing.

Neither of them had wanted to stay in the house with Malia and her parents. The calls are slowing down. People are losing interest, and so far nothing has come in that has been even remotely helpful.

'That was a complete fuck up,' says Mike.

'I know, we should have found another way to do it. Thank God her parents are here now. I think she's ready to collapse.'

'I think you're ready to collapse. Why don't you go home to Reuben and Charlie? I'll stay here and I promise you that I'll call the minute we have anything.'

'Stop babying me, Mike. I can handle this.'

'It didn't look like that in the park.'

'Oh, forgive me for showing some emotion.'

Mike sighs. 'I think this is too much for you, Ali.'

'Abigail died four years ago. I took nearly a year off and all Ossie let me do was paperwork when I came back. If I hadn't fallen pregnant with Charlie I think I would have resigned. I understand I looked a little shaky when I started work a month ago but I feel like I'm really ready to be here. I know that this case is making me a little emotional, but it's not because of Abigail. It's because I'm a mother and I'm watching another mother go through everyone's worst nightmare. I can promise you that all across the country there are mothers glued to their computers and televisions waiting for news of Zach and it's not because they've lost their own children. This is something that could happen to any of us. So, please, spare me the lecture.'

'Okay, okay,' says Mike, lifting his hands in the air. 'I'll shut up about it.'

'Thank you,' says Ali. 'How long has it been now?'

Mike looks at his watch. 'Nine hours.'

'If we don't find him soon ...'

'I know Ali, I know. It's all over Facebook and Twitter and Instagram. It's fucking everywhere. How can he have disappeared so completely?'

'Someone, somewhere, must know something. Maybe we should call in the news crew again, get Malia to do another appeal?'

'What for? They're screening the one from this morning over and over again.'

'That feels like a lifetime ago,' says Ali, chewing on a nail. 'I can't believe it's only been one day.'

'Feels like forever,' says Mike.

'Are they still searching the park?'

'Yeah, but Ossie says he's going to scale that back soon. Garnet was just a nut case who saw an opportunity.'

'Or she thought she really had the baby.'

'That's even sadder,' says Mike.

'Yeah,' agrees Ali.

'Do you think we'll find him—gut feel?'

'I don't know. This morning I was completely sure that it would only be a few hours. I mean, who takes a baby who's still being breastfed? It's not something I've ever seen. You?'

'Yeah, I'm not sure either. I've never come across this unless it's a custody thing with a pissed-off dad and even then they tend to bring back the babies. Too hard to take care of.'

'I think Ian finds all his kids too hard to take care of.'

'He's a superior human being, isn't he,' says Mike, shaking his head. 'Who the fuck walks out on his wife in a situation like this?'

'He did say she told him to go, and I can't blame her. He's only a couple of streets away at a mate's house. Maybe we should have another chat with him?'

'It had nothing to do with him, Ali. Let's not chase ourselves around in circles. We know where he is and he's keeping in touch with me. It was probably best for him to be out of the house. Malia's dad didn't look happy to see him. Imagine what that wedding would have been like. I wish I knew why good women stay with arseholes.' Mike laughs ruefully.

'Well, when you find out you can write a book and let the rest of the world know. I'm sure there would be thousands of women who would thank you for the answer. I suppose he's good-looking. He's smooth and charming when he wants to be, I'm sure. He sells cars, he must be. I think Malia got sucked in and then found herself with three kids. It's a lot harder to go anywhere when you have kids. It's why women stay, even when they're getting beaten.'

Mike shakes his head and touches a button on the side of his seat so he can recline it. 'I hear that. I may take a few minutes' rest. It's probably going to be a long night.'

'Go ahead,' says Ali. She knows she should do the same thing, but she feels jittery, as though something is about to happen. Ossie has told both of them he will replace them with another team, but that's not possible for either of them. They're too invested; they have to see this through until the end—whatever end that may be.

She feels her phone vibrate and looks down at a text from Reuben.

Where is Charlie's ducky for the bath?

Check under the sink, she replies. *He likes to hide it there.*

Got it thanks, comes the immediate text back.

Ali smiles and closes her eyes, leans her head against the window and imagines her son in the bath, hitting the water with his hands and kicking his legs. Reuben will end up getting soaked as she does every night, but it's the best time of the day. Charlie's smile is the last thing she thinks about before she falls asleep.

Chapter Twenty-Eight

'Well, I told them,' says Edna slipping back onto her barstool. 'I may skip dinner, Paulo, and head back home. I'd like to see them arrive and get her to open that door.'

'Did they believe you?' says Luis.

'They certainly did. They asked me a lot of questions, and I even gave them my mobile number. They took it very seriously, I can tell you, and the woman I spoke to said they would send someone over as soon as they could.'

'I'm staying here until it's all over,' says Luis. 'If I give you my mobile number, do you think you can give me a buzz and let me know when they've been and gone?'

'I don't see why not,' says Edna, feeling quite excited at the prospect of using her phone again.

'I'll put it in for you,' says Luis. Edna hands him the phone and watches his fingers move quickly.

'How will I find your number?' she asks when he's done.

Luis laughs. 'You're like my nan. Don't worry, Edna, I had to teach her how to use her phone as well.'

He slides his barstool closer to hers and begins moving through all the little buttons on her phone, explaining each one of them, and then he shows her exactly how to find his number in her contacts. He's very patient.

'How old is your nan?' asks Edna.

'Eighty-five years young,' he says. 'You two would probably get along all right.'

By the time Luis has finished his lesson Edna decides it's time to head home. She doesn't want to miss the arrival of the police.

'Let us know what happens!' shouts Paulo as she leaves and Edna gives a wave, letting him know that she will.

At home she opens the front door slowly, expecting to have her ears assaulted by the music but everything is quiet. There's no music and no baby crying.

'Oh dear,' she mutters as she makes her way through the house. *I might have made a dreadful mistake. I really shouldn't have said anything.*

She realises she should have simply waited for Jackie to turn off her music and then had a chat with her about it.

Perhaps poor Jackie had the music on all day to conceal her own distress from everyone else as she sheds tears over her life? Edna knows that having the police arrive to talk to her will really upset her and she may have done nothing to deserve it.

She feels unusually angry with herself and ashamed for making something out of nothing. *Silly old woman!* The whole thing seems like a terrible overreaction now, especially since there is no baby crying at all, and if Jackie had stolen that baby from the 7-Eleven he would surely be crying for his mother. She acknowledges to herself that she's made a terrible mistake and she should just call the police again and explain, tell them not to come.

She takes out her mobile phone and starts to dial the Crime Stoppers number, but then she thinks it will be better if she tells them in person. She decides to have a lie down while she waits for the police to arrive. She will listen for the knock on the door and then she'll nip downstairs and explain everything to them and send them away again.

If the police insist on talking to Jackie, Edna knows that Jackie will be angry with her, and then Robbie will be furious with her, and he's sure to tell her she's losing her marbles and will try to shift her off to a home.

But after today, that doesn't feel like the worst idea in the world. She has begun to feel very alone lately. If Solomon is no longer living in the house, she's not sure who would notice if she never came out of her room at all. William and Nate are only interested in each other and Albert is always down at the charity shop. The truth is, she spends most of her days alone.

It had been nice to be at the pub, surrounded by people. She doesn't even need to talk to anyone; she just likes to listen.

'What's done is done,' she says aloud.

Once she's in her bedroom Edna takes off her shoes and lies down on the bed. She stares at the ceiling, willing herself to stay awake for the police, but she's had too much gin and she starts to drift into a doze.

Chapter Twenty-Nine

7.00 pm

Malia opens her eyes and for a moment can't remember where she is. She has slept and there is a twinge of guilt at having allowed her body to relax.

Her bedside clock tells her it is already seven. Soon the sun will begin to go down and with a bit of luck the air will cool. Then it will be night and time to unwind from the day, maybe share a glass of wine and prepare for tomorrow. People all over the country will watch the news and shake their heads at the sadness of the missing baby, but then they will change the channel and watch a movie or help their kids with homework and later they will go to bed, safe in the knowledge that tomorrow everything will be exactly the same as it was today.

NICOLE TROPE

The day is nearly over and if Zach is still not home by nightfall then Malia is sure that he will not survive until the morning. He has hated formula on the few occasions she's tried it to make putting him in day care easier. If whoever has him is trying to feed him he may be refusing to drink anything. *If they are trying to feed him. Please let them be trying to feed him.*

She summons an image of his face, of his smile, and feels the physical ache of missing him come over her. She woke up this morning with her head crowded with thoughts of bills and money and the routine of the day unrolling before her. Now everything has changed. Even if they do find Zach safe her life will never be the same—and if he is not safe then she has no idea what will happen.

'I have to get up,' she says, but she can't move. Her body is rooted to the bed.

She closes her eyes again, sees Zach trying to roll over as he did so many mornings, rocking his chubby body back and forth, back and forth before finally managing it and giving her a triumphant gummy smile. 'What a clever boy,' she'd said, clapping her hands. 'Who's Mummy's clever boy?'

'Yay, Zach,' Aaron had said.

'Good Zachie, good Zachie,' Rhiannon had said, jumping up and down.

'One day, Aaron, he'll be able to crawl and then he'll walk and then the two of you can play soccer in the garden.'

'I don't think he's ever going to be big enough to play soccer with me,' Aaron had said solemnly.

'Oh, he will be,' Malia had laughed. 'I promise he will be.'

Malia closes her eyes again, willing herself to go back to sleep. She cannot bear this anymore, simply cannot bear it.

A rush of adrenaline flows through her body and she is suddenly unable to keep still. She moves her legs and arms around, trying to get comfortable again but suddenly sits up and gets off the bed. An urge to speak to the detectives engulfs her. She has no idea why.

She leaves her bedroom and goes to the kitchen where her mother is stacking the dishwasher and Rhiannon is colouring in, singing to herself, 'It's a happy, happy day, when you get to work and play.'

'Oh Malia,' says her mother.

'I'm just taking the detectives some water,' she says, filling two glasses from the fridge.

'I'll do that, you eat, eat and rest.'

'No, Mama, I'll do it, I have to do it ... I ... I have to do it,' she says, hearing a tremor in her own voice. Her mother opens her mouth to say something else but then only shakes her head. 'Okay, I open the door for you.'

Malia holds the glasses of water tightly and makes her way slowly down the driveway.

By the time she gets to the car Mike has gotten out.

'What's happened?' she asks but she knows. She just knows.

Chapter Thirty

It was just before seven when I woke up. I had fallen asleep with the music on. I turned it down little by little, waiting for the sound of screams to assault me. But there was only silence.

On my bed I sigh with relief. The room is very hot, and I would like to open a window but I'm afraid he will start crying again.

I think about what Marcus would be doing now. I wonder if he is sorry for the things he has said to me. I pick up my mobile phone and dial him once more but all I get is his voicemail. I don't mind. I like listening to his voice. I know he won't pick up but I try a few more times anyway.

I would like to lie on my bed until the sun goes down

and the air cools but I should check on him in there because you need to keep checking on your baby. Opening the cupboard I am assailed with the smell of shit and piss and something else, something rotting. Something dying. Something dead.

It's disgusting. I don't look too closely at him, I don't want to see. I close the door quickly. I can't bear it. I recognise that smell. I know what it means. I put my hand over my mouth because it feels like I'm going to vomit. I open the window because I can do that now and pull a chair over to the air. I breathe in and out quickly. I recognise that smell.

I know what it means. I know what it means. Oh God, I know what it means.

Baby killer
Murdering mother
Die you bitch
Rot in hell
You didn't deserve to be a mother
You're impossible to love

I wrap my arms around myself.

It is too much. I have lost too much. I have lost her. I have lost my baby. She's gone. I didn't mean to. It was a mistake. It wasn't my fault. I made a mistake.

I rock back and forth in my chair, feeling pain squeeze my insides. She is gone and because she is gone, he is gone. I will never get Marcus back. I have made too many mistakes and I will never get him back.

He is gone.

He is gone and I am alone again.

My aloneness is a blank space inside my head that grows and grows and fills my whole body until I am nothing but the space.

I am only space, just space, empty space.

Chapter Thirty-One

The simultaneous ringing of both their mobile phones wakes Ali up. She is surprised that she has dozed in the car.

'Hello,' says Mike as she fumbles for her phone, sees it's headquarters, and ends the call without answering because Mike is already speaking to Ossie. Something has happened. Something big. She watches Mike nodding.

'Uh huh, yeah, yeah, no, got it.'

'What?' asks Ali when he hangs up.

'Okay. There was a call from a woman who says that she lives in a boarding house two suburbs away from the 7-Eleven. Apparently she's in her eighties so they didn't want to give it much credence, but she went on and on about someone living there who has had the music turned up all day. The woman wanted to tell the police that she thinks she heard a baby crying in the room.'

'Why do we need to know about another crackpot, Mike?'

'Because the woman says that she thinks the woman with the music turned up has just been released from prison. Her name is Jackie, but she didn't know the surname. Easy enough to dismiss, but get this. At the same time, maybe half an hour after that call came in, there was a call from a guy named Marcus Leogian. He wanted to complain about his ex-wife being allowed to contact him. Complained that he thought the AVO he'd taken out against her would have prevented her trying once she got out of jail. He's worried she's delusional because she believes they're still married, even though he's remarried. He told them that her name is Jackie.'

'What was she in prison for?'

'She left her ten-month-old baby in the car for a whole day in the middle of summer. The kid couldn't be saved. She claimed it was a mistake, but her computer turned up some really weird searches. The husband and the jury think she did it on purpose.'

'On purpose? That's … that's …'

'Yeah, pretty fucking horrible, but there wasn't enough evidence to prove murder so they had to settle for manslaughter.'

'So she spent a few years behind bars and now she's out again, free to have another baby and do who knows what with it.'

'That's not what I'm trying to tell you,' says Mike, growing impatient. 'The husband said she kept going on about having a new baby so they could be a family again.'

'So she wants to get back together and get pregnant? I'm not sure how …'

'No, Ali, she wants to get back together and she has a baby already. A boy. He also said there was music playing in the background but it took a while for some genius to put two and two together. Ossie has already sent everyone he can over there, including an ambulance, but he says they'll wait for us.'

Ali touches her chest. 'This is it. Oh my God, I can feel it. Let's go.'

'Should we tell Malia we're leaving?' asks Mike.

'I don't want to. If this is another false lead, I don't think she can handle it.'

'Yeah, but what if it's not, what if it's him and she can feed him?'

'Fuck, I don't know what to do,' says Ali.

Just then the front door to Malia's house opens and Malia comes down the driveway holding two glasses of water.

Mike gets out of the car. 'You didn't need to do that.'

'Oh I just thought … it's so hot. I had to get myself off my bed … I had to …' Malia is silent and she looks from Ali to Mike, perhaps sensing the energy between them.

'What's happened?' she says.

Mike hesitates and then he runs his hands through his hair. 'Nothing, but we have to go …'

'You're lying,' says Malia, narrowing her eyes. 'They've found him, haven't they?' Her voice is high and her hands holding the glasses of water start shaking.

'Okay, you need to stay calm, Malia, but we've had another call about a baby,' says Ali. 'You need to let us check it out first.'

'I'm coming with you,' insists Malia, setting down the glasses on the side of the driveway.

'I don't think you should,' states Mike.

'I'm coming with you,' repeats Malia, opening the door to the back seat of the car and sliding inside. She pulls her mobile phone out of her pocket. 'I'll call my mother and tell her.' Ali knows they could force her out of the car but the determination on Malia's face stops her. They don't have time to argue the point anyway. Mike shakes his head and gets back into the car.

'Fine,' says Ali, looking at Malia, 'but you stay in the car.'

Malia nods like she agrees but Ali knows she probably won't do as she's told. *You wouldn't keep me from my baby either.*

Chapter Thirty-Two

Edna dreams she is on a picnic with Harry. They are sitting in a park by the harbour, looking at a giant cruise ship. There is a light breeze blowing and all around them are butterflies. They are on the grass and in the trees and on Harry's hand. Edna feels their touch as they alight on her hands and face.

'I've booked us a trip on that, love,' Harry says, pointing at the ship, and Edna begins to laugh with joy.

Her dream is interrupted by the noise of fists drumming on the front door downstairs.

'Police, police! Open up!' she hears.

Edna struggles to sit up. 'Coming!' she calls as she pushes her feet into her shoes.

Before anyone can open the door there is a tremendous cracking and splintering of wood and pounding footsteps through the house. There is more knocking on doors downstairs. 'Police, police!' they shout, their voices loud and commanding, and then if the door isn't opened, 'Police, get back! Police, get back!'

The sounds of a door being smashed open follows. Edna's heart races as the house fills with noise.

'Oh dear, oh dear,' she says, wringing her hands. She's heard that people can get into a lot of trouble for giving police false information.

Edna gets off her bed as she hears footsteps up to her room. She doesn't need her door smashed in. She opens up and moves back to allow the police to see inside her room. A man dressed in black and holding a gun steps into her room, looks around, then flings open the cupboard.

'Clear!' he shouts.

'Her room is the next one,' stutters Edna, but she can already hear banging on Jackie's door, and then a moment of waiting, and then the sound of a door being bashed in.

Edna is really frightened now. What has she done? She steps out into the hallway that is filled with police.

'Oh my,' she breathes.

A policewoman spins around. 'Stay in your room, ma'am,' she says, holding her hand out to prevent Edna going any further.

'I will not,' says Edna, standing up straight. 'I'm the one who called you. I want to see if she has that baby.'

She has a terrible thought: she hopes Jackie *does* have the baby otherwise she's in a dreadful fix.

The policewoman has already turned back around. Edna stands on her tiptoes and tries to peer over everyone's heads, but she can't see a thing. She shuffles forward and pushes through. Everyone is looking into Jackie's room, where it's dark and silent. The police hush their voices down to whispers.

Edna pushes further forward and then she sees the mother, the baby's mother, standing next to a policeman. She is crying and hugging herself.

Edna would like to go up to her, but someone says, 'Step back, please,' and so she does.

'What's going on?' she hears Robbie say. He comes up the stairs and pushes into the throng of police. 'Edna, what's happening?'

'I think she stole the baby,' says Edna. 'I called the police.'

Her voice sounds certain, and she is pleased that she doesn't sound unsure or regretful—there will be time for that later.

'Oh Jesus, Edna, what have you done?' says Robbie.

Edna has no interest in replying. She squeezes herself forward once more. There are two people standing at the door to Jackie's room. They're not dressed in uniforms, but they look like they're in charge. There's a big man and a woman with red hair. The man takes his gun out of his holster and Edna steps back. She hopes no one is about to get shot. It's like something out of a movie.

I really should have kept myself to myself, she thinks.

Chapter Thirty-Three

7.30 pm

Malia stands next to the room that Ali and Mike have forced their way into. Suddenly, it is very quiet despite the hallway being filled with at least twenty people. Everyone has been rendered mute by Ali's signal.

It had only taken minutes for her and the detectives to get here. Malia had held onto the handle of the car door as Mike sped through suburban streets, mounting pavements and going the wrong way down one-way streets with lights flashing.

'It's not a guarantee,' Mike had said on the way. 'I don't want to get your hopes up, but it's the best lead we've had all day.'

'Is it a better lead than the crazy old woman?' Malia had asked.

'It's come from two different sources,' said Ali. 'But I need to know that you're going to be able to handle it if it's another dead end.'

'I can,' Malia had said. 'I can handle it,' and she had felt something inside herself unfold. The whole awful day had flashed in her thoughts, but she knew that she would not break. Whatever happened now, whatever happened tomorrow or next week or next month, she would stay standing. She would stay standing for Aaron and Rhiannon and, please God, for Zach.

She sat up straighter in the back of the car. *I can handle it*, she thought. *I can handle anything*. She had looked behind her while Mike turned another corner, and as her body slid across the back seat and was yanked back by her seatbelt, she had seen an ambulance, its lights and sirens screaming, swing into the road behind them.

'An ambulance?' she queried.

Ali had turned around. 'Just in case, Malia.'

Malia hadn't had time to ask anything else. Mike had screeched to a halt in front of a large house surrounded by a wrought-iron fence covered in peeling white paint.

They all got out of the car at once and Malia had run up the front path, not even giving Ali the chance to tell her that she had to stay in the car. There were police everywhere in black riot gear. At Mike's command to 'Go, go, go' they had charged into the house with guns drawn, shouting and battering open doors.

'What are you doing?' Malia heard a man say, and then she felt like she was carried up the stairs by a swarm of police. An old woman stood in an open doorway, bewilderment across her flushed face. They had knocked on the door of the room belonging to the woman they suspected had Zach, and when there was no answer they had bashed it open, shouting, 'Police, police! Get back!' the whole time.

Malia hadn't at first been able to see inside the room, but now Ali has held up her hand and everything has gone silent.

Malia tries to move forward, but one of the constables holds onto her arm and puts her finger to her lips. Malia can feel her whole body fizzing. Her muscles are cramping and shaking. They have only been in the house for a few minutes, but she feels as if she has been standing in the dimly lit hallway forever.

'Jackie?' she hears Ali say quietly. 'Jackie?'

Chapter Thirty-Four

The room is dark. The only light is coming from a lamp on a side table.

A woman sits in a chair over by the window, staring out at the setting sun. There is a slight breeze moving through the room from the open window, but it's not concealing the smell. Something is rotting somewhere.

The woman is not moving, although Ali thinks she must have heard them entering the room. The whole suburb must have heard them, and Mike's first instinct had been to switch on the light, but something in Ali knew they now had to proceed slowly. She had given her head a shake and Mike had dropped his hand and pointed his gun down.

They made a lot of noise when they smashed down the door. Ali can't see if the woman is holding anything and her stillness is worrying, as is the open window, just big enough to push a baby through onto the ground two storeys below.

'Jackie?' says Ali softly, moving one foot forward slightly.

The feeling of many people trying to keep quiet nudges at Ali and she can almost hear their collective breathing. The residents who were found at home have been ordered to stay in their rooms, but Ali knows they have followed the police upstairs. This is no ordinary visit from the police and everyone wants to know exactly what's going on.

In the car on the way to the property, Ali had glanced at the file on Jackie Leogian that had been sent through to her mobile phone. It was gut-wrenching reading. Jackie had left her child in the car for an entire day in the middle of summer. The baby, Ella, had died, trapped in a car that had effectively turned into an oven. At first everyone, including her husband, had assumed that it was a case of Forgotten Baby Syndrome, but then detectives had found the searches on her computer.

Jackie Leogian had been searching how long it was legally acceptable to leave an infant in a car. If that had been all she looked up her life would have turned out differently, but the tech guys had found deleted searches on legal cases where Forgotten Baby Syndrome was used as a defence, as well as searches on personal stories of people who had forgotten their babies in cars, searches on how hot a car got, depending on the temperature outside, and how quickly the car would heat up.

It was too much to take in, the idea that someone would willingly hurt their child. Ali knew that, as she and Mike and Malia raced to find Zach, it would be better for her to put aside any thoughts on the kind of person Jackie Leogian was. There would be time for that later.

Ali breathes out slowly and edges forwards. 'Jackie?' she says, wanting to run over and grab the woman but knowing that if she is holding Zach in her arms it is possible she will decide to throw him out of the window.

A woman who left her child in a hot car to die is capable of anything at all.

She is in a state of heightened awareness, hearing every small sound in the house. Zach is here, she knows it.

'Everyone move the fuck back,' she hears Mike say in a menacing whisper as she carefully puts one foot in front of the other, taking minutes to cross the space that could be crossed in a few seconds.

'Jackie,' she says again, the word soft on her lips. She knows Mike has allowed her to take the lead right now because a soft touch is needed. Ali has not taken her gun out of the holster. Her instincts tell her to keep her hands free and she's certain that Jackie does not have a weapon.

Although the room is frighteningly silent, Ali is sure the baby is here. He has not been fed for nearly twelve hours and the room, like the whole boarding house and the thick air outside, is stifling. The baby should be howling with hunger and thirst unless she somehow managed to feed him. *Please let her have fed him.* But even then, Ali realises, even then he should be awake and crying. The noise should have woken him.

Ali breathes in a sinking sensation, almost choking on the thick, putrid smell. If he is here—he is dead. *Don't think like that, don't think like that*, she hears in her head as she reminds herself to focus only on what she is doing now.

'Jackie,' she says softly for the fourth or fifth time, still hoping for an answer.

'Don't come any closer,' says Jackie, startling Ali. She hadn't expected a reply.

Ali stops moving. 'Jackie, I'm Ali. I'm here to help you with the baby.'

'I don't need help with him anymore,' says Jackie.

She remains curled in her chair. Her voice is flat. Ali wishes she could see her face. She would know if she could see her face. She needs to get around to the front of the chair.

'Everyone needs help with a baby,' says Ali.

'It's no longer necessary.'

No, no, no.

'I'm sure that's not true, Jackie,' she says, clenching her fist, squeezing her nails into her palms. She would like to grab the woman and shake her until she has no energy left. 'I'll just hold him for a bit,' she says.

'He's a beautiful baby,' says Jackie.

Present tense. 'I'm sure he is, but your neighbour, Edna, says that he's been crying a lot.'

'He's not crying now.'

Enough of this. 'Jackie,' she says, more stridently, 'you

need to tell me where the baby is. I need to see that he's okay. You need to tell me right now.'

'He wouldn't eat,' says Jackie. 'I tried formula, but he wouldn't drink it. He's very stubborn. Babies can be so difficult when they want to be. People don't understand that. They think babies don't know what they're doing, but they do.'

There is no emotion in the woman's voice. She could be reading from a cue card.

'Maybe he's not feeling well,' says Ali. 'I could take him to the doctor for you.'

She shuffles forward another half step. Behind her she can sense the others. They are making sure to stay quiet.

'I gave him some water.'

'I need to see him,' demands Ali. 'Where. Is. He?'

'Go away,' says Jackie. 'Go away and leave me alone. She doesn't deserve to have him back. She just left him there in the car. She didn't even care.'

'She does care,' says Ali. 'She's his mother and she misses him desperately. She just wants him home. She won't make that mistake again. She just wants him home.'

'People should be punished for their mistakes.'

'They should,' says Ali, 'but she's been punished enough. You need to tell me where Zach is.'

'His name is Xander.'

'No, Jackie, his name is Zach and he's not your baby. You need to give him back to Malia. Malia is his mother and he has a brother named Aaron and a sister named Rhiannon

363

and a father, Ian. They all miss him and want him to come home.'

'I was punished for my mistake and now I am alone,' says Jackie.

'I know,' says Ali. 'I know you were punished.'

'I never got him back. I will never get him back.'

'Jackie, your baby was a little girl. Her name was Ella—remember?'

Jackie turns around to look at Ali. There is a final shaft of light as the sun sets, offering a clear look at her face. Her eyes are dark in her face and her hair is matted.

'I'm not talking about her,' she spits.

'Then who are you talking about?' says Ali.

'Marcus, I'm talking about Marcus. I'll never get Marcus back.'

'Your husband?'

'He was. He was everything and now he's gone.'

'Gone?'

'Married to someone else. I told him that I had another baby for him, that we could start again, but he didn't want to see me. He doesn't love me anymore. I didn't need a baby after that.'

Behind her Ali hears a moan, a soft breaking of a heart. *Fuck*, she thinks, *I told them to keep her away*. Ali hadn't realised that Malia was in the room.

'Jackie, I'm going to ask you one more time and you need to answer me. You need to answer me now! Where is Zach? Where is he, Jackie?'

Ali's voice is loud now. Jackie isn't holding Zach. Her arms are empty.

Jackie stands up and steps forward. 'Gone,' she says. 'Gone and forgotten.'

'Please, please no!' wails Malia and then everything happens at once. Malia darts forward and grabs Jackie.

'Where is he!' she screams, shaking the thin woman by the shoulders. 'Where is he? Where is *he*?'

The lights are switched on and the constables rush into the room and separate Malia and Jackie. Malia is screaming and kicking, but Jackie is unresponsive, as though she is under the influence of drugs. Outside the room the other residents begin talking and Ali hears someone say, 'I told you so, didn't I tell you so? That's what happens when you let in the riffraff.'

'Shut up, Edna!' shouts a man.

'Go back to your rooms,' come the voices of two or three constables. The room fills with uniformed police as Malia is pushed into a corner and Jackie is pinned down.

'Move back, move back!' shouts Mike, and amidst the chaos there is a pocket of silence in which Ali hears a sound, a small desperate cry, so soft, so light that she almost misses it.

'Shut up!' she screams, and the room is instantly silent with everyone standing stock-still as though frozen by the magic of a photograph.

Ali looks wildly around her and then darts towards the cupboard. She flings it open and is assailed by the smell of faeces and urine and sweat. Zack is lying in a nappy at the bottom of the cupboard on top of some shoes, a rag doll flung away by an uncaring child. His little legs are still and only one hand opens and closes slowly.

The cupboard is sweltering. Ali slides her hand under his head and lifts him out gently. His body is limp, but his eyelids flutter.

'Paramedics!' yells Ali.

'Zach!' shouts Malia and she wrenches herself out of the grasp of a constable and launches herself at Ali.

The paramedics who have been waiting outside come into the room.

'Ma'am please, please don't,' says one of the paramedics as Malia prepares herself to feed Zach. 'He won't be able to. Give him to us, he's too dehydrated.'

But Malia won't let go of her child, so Ali steps forward and helps the paramedic release her hands from around Zach's body. When her arms are empty Malia wails like a child.

Ali grabs her shoulders. 'Malia, he needs to get to the hospital. He needs help from doctors.'

Malia turns to look around the room. She looks dazed.

'Come with us,' says the other paramedic, and finally Malia seems to understand and she follows him out of the room.

Ali breathes deeply. *Please let him be okay.*

And then it is over and the frenzied atmosphere of the room calms.

'Fuck,' says Mike as two constables lead Jackie away in handcuffs.

'Fuck is right,' says Ali, feeling her body sag.

Her phone beeps and she takes it out to look. Reuben has texted: *Just letting you know our boy had a good dinner and he has enjoyed three stories from grandma and one from dad. He has his blanket and his little dog and is fast asleep and I have opened a bottle of wine to breathe. Will wait to hear from you.*

Ali sinks down onto the bed in the stinking room and lets go. She buries her face in her hands and gives into the distress that has been pushing at her all day.

'Get out now!' barks Mike at everyone, and then he sits down beside her on the bed. 'It's okay,' he says, holding her tight. 'It's okay.'

After a few minutes Ali takes a shuddering breath and wipes her eyes.

'I'll get started on interviews,' says Mike. 'But I think your day is over. Start again tomorrow, eh?'

Ali thinks briefly about telling him that she will stay to finish up, but then she nods. She will start again tomorrow.

She looks at the screen of her phone and texts her husband.

Will be home soon.

Chapter Thirty-Five

Melbourne, eighteen months later

The doorbell peals through the house and Malia glances desperately around the kitchen for someone else to answer it. Her hands are covered in the olive oil and herb mix she had been rubbing into the lamb. *Surely they can't be here already? I told them to come for dinner*, she thinks.

'Sean!' she shouts, and then, on receiving no answer, 'Aaron, Rhiannon … Can someone please get the door?'

The bell rings again, but this time she hears running footsteps from all over the house.

'No, no!' shouts Sean from wherever he is. 'Only grown-ups answer the door. Only grown-ups. I'm changing a nappy, Malia.'

'It's just my parents … Oh shit, never mind, I'll go.'

Malia rinses her hands and leaves the kitchen for the front door that Aaron has already answered. Aaron is standing, frozen in the doorway, staring at a man dressed in faded jeans and a T-shirt. Malia steps forward quickly, intending to get Aaron behind her, when she recognises him.

'Ian.'

In her head, whenever she pictures Ian, he is always dressed in a suit with his hair neatly slicked back. The man in front of her is casual, relaxed and sunburned.

'Hi, Malia. Hey, Aaron. Hello, Ri Ri,' Ian says.

Rhiannon is standing behind Aaron with her thumb in her mouth.

'Ian … I didn't …'

'Can I come in?' he asks.

Malia would like to say no. She would like to say, 'Go away.' Would like to scream, 'Get away from us.' But her children—Ian's children—are standing right next to her. So instead she says, 'Of course,' and she steps back to let him inside. 'Say hello to … to Dad, kids.'

'Hello,' says Aaron warily.

''Lo,' says Rhiannon.

For a moment Malia feels rooted to her spot at the front door until she recovers herself, turns, and walks towards the living room, talking as she does.

'Come through, Ian, and sit down. I'm just … I was getting some lamb ready to go in the oven. My parents are coming over for an early dinner. They come every Sunday, or we go to them. Usually Mum has a huge family gathering …' She stops speaking, aware that she is babbling.

'This little man is all clean,' says Sean, coming into the living room where Malia, Ian and the children are standing, all unsure of what to do next.

'Ian,' says Sean, and he puts Zach down on the floor. He sounds as flabbergasted as Malia feels.

'Aw ceen,' says Zach to Malia.

'Yes, baby, all clean.'

'Dada aw ceen,' says Zach to Sean.

'Yeah, mate,' says Sean, 'all clean.'

Zach, satisfied that everyone knows his nappy has been changed, goes back to playing in the kitchen where he is busy with the serious business of making play dough cakes. 'Patty cake, patty cake,' he sings.

'Sit down,' says Sean as though he has just thought of the idea—gesturing to the sofa. 'Do you want a drink? I've got beer and wine and um …'

'Mineral water,' says Malia. 'Would you like a mineral water with some juice?'

'I'd like a mineral water,' says Aaron.

'Me too,' says Rhiannon.

'Aaron, can you go and sort out drinks for you and your sister, please,' says Malia.

'Okay.' He grabs Rhiannon's hand to pull her out of the living room. Usually he would argue that he didn't want to have to get one for Rhiannon, but the tension between the three adults can't be concealed and Malia knows that her son is grateful to get away.

'I'm not thirsty, but thanks,' says Ian to Sean as he takes a seat. Malia and Sean sit as well, awkwardly. Malia would like to take Sean's hand but she resists.

'I didn't expect to see you,' says Malia. She doesn't add *ever again*, but she thinks those words, turns them over in her mind and realises that it's what she's been hoping: for him to simply disappear and never come back.

She studies him, trying to see what it was about him that had once made her stomach flip, that had once made her the kind of woman who forgave and forgave and forgave until it was too late. She shakes her head. The idea of falling out of love with Ian was once an impossible concept, but here she sits and she may as well be looking at a stranger.

'I know, it's been a long time. Zach's so big. I can't believe how big he is. How old is he now?'

'Almost two,' says Sean and he puts his arm around Malia's shoulder and squeezes. Malia knows he's trying to keep her calm. She can feel herself getting angry and she doesn't want to feel that way. It doesn't do her any good. It gives her reflux and makes her head ache.

Ian should know how old his son is, of course he should, but there is no point in getting upset that he doesn't, or that he hasn't seen his children since the day they found Zach.

Images from that day flash in Malia's mind and she bites

down on her lip because she has worked so hard not to let that one day affect every day since. *Silly woman*, she thinks to herself. It had changed everything.

Malia remembers the ride in the ambulance with the paramedics struggling to find a vein on Zach's body so they could begin rehydrating him. She had wrapped her arms around her aching breasts as her precious milk leaked away, failing to save her baby. The small sound Zach made when the paramedic did finally find a vein ripped at her heart: he was so close to death that the pain barely registered.

The memory of the serious faces of a team of doctors waiting for them at the hospital makes her squeeze her eyes shut. She had been pushed out of the way and directed to wait.

Hours later Ian had arrived at the hospital. By then, Malia had spoken to her parents and asked every doctor and nurse she saw if her child would survive. No one had been able to give her the answer she wanted.

When Ian had walked into the hospital room Malia had been surprised to see him. The one person she had not thought about was Ian. She had felt momentarily abashed for not calling him.

Malia had been sitting next to Zach's cot. He was being rehydrated with fluid and given antibiotics. Malia was holding his hand, stroking his little fingers and concentrating on not pulling out the IV lines that were bruising his tender skin. The nurses had wiped him down and put on a clean nappy. On the way to the hospital Malia had watched the paramedics' faces and she had known that there was a good chance Zach would not survive.

Malia has thought about the woman who took him many times since that day. Thought about her, been furious with her, hated her, planned to execute terrible acts of revenge on her and eventually forgiven her because she knows that Jackie has lost her mind and will live out the rest of her days in a psychiatric institution. Malia's revenge could not be any greater than the torment she must be going through in her tortured head.

Ian sitting on her sofa brings back some of those thoughts and Malia imagines a hand pushing away the darkness of that day, pushing it far away.

'Is he going to be okay?' Ian had asked in the paediatric intensive-care section.

'They don't know,' Malia had replied. 'If he starts to perk up in the next few hours he'll be fine but otherwise ... they don't know.'

'I'm sorry, Malia,' Ian said.

She had sighed. She couldn't believe how tired she was. She knew that if she even so much as rested against the back of the chair she would fall asleep for days. 'It's the shock,' one of the nurses had said.

'Leave it now, Ian,' said Malia. 'We've found him and all that matters is that he gets better. Maybe later you could go home and get some stuff for me. I need a shower and I need to change.'

'You should go home. I'll sit here. Go home and get some rest.'

'I'm not leaving my child.'

Ian had pulled up a chair and sat down next to her. 'I fucked up,' he said. 'If I'd gotten the milk we wouldn't be here.'

'I don't want to discuss this now. I can't discuss this now. I need to concentrate on Zach and we can sort out everything else afterwards.'

'Yeah, I know, and I don't want to push you to talk, but I need you to know that I understand a lot of this was my fault. I'm not a good husband and I'm not a good dad.'

'Ian, please,' said Malia, wishing that he would just keep quiet so she could focus on watching Zach's chest move up and down.

'No, Malia, I know this isn't the best time, but I need to say this. I'm going away for … for I don't know how long … But I need to get myself sorted out. I need to figure out who I am in all this and why I do the things I do. I came to see that he's okay, but I also came to say goodbye.'

Malia felt a sudden urge to laugh. What Ian was saying could only be a joke. 'You're joking, aren't you,' she said, trying and failing to keep her anger at bay.

'I'm not, I'm sorry. I've realised that I can't do this. I've been … I've been playing along at being a husband and father, but none of it was ever what I wanted. I'm not cut out for this. I'm no good at it. I know this is the worst possible time for me to do this, but there never would have been a good time and I need … I have to go away.'

Malia could not comprehend what Ian was saying. It was too much to process, and too hard to believe that at a time like this he was actually telling her he was leaving.

'Just go then, Ian,' she said. 'Just fucking go.'

Ian had waited a moment and Malia had been sure that he would say, 'Of course I'm not going anywhere. I'm just upset about this and I know we'll sort it out. I'm here to stay.'

But Ian didn't say anything like that and the silence between them grew until he said, 'I'll let you know where I am. I'll send as much money as I can.'

'Go.'

'Malia, I'm …'

'Just go, just go, go, go!' she yelled, bringing nurses running. All her frustration and anxiety and fear and despair of the awful day came roaring up and she felt as though she were in the middle of a storm. 'Go!' she kept screaming. 'Go, fucking *go!*'

'Mrs Ellis, calm down, calm down,' said one of nurses, putting her arms around Malia, who was shaking and crying. 'This does no good. If you can't be calm we will have to sedate you. Now breathe in and out and relax. That's it, that's it.'

When Malia had composed herself she looked up to find Ian gone, almost as if he'd never been there at all. For days afterwards she thought she had imagined his presence in the hospital, dreamed the words he'd said.

Now Malia looks at her husband—ex-husband, whom she has not seen for a year and a half—and feels that she has nothing new to say. Sean's comforting arm reminds her to keep breathing and that everything will be fine, just as his presence has done since Ian left.

'Why have you come back?' she asks.

'I want … I want to see the kids again, to be part of their lives.'

'You lost that right the day you walked out of the hospital, leaving me to care for a baby who might have died. Leaving me with three children to raise on my own.'

Ian puts up his hand. 'I know. It was a crappy thing to do, but I had to get my head right. I had to do it alone. I know I don't deserve to see them, but they're my kids and I want to try and do it better. I want to be a good father to them. I've stopped gambling and I've got a job in Melbourne. Please don't send me away. I won't fight you if you do because I know what an arsehole I've been, but I'm better now and I want to be part of their lives. Please, Malia, please give me a chance.'

Malia is unused to this Ian. In fact she has never met this Ian. His blue eyes are earnest and, despite his weathered skin, he looks younger than she remembers him. Malia knows that people change, that there are catalysts in people's lives that forever alter who they are. She is a very different woman to the mother whose son was taken from her car all those months ago. She surprises herself these days with her ability to state exactly what she wants, to not give in or compromise on the things that are important to her.

'Sean and I are married now, Ian. He's been taking care of the kids with me. He's been their father for the last year.'

'But Ian *is* their father, Malia,' says Sean, quietly. 'I'm sure we can work this out. We can all work together to do what's best for these kids. I know that's what you want.'

Malia shakes her head. As usual Sean's measured tones make her see reason. He is, as her father likes to say, 'a man among men'.

Once Zach was released from the hospital, Malia had begun packing up her house so she could move back to Melbourne. There was no question of her staying in Sydney. Her father's rage at Ian's disappearance had been frightening, but it was never directed at her. Malia knew that his heart broke for her.

At least twenty family members had arrived in Sydney to help pack up the house and send all Ian's things into storage. Aaron and Rhiannon had been upset and confused, not to mention devastated at having to leave school and preschool, but Malia had known it was the right thing to do. The only regret she had felt was at the thought of leaving Sean, who called every day even though she hadn't found the energy to speak to him.

A few days before she was due to leave Sydney Malia had left the children with her family and gone in to explain everything. She had told Sean about Ian leaving and she had talked about how it had been with him. She had told him she was going to live in Melbourne because she needed to be with her family so she could somehow find a way to embrace normal life again after her hours of terror when she believed her son was lost. Hours that still woke her from sleep and sent her running down to his room to check he was in his cot, alive and breathing.

Sean had listened without speaking until she told him she was only days away from getting on a plane.

'Malia, you know … you know how I feel about you, right?'

She had nodded, knowing there was no reason to pretend. 'I feel it too, Sean, it's just not …'

'Not the right time, I know. But you know what? When it is the right time I'll be there.'

'Sean, you live and work in Sydney. I'm moving to Melbourne. I can't live without my family near me. I just can't.'

'Well,' said Sean, 'I can see how that would be a problem, so it's a good thing that Melbourne is full of hipsters and I can make a cookie brownie combination they'll just love.'

'Oh Sean, you can't …'

'But I can, Malia. There's nothing for me here, really. My parents are gone and I don't have kids. A change might be good for me. You're the reason I love coming to work each day, Malia—you.'

'Sean, I can't ask you to uproot your life, and even if you

do I can't promise you anything. I don't know how I'm going to feel next week or next month.'

'But we'll be friends no matter what, right?'

Malia had smiled. 'No matter what.'

Six months after Malia had arrived in Melbourne Sean had appeared on her doorstep. They had been skyping nearly every night, but Sean had not mentioned his move or that he had opened a bakery in Melbourne.

'I wanted to make sure it was the right thing to do first,' he told her.

Zach had bonded with Sean immediately. Aaron and Rhiannon had taken a little longer, but Sean was patient with them and eventually they responded.

'I don't want to get in the way of what you two have,' Ian says now. 'That's why I agreed to the divorce. I know we can't go back, but I would still like to go forward.'

Malia can hear more changes in his words. She knows he has spent long hours thinking about this. Her heart relents. He is still the father of her children and she will always hold some love for him because of that. She can't look at Aaron, Rhiannon and Zach with anything except grateful joy. She decides to give the man who helped create them one last chance. When the children are older they can decide whether or not they want to see him but she would never want them to be able to accuse her of keeping them away from their biological father.

'You'll have to let them get used to you again,' says Malia. 'You hurt them by going away. They're not going to forgive you so quickly, especially Aaron.'

As though summoned, Aaron comes back into the living room with Rhiannon. Malia knew that they would stay in the kitchen to have their drinks. It was a rule of the house and she knew she needed time to figure out what Ian wanted. He had, true to his word, sent money every month. It hadn't been much, but it had been something.

'I'll do whatever you tell me to do,' says Ian.

'I think that's fair,' says Sean.

Aaron sits down on the couch next to Malia and puts his hand on her knee in what Malia is sure is a protective gesture, and her heart breaks for him. Rhiannon climbs onto Sean's lap. Both children regard their father with impassive faces. Malia can't imagine what they must be thinking. She runs through a list of possible things to say, but then Aaron speaks for her.

'You're my dad,' he says quietly.

'Yes,' says Ian, 'of course I'm your dad.'

'You went away.'

Aaron is at the age where he likes to collect facts. The solar system was formed 4.6 billion years ago. The human body has two hundred and seventy bones at birth. His father leaving is just another fact that Malia knows makes his departure easier to deal with.

'I did, mate, but I'm here now and we can have a talk about that. I'm happy to answer all your questions.'

Malia feels herself holding back. She would like to jump in and smooth things over, make everything all right again, but she knows that it's not up to her. It's up to Ian and his children.

Aaron looks at Sean. 'He's our dad, too,' he says in the casual way that children have, not meaning to be cruel, just stating another fact.

Malia holds her breath, aware of how difficult this will be for Ian to hear—regardless of his poor performance in the past, he is still Aaron's father.

'He is, Aaron, which makes you really lucky because you have one great mum and two great dads.'

'I guess,' says Aaron, and then, 'Want to see my Xbox?'

Ian looks at Malia, who nods. She will have to make sure he is gone before her parents arrive for dinner, but for now she can let him play with the children.

As Ian, Aaron and Rhiannon leave the room a feeling of peace settles over her. She drops her head onto Sean's shoulder.

'It'll be fine, love, I promise,' he says.

The peace Malia feels is hard-won, the result of many hours of anger and despair, many long talks with Sean and her sister and her mother, as well as many months examining how she came to find herself sitting on the ground at a petrol station with her baby missing. She is not sure that letting Ian see the children is the best thing to do, but she feels it is the right thing to do, and so she gives Sean a quick kiss and goes back to cooking her lamb.

Chapter Thirty-Six

Sydney

Ali stands up from her desk to stretch the kink out of her back. Her paperwork has been piling up and today Ossie told her that it would no longer be tolerated, so she's been at her desk for hours.

Mike is out sick so it's a good time to get things done. 'More like hungover,' she said to him on the phone, knowing that he'd been out celebrating his anniversary the night before.

'You're just jealous because you can't drink anymore,' he had said, and she had laughed because she was a little jealous. She had not expected to fall pregnant. They hadn't been trying, but they hadn't exactly been not trying.

Charlie will be close to three when the baby arrives, which isn't a bad age gap.

And Charlie will be at preschool full time by then so she will be able to have some time alone with the baby. It's another boy, for which she is very grateful.

Even though Abigail's death feels like it was so long ago it may have happened to someone else, she still feels a pang whenever she sees a baby girl who is around the age Abigail was when she died. She never wants to feel like she is replacing her little girl. When she meets people for the first time she always hesitates when they ask her how many children she has. Usually she answers *one*, but sometimes she meets someone she feels will understand and answers *two, but one living child*. What amazes her is how many women she meets who not only understand her experience but share it as well. Her baby son gives her a quick kick, forcing her to push away dark thoughts.

'Hungry, baby?' she whispers.

Her phone buzzes with a text from Malia: *Ian's back.*

'Wow,' says Ali.

She hadn't expected Ian to ever turn up again. She grabs her bag to go outside and give Malia a call on the way to the corner cafe.

Her friendship with Malia had come as a surprise. She had called a few days after Zach had been released from the hospital to check up on how he was doing, and for some reason the conversation had veered away from a professional courtesy call into a discussion about Ian leaving, and then about both their lives.

They had met for a quick coffee and then they had met for dinner, and after Ali told Malia about Abigail she knew that the bonds of friendship were forming. She and Reuben had taken Charlie down to Melbourne to visit with the Ellis kids. They had even snatched a wonderful child-free weekend away to attend Malia and Sean's quiet wedding, although it had been the biggest quiet wedding Ali had ever attended.

Outside the station Ali pops a piece of gum into her mouth and dials. 'So,' she says when Malia answers, 'what did Sean say?'

Chapter Thirty-Seven

Sydney

Edna has never been one to be rude for no reason, so she's struggling to think of a polite way to tell Lottie from next door that she's never going to learn how to knit, no matter how enjoyable she says it is.

Lottie is her best friend in the aged-care home and Edna doesn't want to upset her, but there are too many things for her to do other than learn to knit. For a start, the home has cable television and she and Solomon and a few others have worked out their entire month's viewing. They're all fond of period dramas. She also now goes to water aerobics twice a week and there's a nature walk every Wednesday. By the end of each day she is tuckered out, and learning to knit seems like more trouble than it's worth, although she supposes she could knit jumpers for Aaron, Rhiannon and Zach.

She would have to get Malia to send their sizes up, but she's sure that would be no trouble. Malia sends an enormous basket of wonderful cakes and cookies from Sean's bakery to the home every month, and the whole family has been up to visit so many times that Edna has lost count.

Edna doesn't think much about the day Zach was stolen, but sometimes she feels guilty for thinking that she's pleased it happened; that she's glad she was the one to help Malia find her baby. She wouldn't have a whole new family otherwise, and they are her family. Zach calls her 'Gamma' now that he's begun to speak, and every time he says it Edna can't believe how lucky she is.

Sometimes Edna is woken by a nightmare in which she decides not to call the police because she doesn't want to interfere and little Zach dies in that dreadful woman's room. Edna wakes up shaking and sweating and has to turn on her light and read until she feels better. Perhaps learning to knit wouldn't be the worst thing in the world. She could knit away her nightmares.

Edna enjoyed her fifteen minutes of fame after Zach was rescued. First, she'd had to explain to that nice detective everything that had happened that day, and then she'd had to go down to the police station and explain it again. She was considered a 'very good witness' because she never forgot anything and her story always remained the same, never mind the fact that she was eighty years old.

Edna had not imagined she would hear from anyone else about that day, but she'd been wrong about that.

The police had let her know that Zach was well and that he had survived his ordeal, and Edna had been so grateful to hear it. But then Malia had tracked her down to the home where she'd moved soon after the incident and flung her arms around her right there in the visitors' room.

'You saved my baby,' she'd said over and over again, and they'd both had a good cry together over that. Edna hadn't minded crying in front of someone else because Malia was crying too.

Edna heaves herself off her bed and goes to find Lottie, who will be having tea in the common room now, just as she does every day at this time.

'I'm going to make jumpers for my grandchildren,' she'll tell her. Lottie has assumed, as most people have, that Aaron, Rhiannon and Zach are her grandchildren, just as they have assumed that Sean is their father and Edna's son. Edna likes to pretend he is. He doesn't have a mother after all, so it's nice for him as well.

She'll take her bag and coat with her to find Lottie, she decides, because it's close enough to the time the shuttle bus takes her and whoever else wants to come for a visit to the pub. Edna is pleased that she's still allowed to go to her old pub. She would have missed Paulo otherwise. He always says, 'Hail the conquering hero,' when he sees her now and gives her a double G&T on the house.

She and Paulo and Luis were in the local paper together after Zach was found, and a very pretty young woman came to the boarding house to interview her about what happened. Robbie had been impressed, and Edna knew there was no way he would push her out of the house after she'd become famous, but it didn't take long for everything to go back to the way it had been and for another resident to move into Jackie's old room. Edna knew she'd had enough of the boarding house. She wanted something more.

It hadn't been difficult to move into the same aged-care home Solomon was living in, and although Edna had intended to only leave her room when she was desperate for company and for meals, she now found that she was out doing things all day.

She makes her way down the hall to the common room and she can't help but smile when she thinks of her father. 'Keep yourself to yourself, Edna,' she hears him say. 'Stay out of other people's business.'

Edna walks into the common room and looks around.

'Edna, over here!' calls Lottie. 'Over here!'

Chapter Thirty-Eight

Sydney

'So how have you been feeling this week, Jackie?' asks Dr Atlas.

'Oh, I'm really well, thank you. How about you?'

Dr Atlas smiles at me. I know he likes me, even though I'm a bit fat from the all the pills I have to take these days. He's older, more settled, and I think he'll make a wonderful husband. I like his soft brown eyes and the way he keeps pushing his hair out of his face. He's interested in everything about me, just as a good husband should be.

'Is there anything you'd like to talk about? I know that some of the group leaders are worried that you don't spend much time doing activities.'

'Well, I'm too busy for activities,' I laugh. 'How can I go to an art class when I have my baby? He's very patient, but I don't think he would enjoy it if I left him to do an art class.'

'Yes,' says Dr Atlas. 'I can see that you've brought …'

'Marcus,' I say, upset that he's forgotten my baby's name. I tell it to him every time I see him. He's not going to make a very good father if he can't remember his own child's name.

'I see you've brought Marcus with you. Do you think you could put him down for a few minutes so we can talk?'

'Of course,' I smile. I want Dr Atlas to like me. I put Marcus on the floor and brush my hand over his face and he instantly goes to sleep. He's such a good baby. He is so well behaved and he never keeps me up at night or makes unreasonable demands. He is the kind of baby I've always wanted.

'Jackie,' says Dr Atlas, 'I want to talk to you about maybe leaving Marcus in your room during the day. I think it would be very good for you if you could spend a little time without him. I'm sure that you could do a lot more with your day if you didn't have him with you.'

'Don't be silly, Dr Atlas,' I say, wagging my finger at him. 'A mother can't simply leave her child somewhere, a mother doesn't expect her child to fend for himself. Only a bad mother would leave her child alone, and I'm a very good mother, Dr Atlas. Don't you think I'm a good mother?'

'Oh yes,' says Dr Atlas, smiling thinly. 'You're a very good mother.'

'Yes,' I repeat, 'I'm a good mother, a very good mother.' I look down at Marcus lying peacefully on the floor. 'But, then, Marcus is such a good baby. Aren't you a good baby, Marcus?'

'But Jackie . . .' says Dr Atlas.

I look at my beautiful boy lying still on the floor. He won't wake up until I want him to wake up. He doesn't cry at night and drag me from sleep. He doesn't need anyone to look at him or smile at him or feed him or change his nappy. He doesn't need much at all. The only thing he really wants is to love me and have me love him.

He really is the perfect child.

I love holding him and taking care of him. We're so lucky to be able to live here in this lovely home with its beautiful gardens and giant old trees. I walk around the gardens with Marcus every day. I introduce him to everyone else here in this ... in this place. I know, from the smiles I receive, that everyone I meet can see what a wonderful mother I am.

I am never lonely when I am with Marcus, never alone. I love him and he loves me and that's exactly the way it should be.

Dr Atlas keeps wanting to talk about the past and all the things that have happened to me but I have no interest in that. When I first came here I had nightmares every night. Strange visions of a baby's hand reaching out to grab me and pull me down into nothingness. They gave me pills to make the dreams stop and then Marcus came and now I cannot imagine ever being unhappy again.

'It's all over,' I tell Dr Atlas when he tries to talk about who I used to be.

'I can't remember most of it.'

I don't like the fact that he keeps bringing it up again and again so most of the time I don't answer his questions. He says I would feel much better if I understood how I got to where I am today but I don't think that's true. I'm happy enough without thinking about anything except my baby.

'I've forgotten,' I tell him when he talks about other parts of my life and about other babies I can't remember.

'I've simply forgotten.'

Acknowledgements

Thanks to Rebecca Starford for her very detailed first edit, and to Sarah Baker for talking me through every query, getting back to me at lightning speed and generally being nice to me. To my publisher Jane Palfreyman for her continuing support after six years, and to my agent Gaby Naher, who loved this novel from the start. Thanks also to the whole team behind the production of every novel at Allen & Unwin, including Louise Cornegé and Emma O'Brien.

Thank you to the usual suspects—David, the cherubs and my mother, whose name I do know; see, it's on the front page. And, of course, to all the readers who have embraced, reviewed or complimented me on my work and who continue to be excited about each new novel—thank you, thank you, thank you.

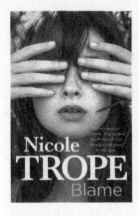

'I am here because they suspect me of something. I am here because I am a suspect. I know that, she knows that. Everyone knows that.' *Anna*

'It wasn't my fault. None of this is my fault!' *Caro*

Caro and Anna are best friends ... they *were* best friends. Over a decade, Caro and Anna have bonded while raising their daughters, two little girls the same age but living two very different lives. The women have supported each other as they have shared the joys and trials of motherhood, but now everything has changed.

There's been a terrible car accident, an unimaginable tragedy that leaves both families devastated. Over two days, as Caro and Anna each detail their own versions of events, they are forced to reveal hidden truths and closely guarded secrets.

The complicated lives of wives and mothers are laid bare as both women come to realise that even best friends don't tell each other everything. And when hearts are broken, even best friends need someone to blame.

A hard-hitting, provocative and gripping read from the queen of white-knuckle suspense and searing family drama.

Praise for *Blame*

'*Blame* is ... honest and searing and examines the many issues of motherhood and marriage, especially when it's not picture perfect.' *My GC*

'A hard-hitting, provocative and gripping read' *FeMail*

'This story blew me away! I never saw the end coming. A first-rate read.' *For the Love of Books*

'If you're looking for a book that packs a punch, pulls you in and makes you think long after you are done, then *Blame* is your book. Five stars.' *Laura's Book Blog*

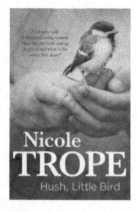

Birdy thought she would have to wait until she was free again to see Rose, but now Rose has been convicted of a shocking crime and she and Birdy will be together. Birdy has been saving all her anger for Rose. It is Rose who should have protected her and kept her safe. Birdy was little but Rose was big and she knows Rose could have saved her.

This is a story about monsters who hide in plain sight and about the secrets we keep from ourselves. It is about children who are betrayed and adults who fail them. This is the story of Birdy who was hurt and Rose who must be made to pay.

A provocative and compassionate read from the queen of white-knuckle suspense and searing family drama. You won't be able to put it down.

Praise for *Hush, Little Bird*

'You'll love the characters and hope for redemption.' *Canberra Times*

'… a thought-provoking and heartbreaking story … A story of innocence betrayed, regret, forgiveness and revenge, *Hush, Little Bird* is told with keen insight and compassion for the victims of abusers … a story that needs to be told.' *Book'd Out*

'*Hush Little Bird* really hooked me … The characters felt realistic not caricatures of what they might be … Trope's writing is engaging and she deals with difficult topics with sensitivity and in a gentle way.' *Create Hope Inspire*

'Trope expertly unpicks at the edges of the plot so it unfolds slowly and elegantly. *Hush Little Bird* is a beautiful (contemporary) novel about innocence, regret and revenge.' *Debbish*

'… *Hush, Little Bird* … is a good, easy read of a complex topic and will reach the heart of readers. Thought-provoking… *The Compulsive Reader*

A stunning novel about secrets and silence—and how sooner or later the truth must be spoken. Another hard-hitting, gripping and unputdownable read from the queen of white-knuckle suspense and searing family drama.

There was so much anger brewing in the child that sometimes Alicia feared for all of them. And now she had gone and done this terrible thing. This terrible, terrible thing.

Tara has lost her voice. She knows there was pain and fear but she cannot remember anything else. Now she can only answer the questions with silence.

Minnie has buried her voice for years, losing herself in silence and isolation, keeping her secrets safe and her broken heart concealed.

Liam finds refuge in silence; it is a place to go to when he cannot get the words out.

Kate cannot speak for herself just yet.

People are only separated from each other by moments, by fate and coincidence.

One teenage mistake, one shocking choice and one terrible night will lead to courage found, voices raised and the truth finally spoken.

Praise for *The Secrets in Silence*

'Powerful and thought-provoking writing with a telling edge of reality' *Women's Weekly Pick of the Month*

'If you like knuckle-biting suspense, you will thoroughly enjoy this latest novel from one of the fastest-rising Australian writers of thrillers.' *Ballarat Courier*

'I loved this book, devouring it in one long lazy afternoon. You will too.' *Geelong Advertiser*

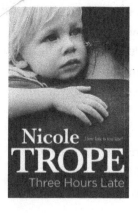

The terrible secrets of a marriage, the love that can turn to desperation, the refuge and heart-break of being a parent, the fragile threads that cradle a family. *Three Hours Late* is the second heart-wrenching novel by author Nicole Trope.

Once, so very long ago, she had watched him like this when he came to pick her up from a date. Her stomach fluttered and burned with infatuation and desire. She would watch him walk up the path and think, 'This must be love.'

But that was so very long ago. Now Liz is wary and afraid. She has made a terrible mistake and it cannot be undone.

Alex believes that today will be the day she comes back to him. Today will be the day his wife and young son finally come home. Today they will be a family again.

But Liz knows that some things can never be mended. Some marriages are too broken. Some people are too damaged. Now the most important thing in her life is her son, Luke, and she will do anything in her power to protect him.

So when Alex is a few minutes late bringing Luke back Liz begins to worry and when he is an hour late her concern grows and when he is later still she can feel her whole life changing because: what if Alex is not just late?

Praise for *Three Hours Late*

'A gripping and deeply emotional novel of almost unbearable suspense from a writer of great insight and empathy.' *FeMail*

'*Three Hours Late* is loaded with tension, bristling with suspense and blanketed with empathy—all in all, an enthralling read.' *WriteNote Reviews*

'A fast-paced page-turner' *Culture Street*

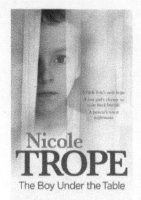

Nicole
TROPE
The Boy Under the Table

From the queen of white-knuckle suspense and searing family drama comes a harrowing glimpse into the real world behind the headlines. This is a novel of immense power and compassion—one that will move all who read it.

Tina is a young woman hiding from her grief on the streets of the Cross. On a cold night in the middle of winter she breaks all her own rules when she agrees to go home with a customer. What she finds in his house will change her life forever.

Across the country Sarah and Doug are trapped in limbo, struggling to accept the loss that now governs their lives.

Pete is the local policeman who feels like he is watching the slow death of his own family.

Every day brings a fresh hell for each of them.

Told from the alternating points of view of Tina, Sarah, Doug and Pete, *The Boy Under the Table* is gritty, shocking, moving and, ultimately, filled with hope.

Praise for *The Boy Under the Table*

'Impossible to put down once I had started—the pace is unrelenting and the story is utterly engrossing. I held my children a little tighter and a lot longer when I had finished.' *Great Aussie Reads*

'A gripping read that's difficult to put down' *Melbourne Weekly*

'A nail-biting, harrowing drama of a world behind the headlines' *Pittwater Life*